HAVOC

E. G. KEITH

GREMLYN PRODUCTIONS
2022

Manuscript is printed in Amiri, 11 pt

For information about Gremlyn Productions

and/or E.G. Keith, please contact PO Box 312,

Lincoln, Illinois 62656

or egkeith.com

Cover design by Damon Freeman

Manufactured in the United States of America

ISBN 979-8-9852725-0-5 (pbk)

ISBN 979-8-9852725-2-9 (ebook)

ISBN 979-8-9852725-1-2 (hbk)

Library of Congress Control Number: 2022903269

DEDICATION

TO MY MOM

Thank you for your endless support and evident pride.

I love you.

PRONUNCIATION GUIDE

Elysian [ih-**lis**-zh-uhn]

Ashlyn (Ash) [**ash**-lin]

Sage [seyj]

Sorin [**sohr**-in]

Milo [**mayh**-loh]

Ameer [uh-**meer**]

Everett [**ev**-er-it]

Finn [fin]

Xelma [**zel**-ma]

Malikah [**mah**-lee-kuh]

Buit [byoot]

Happy reading!

HAVOC

E. G. KEITH

E. G. KEITH

PROLOGUE

ELYSIAN

My nightmare starts like this:

A little girl—about seven years old—stands on a beach. Her hair is combed and perfectly styled, twin buns with fake purple flowers stuck in them. It's a nice contrast, the light purple with the deep, depressing brown of her hair. She has light brown skin, smooth and flawless. She wears black jeans and a black T-shirt, an outfit unusual for a trip to the beach, and her back is to me.

The water licks at the shore, clapping against the dunes. The girl is surrounded by darkness, but I can see everything perfectly.

I wonder who the girl is.

I don't have much time to ponder that, though, before an older version of the tiny girl—purple flowers and all—appears from the shadows.

"Hello, darling," says the older girl, her voice filled with emotion. It's smooth and silky, the perfect kind for telling you bedtime stories that will put you to sleep in a matter of seconds. "I see you've found a liking for the water. It's ironic, considering your powers."

"I know, Mother," responds the girl. She sounds much more

1

grown-up than I expect her to. "Why did you call me here?"

A pained expression forms on the woman's face. "My dear, your father is one of the Plenty."

The girl looks up at her mother. "I know." Her voice is faint, being swallowed by shadows.

"And you have unimaginable powers."

"Yes, Mother." The girl sounds as if she's becoming annoyed. "What is the point of this meeting?"

"Be patient, dear." The woman sighs and steps forward. I'm instantly hit by her beauty. Sharp, chiseled features, brown skin, intimidating eyes that reflect so many past miseries. Her long black dress sways in the nonexistent breeze. "Do you know about the kingdom of Buit?"

The girl looks at the ground like she's ashamed of herself. "Yes, Mother."

The woman chuckles. "I knew you would go sneaking through your father's old photography books. And you are aware of the rulers, King Cirillo and Queen Malikah?"

The girl nods, and a tear slides down the woman's face. Neither seems to notice. "They are good friends of your father, as you know."

The girl sighs. "Mother, is there a point to this?"

"Of course, dear," the woman replies, way too quickly. I have reason to believe she's hiding something. If I suspect her, I wonder how her daughter is feeling?

2

The girl's hand hovers over to her back pocket, where something sharp pokes out. It takes a second before I realize it's a blade. Not at all bad parenting if you give your child a knife.

"Darling," the woman starts, stepping toward her daughter, "you know this is best."

The girl takes a shaky breath. I hope the woman isn't talking about what I think she's talking about. "What do you mean? I never saw anything about the kingdom of Buit being hateful against Magics in Father's books."

The woman's airy dress swishes as she smiles sadly at the little girl. "Well, they don't exactly pride themselves on that, do they?"

"You're trying to make a joke when I'm about to be executed?"

In a flash, the woman removes something just as sharp as the little girl's and has it pointed above her daughter's heart. Another tear slides down her face as her eyes reflect the scene: a pure black dagger, the terrified face of a seven-year-old child, and ... is that fire?

"Just trying to lighten the mood." The woman eyes the fire and smiles coldly.

The girl lets out a strangled sound, then swiftly regains her composure. "How much did Buit pay you?"

Her mother scoffs. "You think that I can be bribed into killing my magical daughter? It was more of a voluntary job. I've always disliked you, my dear."

"But I'm guessing finances still weren't off the table?" the girl asks, and I have to resist the urge to vomit. What kind of mother would be paid to kill her very own daughter, yet do it voluntarily? This mother, apparently.

"Your father's money definitely … interested me," the woman agrees. "A small part of his salary for a few months, just for my services killing a Magic … we both know that is not much when it comes to having your valuable blood on my hands, but Cirillo and Malikah appreciate jobs as hard as this. Their recognition of me in their kingdom was more than enough to get me to agree."

I realize the girl's strategy. Keep her mother talking, and she'll have longer to live and form a plan.

"And the king and queen were the ones who proposed my assassination?"

"Oh, please, darling. Only use 'assassination' when someone important is being murdered brutally." The woman flashes perfect teeth, then continues. "But, yes, when I went to their castle in the heart of Buit—gorgeous, by the way—I told the king and queen that I had a Magic in my hands, the daughter of a Plenty, and they immediately agreed to your … elimination. Now, any further questions before you're dead?"

The girl carefully unsheathes her dagger, so quietly her mother doesn't notice. She holds it behind her back casually, and while her mother is rambling on about the wealth she will have after the girl's death, a ball of flames springs to the girl's hand, again, surprising me.

4

What was that she'd called herself? A Magic? That would explain the fire that appeared out of thin air.

"Ah, smart move, summoning your fire," sighs the woman. "You always know how to use it in desperate times. I applaud you for that. Fortunately, the king and queen of Buit have foreseen you might try to use your insufferable magic when we both know killing you and the magic itself would help humanity."

She shows a piece of what looks like black silky fabric from her dress, but I have a feeling it's more.

"Fireproof fabric, Mother? Really?" complains the girl.

Her mother looks down at her with utter hatred. "Oh, dear, don't you understand? I always come prepared."

The girl suddenly erupts in flames, from head to toe, surrounding her like oxygen. She yells in agony and throws herself at her mother, who stares at her in shock, and as her shout echoes throughout the dunes and across the dark water, I feel her pain. Her mother. Her own mother.

For a second, both of the females are coated in flames. I figure the woman must have been reduced to an ember, fireproof fabric or not. There's no way any human being—except those immune to fire—could survive that.

The girl emerges, sweating and breathing shakily. Summoning all that fire must have been exhausting.

A minute goes by. It seems like years as the little girl stares at her lifeless mother. Heavy breathing fills the quiet content of the beach, coming from me or her I can't tell. The little girl reaches down to stroke her mother's singed hair, and pulls a piece of fabric from her burnt hand, a fragment of the woman's dress. The girl runs her thumb over it as a choked sob sounds from her.

Once the girl is on the floor, crying and sobbing, I know it's over. Her mother is dead. And she's the one who killed her.

"Why did you do this, Mother?" The pathetic attempt at a whisper makes me want to cry. "We could've been together. We could have been powerful. That was all you ever wanted, wasn't it? To have power?"

I want to comfort the girl, but she's beginning to pull herself together. She stands from the scene and brushes burnt hair from her mother's face. "I truly am sorry, Mother. I hope you can forgive me in the afterlife."

The little girl brushes sand from her jeans and wipes tears from her eyes, clutching the fireproof fabric so tightly that her knuckles turn white. She breathes in deeply and urges a ball of fire to ignite in her palm, but it never comes. Her powers seem to be drained along with the life of her mother.

As the girl is leaving, I hear a faint voice, one I have never heard before, calling something that sounds like, "Lys—Lys, wake up!"

She turns toward me and smiles sadly.

"Is that your name?" I ask, surprised I can suddenly talk. My mouth seems to be working on its own, opening and closing when it wants to.

"No," the girl answers. "But it's yours."

And then everything goes black.

CHAPTER 1

ASH

I spin my sword on the tip of my finger, bored.

We are all gathered in the meeting room at my camp, Camp Havoc. The meeting room has to be the brightest place at camp. Sunlight bounces off wide windows positioned along the back wall; a water cooler and fluffy couches sit next to us, inviting us to sit and take a long drink; paintings of winter hang above the furniture. Let's just put it this way: I didn't design it.

"*On n'a pas le temps!*" shouts the old man across from me. His name is Everett Nightgale, and he's our supervisor. Funnily enough (hilarious, as Milo loves to remind me), he always speaks in French, the only language that confuses me.

Luckily, his bodyguard is translating. "He says you don't have time," the bodyguard reports.

"Our deadline is in a few weeks," Milo agrees. He leans forward on the table. "If we don't get a good story quick, we're on a run for our money."

We get all our income from newspapers.

"*Exactement,*" Everett grumbles under his breath. "*C'est ce que j'essaie de vous dire*, Ashlyn!"

"Exactly—that's what I'm trying to tell you, Ashlyn," his bodyguard explains.

I ignore him.

"Where are we supposed to find a story when Camp Serenity has gone quiet? No mocking letters, inappropriate comments on sticky notes, or annoying floods in our forest."

Everett's bodyguard raises an eyebrow at my statement. I send a glare his way.

Camp Serenity, another Magic camp, has been our rival for years. Ever since that unworthy, ungrateful "leader" Elysian Viggo took over the camp, we've been attacked by them. It's become a frequent event in our day, so frequent that some of us keep calendars. Thinking about this, my eyes drift to the calendar on the wall of the meeting room, today's date crossed out in red ink. Behind the markings, I can barely make out the words: WATER BALLOON SHOWER—11:30.

"We don't get all of our stories from them," Milo assures the supervisor. He sends a warning glance my way, his brown eyes that are usually filled with warmth shooting daggers at me. "We are rather independent. That is only when we are in desperate times."

"*Les temps désespérés*," Everett mutters. "*C'est ce qu'il tous disent.*"

Everett's bodyguard shrugs. "That's what they all say."

"Reporters are being sent all over the kingdom," he continues.

9

"We will find that story, I promise you."

The supervisor sighs and waves his hand, exasperated. His bodyguard stands, ready for movement from the old man.

"*Bien sûr que nous le ferons, mon garçon. J'aimerais parlert avec Ashlyn avant de disperser, si vous me le permettez,*" Everett says to us, although he knows we have no clue what he just said.

"He wants a word with you," the bodyguard says to me. I'm guessing by the look on his face, that isn't such a good thing.

Milo stands from his chair and motions for me to do so as well, and then he straps his dagger to his belt before glancing at me uneasily and leaving the room.

"What's up?" I ask the supervisor.

"*Quoi de neuf?*" he repeats icily. "*Quoi de neuf est votre paresse quand il vient à ce camp!*"

The bodyguard translates: "What's up? What's up is your laziness when it comes to this camp?!"

"My laziness?" I say, annoyed and angry. "In case you have not noticed, sir, I have put my heart and soul into this camp, and I intend to keep it that way." My voice is level, but as hard as steel. "Just because I don't have a few measly stories to put into the mortal newspapers, which, news flash, no one is ever going to read, it doesn't mean I am lazy."

"For your information," the bodyguard says while Everett advances on me, "I am the supervisor of this camp. You will not disrespect me in any way, or I will suspend your privileges."

"What privileges?" I shoot back. "All I get as a thank you for building the foundation, the image, the idea of this camp is an extra bagel at breakfast. If I'm lucky, I'll get some butter on it."

"It was your idea to start this camp, to run it in chaos." The old man is yelling so loud I can barely hear his bodyguard. "Do not attack me for your foolish mistakes. Milo Belittle does much more than you to support this place you call home, and I suppose that's the way it will stay. But if and when this experimental project of yours fails, do not come crawling to me for help. And get a story on the board!"

The old man huffs and turns toward the door, muttering in French while his bodyguard scrambles to keep up with him.

My hand clenches around the hilt of my sword. It's my favorite sword to use: steel silver blade, red hilt, fake flames dancing across the bottom of the blade. Milo got it for me when I first became the leader of Camp Havoc. That seems so long ago ...

I pull myself out of *those* thoughts and force my feet to move. Eventually, I shuffle to where Milo's waiting, tapping the butt of his hilt like a drum.

"Thank gods," he says, relieved. He knows how tough Everett Nightgale can be, especially when it comes to me. "Did it go well?"

"As well as it could," I mutter, trying not to convey too much emotion. I tell him about our conversation, and his jaw drops.

11

"*I* do everything? Did you tell him about what happens, well, every day?"

"I tried," I retort, "but he's hard to convince when he's angry. His French sounds even more jumbled than usual."

He laughs. It's a nice sound, reminding me of my father, and where we lived in the forest after Mother … "Hey, Ash, you okay?"

My eyes flick over to Milo, and I realize I'd zoned out. "Oh, yeah, sorry."

He checks his watch and smiles lightly.

We speed off in the direction of the forest.

At Camp Havoc, we have a huge forest with tons of equipment. There are mortal basketball courts and soccer fields, footballs and helmets, bicycles, armor, and a trunk where we store extra swords. There's a riverbed along the left side of the grove of trees, which Camp Serenity always uses as the butt of their pranks. When Everett Nightgale hasn't demanded a meeting, the campers aren't on our backs about every little thing, and everybody's in their cabins, Milo and I like to spend our time here, relaxing and wasting time.

Only a few campers are in the forest when we arrive. Milo shoos them away while I ready the practicing range. When I first made the camp, I told the designers how I wanted a place where Magics could practice their powers. Luckily, these woods were perfect.

The practicing range is a huge clearing in the forest, equipped with all sorts of things: a body full of clean water, a wall full of fireproof fabric, rocks for telekinesis, and more. Milo helped me with the design.

I pull out my sword and stare at the flames. I'm a Magic, of course. I am a firebender. Sometimes it hurts me to say that, especially since that was the way my mom … but I am. I'm a firebender, and everyone knows that.

Fire is known to be uncontrollable. Maybe that's why I am the way I am or maybe it's another medical reason. Honestly, I don't care.

Milo throws his dagger at a target on a tree. It hits a little off to the middle. He glances at it, unsatisfied.

I practice sword fighting with a dummy. It feels nice to be violent, to let out the anger Everett Nightgale gave me. Once I've finished, I burn the fluff that comes out of it for fun. The smell of smoke begins to rise in the air.

Milo yanks my hand away from the cotton after a few minutes. The cotton has turned to an ashy pit of smoke and my anger.

"You were doing the thing again," he tells me, and I wince.

Sometimes when I get bored and start to burn things, I zone out, making me think when I snap out of my trance, I've only been burning something for a few minutes, but it's been almost half an hour.

"It's about dinnertime, and then we've got archery first thing in the morning." He looks at his watch, and I wince again. I've always been terrible at archery. Milo excels at it. The arrows will respond to him. They will burst into flames whenever I approach.

"I don't understand *why* I still have to go to that class," I complain. "It's not like I'm good or anything."

"Venus enjoys having you," Milo chides.

Venus, a seventeen-year-old girl with archery powers, teaches the class, and she's always ecstatic when I show up. I mean, who wouldn't be? I'm amazing. Well, at everything except archery.

"You mean she loves being *better* than me," I grumble, and Milo chuckles and shrugs.

Before we leave, I burn some of the fireproof fabric on the wall.

* * *

I calm my stance and position my bow. Archery. The scum of the earth.

Venus glides past different archers, smiling with all the charm she can muster. Her bright blue eyes turn even bluer as they hit sunlight. They seem to dim, though, when she reaches me.

She smiles that sad smile that always means she's about to say something you're not going to enjoy, and I can read her expression perfectly.

"What have I been doing *this* time, Venus?" I demand.

"O-oh," she stutters. Then she smiles. "You're doing perfectly

14

fine. I just have one adjustment to make …"

She grabs my hand and moves it up the bow, grabbing an arrow and notching it in against my will. I feel heat rising up my cheeks, and prickling in my hands. *I will* not *let Venus Zaran teach me how to do something.*

I take it from Venus. She jerks her hands back. I probably burned her.

"Sorry," I grumble, and I reposition my arrow. Milo watches me from his station.

When we're back in the meeting room for a meeting with each of the campers, he corners me.

"What the hell was that?" Milo glares at me. "She's seventeen, an archer. You're nineteen, a firebender. She's probably terrified of you now."

Good.

"You don't know that."

He sighs.

"Get your anger under control. You want to be a leader? Don't take everything out on the kids you're trying to lead, Ash."

He continues the meeting as if nothing happened.

* * *

I get the message that evening.

I'm working on old newspapers, reading them to see if we've

missed anything. Then, I hear a loud call boom from outside my cabin.

"WHERE IS ASHLYN KAVE?"

I jump out of my skin as the voice rolls across camp. Realization dawns on me. That deep, monotone voice that holds way too much power ... is looking for *me*.

Now's your chance, a voice inside my head whispers. *Let whoever's behind this act know who you are, that you are in charge of this camp.*

I agree with myself silently and storm out of my cabin, grabbing my sword on my nightstand, the wooden door slamming against the wall behind me.

"Looking for me?" I shout, trying my best to look intimidating. I'm terrified.

A giant holographic picture of a burly man's face hangs above the mess hall, glaring down at the remaining campers. Most of them are at the campfire in the middle of campus, trying to protect themselves from the unusually cold night.

The man has a scar the length of his nose under his left eye. The skin around it has healed poorly, for it's raw and red. However he got that scar, the event happened recently. His eyes are far apart on his face, and the little facial hair he has is patched and only stubble. He is young from his voice, but his cruel expression hides his youth behind layers of evil. I can easily mistake him for a forty-year-old man and not think twice about it.

"Ah." He relaxes. "There you are."

How does he know my name and location? is the question I ask myself. I know his voice from somewhere, but I can't put my finger on it.

"Who are you?" I shout. I probably look pathetic in only my pajamas, but the man raises his eyebrows and chuckles.

"Still surprising as always," he mutters. "I see you still have that little sword I sold your friend, my dear."

My hand clenches around the hilt of my sword as I realize who he is. My fingers find the distinctive bump on it.

"F-Finn?"

"The one, the only, darling."

Hundreds of memories rush into my head: the comfort Finn offered me several years ago after my mother's death; his kindness toward me that quickly turned into something else; his jealousy when it came to me saying anything about the people I was interested in; watching Finn surrender to the man dressed in dark clothes before him, talking about a group he had asked to be in. I grip my sword tighter.

"What are you doing here?" My voice is barely a whisper, but Finn hears. He smiles without it reaching his eyes.

"I could ask you the same thing," he says. "You are meant to be my wife. We will live together, have a future together, a family. All you have to do is tell me your location."

"How can I see you if you have no idea where I am?" I see campers scatter into their cabins out of my peripheral vision.

"I'll explain later, darling," he teases, smirking. "You just have to tell me your location."

"I am never going to tell you where I am, not after you did that to me." I feel tears pool in my eyes, and it becomes harder to see because my vision is blurry. "That is a promise."

"Oh, but, darling," he says, moving out of the way so I can see something, "you must."

Ameer.

Ameer Domhnall is sitting in a filthy jail cell. Barely any light comes through the bars, and his frame is weak. In front of him sits a bowl of … dog food? His skin is deathly pale and his eyes are sunken and dark.

"No," I croak. "You can't do this."

"You have until August fourth, my birthday, to come to me. Our last meeting place. I will wait. If by then you manage to find me in time and refuse to accept my hand in marriage, you can kiss your little friend goodbye. Or, rather, shake hands. I would much rather you do that than *kiss* this boy."

I blink tears from my eyes.

"I accept your challenge."

Finn smiles.

"See you soon, my darling."

The hologram disappears, leaving a dark sky speckled with white stars in its wake.

CHAPTER 2

ELYSIAN

My eyes open so suddenly that I think my eyeballs are going to fly out of their sockets.

A redheaded girl leans over me, her startling green eyes staring at me intently. She gasps with relief as I regain consciousness and she leans back against a tree.

"Thank the gods, Lys, I thought you were dead," she says.

I try to sit up, but it's ridiculously hard. My head is throbbing, and when I reach back only to feel a big knot on the back of my skull, my limbs feel heavy. I'm groggy, and tired, and in pain everywhere.

The redhead notices my expression and worry lines appear around her eyes. "Lys? Are you okay?"

"Of course she's not, Sage," calls a voice to my left. "She almost just drowned."

The girl, Sage's, cheeks redden. "I wasn't asking you, Sorin."

I finally manage to sit up and rest my head against a tree. We're in a clearing, tall oaks surrounding the rather large amount of people gathered around me and Sage. A creek runs past the clearing, water catching on the jagged rocks poking out from under the surface.

A boy with dark brown hair and a bright smile appears from behind the trees, holding a jug of clear liquid. I don't entirely trust him, considering the long sword strapped to his belt, but he seems friendly enough.

"Drink," he tells me, motioning to the jug.

I take a cautious sip, and immediately my bones are filled with relief. The throbbing in my head subsides and my senses become sharper. I'm aware of more things, like the dagger strapped to my thigh, my soaked green T-shirt and jeans, and the cold badge stuck to my shirt.

The magical water tastes like a mixture of red Gatorade and lemonade. It's wonderful.

What is this stuff? I want to ask, but my voice fails.

"How does it taste?" the boy asks me with a grin. Sage shoots him a look that quiets him.

"Thanks, Max," she snaps sharply, and her eyes tell Max to leave. "We have to get her back to camp," a voice says from deeper in the forest.

Max bows, which confuses me, then hurries back into the trees.

Sage sighs and glances at me, as if trying to communicate silently. She seems to say, *You okay to walk?*

"And how do you suppose we do that?" argues another voice to my right.

"All this training and we can't even carry our leader fifty feet—"

Sorin's voice makes Sage grumble under her breath and absentmindedly reach for her dagger.

"You are not carrying her," Sage interrupts. "Elysian can handle herself. Can't you?"

She looks at me expectantly, and I nod hesitantly, even though I'm not sure who she is, where I am, or why Sorin called me their "leader."

I try standing, and my legs collapse. I barely know Sorin, but I have a feeling he's eyeing Sage triumphantly.

"Still," Sage growls, "nobody is touching Leader Viggo."

I squint, remembering vaguely that *viggo* means "lightning."

Seriously? My name is "Leader Lightning?"

"You're just saying that because she favors you," complains Sorin's voice.

"So? I'm her best friend."

As they continue to bicker back and forth, acting as if I'm not even there, I manage to stand, but I'm using the tree behind me for balance. The Gatorade-lemonade hasn't really helped my weak joints, just the pain in them. Luckily, my voice comes back in that moment, so I croak, "Hush! Both of you!"

Sorin and Sage immediately shut up.

I clear my throat and try to speak again, but I sound like I have repeatedly scratched my vocal cords against sandpaper.

"What and where is this *camp?*"

Everyone looks at me like I've gone insane. Sage especially looks confused. "Are you feeling alright, Lys?"

I want to say no, but the gods know what kind of damage that would cause, so I nod. "I'm fine. Can you answer my question?"

Sage glances around cautiously, then announces, "Everyone, stay here. I'm going to take Leader Viggo back to camp for an inspection. *Stand guard.* Direct orders from Junior Leader Jobbs."

"I'm coming, too," Sorin announces. "I'm the best Healer at camp. If there's something seriously wrong with her, I can heal her."

Sage takes a shaky breath but doesn't object. Instead, she wraps an arm around me as I stabilize myself against her, and we walk like that until we come across a wooden bench, surveying a sort of little town. There are wooden cabins, all painted the same solid white; a big marble building labeled MESS HALL; an educational center, decorated with funky couches, papers, desks, and everything else an average classroom would have, except the chalkboard reads THE MAGICS REBELLION OF 1786; and an infirmary, where a few teenagers sleep in white beds, a clear jug of that Gatorade-lemonade on each side table next to every bed. Apparently that drink is how they heal a lot of people.

Sage sets me down on the bench and sits herself. Sorin follows suit.

"Are you being serious, Lys, or is this an attempt at scaring me?" Sage asks me, a stern expression plastered on her face. It looks intimidating, especially since her red hair is flaming in the sunlight. She looks about ready to become a firecracker and zoom off into the distance.

"What do you mean?" I ask her, my mind blanking. "I've never heard of this place, or of you, or you."

I point to her, then to Sorin, who has somehow gained a clipboard made of blinding light, almost like sunlight has morphed into a clipboard.

"Are you kidding?" Sage looks heartbroken.

Meanwhile, Sorin takes notes on his clipboard.

I turn away. Her expression is too painful. I feel like I've just stabbed her heart with my dagger, and now I'm stomping on it. "I'm sorry," I choke out.

"Amnesia," Sorin declares so suddenly I almost fall off the bench. He reads Sage's expression, then clicks his tongue. "Sorry, am I interrupting something?"

"Continue," I tell him, eager to change the subject.

"Right. So I'm guessing you have amnesia or memory loss." Sage glares at him, and he raises his hands in surrender. "Don't be offended. I'm just saying it how it is."

"I think we figured that out," Sage snaps. "Can you cure her or not?"

Sorin laughs nervously. "The thing is, nobody's made a memory loss potion that works on Magics. We're so powerful that mortal drugs won't work."

"Magics?" I ask, remembering my strange dream. "You mean, people with magic powers?"

Sage looks so relieved that I'm afraid she's going to suffocate me in a bear hug. "Do you remember that?"

I don't want to crush her spirit, so I nod.

Sorin looks bewildered. "Okay, so that means it's not as bad as I calculated."

Sage is smiling harder than I ever thought someone could smile. "Maybe after a few days in the infirmary, she'll have her memory back?"

"She's a leader, though," Sorin says with a sigh.

"I'm the junior leader," Sage argues. "I'm responsible. I could take care of you."

He glances at her skeptically, and she blushes. "I mean, not *you* you. The whole camp. Not just you. I'd never take care of *you.*"

Sorin grumbles something that sounds suspiciously like, "Thanks," but it doesn't matter. His head pops back up and he snaps his fingers. Instantly, the clipboard vanishes.

"How did you do that?" I ask, astonished.

"Sorin's a sun-related Magic," Sage mutters. "Loves reminding me of it."

Sorin grins, as if thrilled to be able to share this story. "I can manipulate rays from the sun. Pretty cool, huh? Especially since it's my name."

"Sorin means sun?"

"You got it." He leans back and crosses his legs. I stand, trying to take in the camp.

"What do you call this camp?"

Sage glances uneasily at Sorin, then stands and grabs my arm. "I'll take her from here. Sorin, go check on the others. When you get there, *stay there*."

He looks annoyed, but he jogs off in the direction of the forest, his blond hair bouncing with each step.

"I don't get what's so bad about him," I tell Sage, and she smiles sourly.

You may not think Sage can be intimidating at first glance, and her name doesn't do her any favors, but when you get up close, she gets scary. Notice those sharp green eyes that can look through your eyes into your soul, her occasional raise of the eyebrows that's enough to convince you to shut up or else, and her silver-bladed dagger with the jagged emerald-green handle, and you'll pray to never get on her wrong side.

"There's a story behind it," she says. "Trust me."

She doesn't meet my eyes, quiet for a moment, before saying softly, "You don't really remember what a Magic is, do you? You were just saying that to make me feel better."

"I'm sorry," I admit.

She doesn't say anything and begins to walk in the direction of the mess hall. Sage motions for me to follow, so I do.

It's a lot bigger than I expected. The concrete flooring is spotless, not a speck of filth on it. I instantly feel bad about the water on my shoes. The tables are decorated with glassy white plates, cloth napkins, all the necessary silverware for that meal, and name tags. A chalkboard is stapled above the kitchen door, displaying what the mess hall is serving that night for dinner.

Sage leads me over to one of the many tables. "So we can talk in private. Sorin doesn't need to diagnose you with anything else."

I sit down and blurt out the first question that comes to mind: "Where am I?"

Sage places her hands in front of her and folds them. "Camp Serenity. The mess hall."

"You keep calling me Leader Viggo. Is that how I'm known around here?"

"Well, yes." Sage takes a deep breath, getting ready to tell a long story. "You made Camp Serenity, based on our group, I guess you could say. You started Serenity for teen and kid Magics who didn't want to riot to be known, but to just be recognized. To be *seen*. Not to cause fights or draw attention to ourselves in any other way except nonviolence. Immediately, you became the leader. I mean, *you* were the one who started the group. You made me junior leader, out of pity, maybe. Sorin was outraged. He thought it was obvious you would pick him, yet he was the second choice. Or, third, I guess." She paused to take a quick breath.

"Point is, he wasn't happy. He left the group for a while, but eventually came back with news. There was another group named Havoc, a group of Magics that wanted to cause chaos, that were so mad with the mortals for neglecting and abusing their power for so many years that they were willing to do anything to be recognized."

The name Havoc sounds slightly familiar, like a name I placed at the back of my mind for years and suddenly remember.

Sage continues.

"Apparently the leader's mother had tried to kill her just for being a Magic, ordered by the king and queen of Buit." She says 'Buit' like it leaves a disgusting taste in her mouth. "King Cirillo and Queen Malikah."

I think about my dream. That little girl has to be too young to lead a group called Havoc. But everything matches. Even the names of the king and queen.

"What caused me to lose my memory?" I ask.

"We were swimming in the creek by the clearing," Sage tells me. "You must've hit your head on a rock, because you were out for about three hours."

"*Three hours?*"

She shrugs. "It wasn't bad. By the time we got you out, you were already starting to regain consciousness."

I clear my throat and wish I were anywhere but *here*, alone with Sage. It's not that she's unenjoyable—she seems nice enough—but I have no idea who she is. She thinks I'm her best friend, and I barely even know my own name.

"We should get back to the others," I say, shifting uncomfortably. I stand from my chair and eye my name tag. Leader Viggo. *Leader.* I hurry out of the mess hall with Sage trailing behind me.

"Did I do something to offend you?" she calls. "Elysian?"

"No," I say under my breath, feeling bad.

When I reach the clearing, everyone's staring at Sorin expectantly, as if they're children waiting to hear a story.

"Just something she can't control—" Sorin's saying, patiently.

"Camp Serenity," I call, interrupting.

Sorin jumps out of his skin. The other campers just shift their eyes to me, like they're used to me appearing suddenly.

I study their faces. "Everyone to the cabins. I will see you all at dinner."

And then I turn back toward camp and stomp away.

* * *

It's a lot.

I look through the doorway of my cabin, taking it in. The walls are a baby blue, decorated with white puffs I think are clouds. My bed is pushed against the back wall, as if I barely do any sleeping. Charts, loose papers, and books cover the ground. I have a desk in the right corner, cluttered and forgotten in a pile of junk.

The only decoration I have is a sign nailed to my wall that reads *Sky—Lightning—Weather—Leader.*

Sage appears after a few minutes of letting me look. She leans on my doorframe, her red hair tied back into a high ponytail. Her freckles stand out against her pale skin, even paler in the setting sun.

"How are you feeling?" she asks me.

I chuckle under my breath. "Meh."

She sighs and sits down next to me on my bed. "I get it. Most people are overwhelmed when they come here for the first time, even if it isn't really the first time."

She takes my hand reassuringly.

"Do you know what made me start this camp?" I ask.

Sage shrugs. "Honestly? I'm not sure. You told me after making me junior leader that your family had never accepted you for who you were. You didn't ever share any other details, though."

"Oh." I stare at the papers on my floor. "Did I like to write?"

Sage follows my gaze. "Yeah. You never really shared your projects with me, and being a leader of anything is extremely busy, but you spent most of your free time training or writing."

"Huh."

It's so agitating not remembering my own life. I feel like a piece of me is missing with every step, every word, every movement. I'm pretty much physically healed, but mentally, I'm a train wreck.

"Don't be discouraged," Sage tells me. "You'll get your memory back eventually."

Eventually.

"Thanks," I say, trying to keep the disappointment off my tongue.

She just laughs. I hate how she's able to read me.

"See you at dinner, Lys." Sage exits my cabin, leaving the wooden door open. I leave my bed to close it, when I notice my dagger shining. I move toward it, and wonder if this is a prank being pulled by Sorin, using his sun powers to try to scare me.

It's working.

I set the dagger on my bed after changing into fresh, warm clothes and haven't thought about it since before my shower. Now, I can't ignore it. It's glowing a hazy yellow, like it's trying to alert me of something.

I pick it up and weigh the dagger in my hand. It feels familiar enough: the same curves on the hilt, button on the back of the handle that would turn it into a full-fledged sword made to run people through with (Sage taught me that fun little trick), but somehow it's heavier. Almost like it's being pulled down by something.

It suddenly begins to glow bright enough to blind somebody. I shield my eyes but can't resist the urge to look again. Once the light has died down, I stare at the image in the blade, moving so smoothly that it's like I'm seeing it in person. I'm horrified by what I see.

A young man, with brown hair and deathly pale skin, sits in a dark, square room. The walls are made entirely of stone, and the floor is concrete. Along the right wall is a cot filled with what looks like dirt and filthiness. On the left, a security camera is attached to the wall, pointed directly at where the boy sits. Whenever he shifts, the camera inches back, as if getting ready to pounce. It doesn't, thankfully, but that doesn't make the situation any less sad.

The boy looks like he hasn't been fed in several days. He's wearing completely black clothes that blend in with the scenery. They look ratty and used, like hand-me-downs. His arms are covered in red bites, probably from venomous bugs. He takes a shaky breath and tries to stand, but the effort seems to be too much for him in his fragile state.

"Oh, now, don't torture yourself," a voice booms from the wall.

The boy flinches. "Finn."

"Why do you sound so surprised, Ameer? You knew this day was going to come." The voice laughs harshly, cutting through the room like a blade. I shiver at the sound of it.

Ameer doesn't speak for a minute. Then he says, "Why are you checking up on me, Finn? When you put me in this cell, you said, and I quote, 'I will forever be in debt when it comes to my master, so if he commands me, he commands me.'"

"I changed my mind."

"No, you just want to watch my torture." His jaw clenches on "torture."

"Maybe so, maybe not. I am not entirely cruel," says the voice, Finn. "I will let you go, on one condition."

Ameer stares down at his calloused hands. "I told you. I am not—"

"Tell me the location of Ashlyn Kave."

His face turns paler, though I figure they've discussed this before. "Absolutely not."

"You must, if you wish to make it out alive," Finn warns, much more sharply than the other times he spoke.

"I don't know anything about her location, Finn," Ameer snarls. "I cannot tell you anything, even if I wished to, which I do not."

"She is very valuable to the kingdom, Ameer. Surely you know this."

"I am not ratting out one of my friends so you can *slaughter* her."

"It is necessary."

"It is not!"

Ameer picks up a jagged rock and throws it at the security camera.

"I don't care if you don't feed me until the day after tomorrow; I am *not* telling *you* anything."

"Fine," the voice huffs. "But I know we can do better. No food for a week, and then let's see if you know anything about your little *friend.*"

There's a quiet buzz, and then the blade returns to normal.

CHAPTER 3

ASH

The stars sparkle tauntingly as I lie awake in bed. The foam mattress beneath me is comfortable enough, but after what I saw, what my *campers* had to see, I find it hard to sleep.

We have until the end of summer to rescue Ameer, my first friend, the Prince of Buit. I've always had a rocky relationship with Buit, but Ameer is … different. Less self-absorbed, more careful and kind. He is a heater in a room full of ice. The black sheep. I can go on.

Milo knocks on my door late. My eyes are finally beginning to droop as my thoughts cloud my vision, taking over the only thing I have left: a stupid poster of famous firebender Alec Rameriz that I taped to my wall my first summer here. Celebrity crushes really consumed you sometimes.

"Come in," I say groggily, and the door cracks open.

Milo slips inside. He wears a "Kingdom of Ruri" T-shirt and basketball shorts. His messy black hair is pushed to one side of his scalp and his warm brown eyes are wide and alert. He's clearly been up for several hours.

"Mind if I sit?" He motions to the end of my bed, and I nod in affirmation.

Milo sighs. "How are you feeling, Ash?"

I can make out his worried expression in the dark. "Like crap, so, the usual."

He bites his nails nervously. I know what he is craving to ask. I want to ask about the situation outside too, but who better to ask than myself? And self-questioning never ends well. Especially for someone like me.

"You know him?"

I'm silent. Finally, I say, "Yes. I knew him."

"Has—" Milo starts to say something, but stops himself and begins to trace the patterns in my comforter with his finger.

I stare at him curiously. The message from Finn hasn't changed anything. I'm still me. Just more aware of time. "You can ask questions, you know. I'm just not sure that I'll have the best answers."

He brushes a piece of hair out of his face. When he raises his head, his eyes are sad. "We have to save the prince, Ash, or he'll die."

"We?" I say. "I'm doing this on my own. I don't need you to be starved in a cage, too."

He sighs. "What if something happens?"

"Finn won't do anything to me," I assure him. "Didn't you hear him? He wants me to—"

"I heard him." He runs his tongue over his teeth. "Trust me, I

36

heard him."

I take a shaky breath. This is real. Not just a horrible nightmare that I can't wake from. A real, live nightmare.

I let my eyes close. It's a horrible mistake. A horrible, horrible mistake.

A memory swims in front of my eyes. I recognize the setting instantly. The castle of Buit. Dark walls, huge black gates restricting outsiders from the luxuries the castle holds, perfectly mowed lawns and tended-to greenery. The gates open and a tall man, dressed in a crisp black suit, glides past them. His loafers hit the pavement with a loud click every time he moves.

Following behind him is a taller boy with dark hair slicked to one side and a smaller girl with restraints on her wrists. The smaller girl struggles against the handcuffs, trying to break her tiny wrists from the even smaller, tighter restraints. She turns in every direction except where the man is headed, but it doesn't help. The handcuffs seem to be magical, leading her in the direction her captor wishes her to go.

"Calm down," hisses the boy. The boy is Finn.

"He-he's trying to take you away, Finn!" the girl retorts. The girl is me.

The tall man clears his throat. When he speaks, it is a low, intimidating sound. "The boy is right, girl. Calm down and he will be more merciful."

They never told me who "he" was. I was too little. All they told me was that he was powerful, strong, and respected. Not to be messed with. I believed them.

We shuffle along. Finn snaps at me every time I say something or struggle. He's obviously wanting to make a good impression. I know nothing. Finn never told me anything.

The tall man doesn't speak to us again. He leads us to the front doors of the castle and smiles coldly, motioning for us to open them. For once, I don't struggle against my restraints. I stay completely still, refusing to open the doors.

Finn's hand hovers over the door handle as he thinks. I just wish he would hurry up. I don't want to be here. I want to be back home, safe and sound, out of this mess Finn dragged me into.

When he opens the door, the wind trapped inside the house blows out, hitting me in the face. It smells like a beach. I plug my nose to block the smell that triggers my less-than-pleasant memories.

Even the taller man looks surprised, but he leads us through the castle anyway. The halls are dark and empty, lit only by torches pinned to the stone walls with metal brackets. The handcuffs begin to pull me forward with more force. They're obviously ready to see "him," whoever that may be.

The man eventually stops in front of a pair of two huge black doors with ravens painted on them. Finn's jaw drops. I don't know why he's so surprised. *What's his deal with ravens?* I think. The man opens the doors, and another beach smell wafts through them, this time stronger. This is getting annoying.

"This way," the man mutters, leading us through the doors. He turns a corner and the room fades away. When he turns another corner, I'm not surprised. It is a castle. *Of course* it has to be difficult to navigate.

"Are we there yet?" I whine.

Finn slaps my arm so hard it leaves a mark. I wince. "Be quiet," he says nastily. Then, he smiles smugly. "We'll be there soon enough, Ashlyn."

The man leads us down a few more long, dark corridors but stops in the middle of a dining room. I know it's a dining room because of the huge six-foot-long black table, engraved with the same ravens on the doors a few hundred corridors back.

One man, one boy, both with dark brown hair, wearing suits, sit at the table, across from one another, *glaring* at one another.

The man turns his head. "Ah, Julio. About time you show up. I see you've brought our guests." He smiles evilly. "Sit."

Finn and the man, Julio, sit at the table, but I stand still and try my best to cross my arms defiantly.

When the man notices I don't sit down, his smile widens. "She's a stubborn one, is she?"

"Yes," Finn grumbles. "Yes, she is."

"And you wish to become her husband, Finley?" The man turns

to Finn.

"Sir, I've told you. My name is—"

He waves his hand dismissively and Finn shuts his mouth. Whoever this man is, he is the boss.

"Unimportant. If you want to be a recruit, never talk back to the one in power. Do you understand?"

"Yes, sir."

"Good." Bossman leans back in his chair. "The cook has made a wonderful meal for tonight's meeting. That is, if you still wish to attend." He glares at the man sitting across from him.

"No, I don't," the boy says. "I told you. I am not in your crazy group where you hate on Magics."

Bossman raises his hands and sighs exasperatedly. "Again with the Magics! Why do you care about them, anyway? They have never done good! Think of the young Magic who killed her mother. And the one who ran away and started a summer camp! They are insane, unpredictable! They deserve to be locked in cages, for all I care."

"Why do you hate them?"

"Why *don't* you?"

Finn clears his throat. "I agree with you, sir. Magics are wild, unpredictable, animals." He sneaks a glance at me while he says this.

"Finally, someone understands!" Bossman slams his hands on the table.

They move on quickly after that.

Once it starts getting late, the meeting wraps up. My eyes are drooping and my feet have fallen asleep. Bossman's son stands from the table and leaves quietly.

"Who are you, my dear?" Bossman says to the air. He turns to me. "Are you a special girl?"

Finn snorts. "She's anything but."

Bossman sucks in a breath. "Yet you wish to have her hand in marriage?"

He shuffles a deck of cards. Finn suggested they play a game.

"Of course. Look at her," Finn says.

I try my best not to look uncomfortable.

"You're right," Bossman agrees. "She is quite beautiful."

I want to throw up.

"Magical."

My breath hitches in my throat. Finn seems just as surprised. His eyebrows shoot up to his hairline.

"What did you say, sir?" he asks.

"Her beauty is … magical." Bossman whips around to face Finn. "Why?" he asks skeptically.

"N-nothing," Finn mutters. As much as Finn doesn't care about me, we both know how dangerous it would be if anyone, especially a man like this, found out about my power. And not just dangerous for me.

"Julio." Bossman doesn't seem convinced. "Did Finley or the girl say anything peculiar while heading here?"

Julio raises his head and shakes it silently. "No, sir."

Bossman's lips twist into a sneer. "You're lying. Guards!"

Rows of armed men close in on every side of the dining room. They all wear the same black raven on their uniforms. I am really getting sick of seeing this raven.

Finn stands from his seat and tries to get to me, but there are too many soldiers. I wait in the middle of them, ready to singe their eyebrows if they get too close.

But that time never comes. I'm whisked off my feet and dragged away, Bossman shouting at the guards to follow and Finn yelling in annoyance. A strong grip around my waist as I'm flung over someone's shoulder leads me away from the commotion, back down the long corridors, and eventually, to the original doors of the castle.

"Run! You'll be safe!" the boy from earlier tells me as he removes the restraints from my wrists. He is about my age, fifteen, if not older, and has hair that's a deep brown. His black suit is wrinkled and covered in rips, as if he purposely tried to ruin it. He looks down at me with such adoration, it makes me want to ask why. Everyone else in my life has betrayed me, left me behind. Why is he different? Why does he care?

"Good luck." He nods to me, and before I sprint away, I ask, "What's your name?"

The boy thinks hard about this question. Finally, he says,

"Ameer. Ameer Domhnall."

"Ash Kave," I respond, and he smiles slightly. "Thank you." I smile too.

He hands me a slip of paper with an address. "Write. Promise me you'll write once you're safe."

I nod again and he urges, "Go!"

So I tuck the paper into my pocket and I go. I run and run and run until my legs get tired and my shoes are muddy and torn. I run and run until I can't run anymore, and just the thought of running aches me to the core. I sit in a dark alleyway and try desperately to stay awake, but it is too much. I close my eyes and lose consciousness.

"Ash!" Milo's harsh tone makes my eyes fly open.

I groan. My head feels awful. "Milo? What happened?"

He shrugs. He is standing over me. "You just passed out. I fed you some *meringue* and you came back to life." Milo winks. "Miraculously."

I can't tell Milo about my flashback. He knows some things about me, not all. I know he wants to keep me safe, and he thinks that means we have to know everything about each other, but this is something I don't have the courage to share with him. It is *my* past, *my* decision to keep it private or public. And right now, all I wish is for that to stay private.

"Miraculously," I repeat, and try to stand. My legs wobble.

Sunlight shines through the cracked-open windows of my cabin, revealing a beautiful day. Almost all of the campers are gathered in the mess hall. It is about breakfast time, after all.

Milo reaches out to support me.

"Race you to the mess hall?" he offers, trying his best not to laugh. "First one there gets the last slice of bacon." He wiggles his eyebrows at me.

I glare at him. He knows I can barely walk on my own. "You're on."

Soon after, I enjoy my extra piece of bacon.

* * *

"*Another* meeting with Everett?" I ask Milo, who walks briskly into the forest. He's teaching healing classes this afternoon, and he swears when he is by the forest, he can think the best. Therefore, the forest is Milo's workplace.

"He wants to hear the new story," Milo grumbles.

I make sure I am hearing him correctly. "Sorry, he wants to hear our new story? Are you forgetting, Milo, that we don't have a story?"

He whips around.

I stop dead in my tracks.

"We do, though, Ash. What happened yesterday, that holographic message, you think that doesn't deserve some recognition?"

I suddenly become very self-conscious. "You're not including the conversation between me and Finn, are you?"

He shrugs. "If you say I can."

I smile reluctantly. "Here's the deal. We put in the big headline 'Prince of Buit Captured,' and we talk about the events shown on the holographic image. But not a word about the marriage stuff. Cut that out."

"And you want Everett to read it?"

"A story is a story," I say. I'm really growing on this idea. The mortals of Buit will go crazy over this. "I *hate* Everett, but if it means we make money by having him read it, then do it."

"Wow." Milo pretends to be awed. "What a wonderful idea. I wish I would've thought of it."

I smirk. "Thanks."

Milo stifles his laugh as he grabs my hand and runs to the practice arena.

I never really understood why people asked if I wanted to hear the good news or the bad news first. Of course I wanted to hear the bad news. The good news could ease the tension of the bad news. Now, I'm sure I would've wanted to know the good news first.

What is that good news? you may be asking.

We have a story.

* * *

The next day, I meet Everett and Milo in the meeting room.

Everett looks bored. He leans on the meeting room table and waves his hand. Immediately, his bodyguard appears holding a platter of oysters. I glance at Milo.

Do we even serve oysters? I mouth.

Milo gives me the same puzzled look back.

"*Belittle a dit que tu avais une histoire, Ashlyn,*" says Everett. "*S'il te plaît, ne me fais pas penser que je perds mon temps.*"

Milo grunts. "Um, sir ..."

Everett rolls his eyes. When he speaks, his words are coated with a thick French accent, the syllables drowning in his voice. "Right. Of course. You said you 'ad a story?"

I raise my hands, almost dropping the piece of parchment I'm holding. "Wait—you speak *English?*"

The supervisor sighs. "Yes, Ashlyn, yes, I do. If it wasn't for Mr. Belittle 'ere, that would 'ave remained a secret." He glares at Milo sideways.

Okay ...

"Yeah, we have a story," Milo says quickly, trying to change the subject. I'm thankful for his people skills, because Everett's glare is lost as Milo begins to talk, turning into a look of curiosity.

When he's done explaining our idea, he glances at Everett, whose mouth is open wide.

"Ze Prince of Buit …" Everett's gray eyebrows knit together. "'e's been captured?"

I nod solemnly, but Everett isn't watching me.

Milo nods instead. He looks at me. "Really, Ash has more information on this topic," he says.

Everett's head snaps in my direction. "Ashlyn, tell me this story."

I swallow. Thanks a lot, Milo. "Right this way … sir."

* * *

Being alone with Everett Nightgale is definitely … intimidating, to say the least. I lead him to the woods, where we've set up our proof on billboards (Milo always has to go big), and wring my hands.

"Where is this evidence of yours?" Everett's eyes gleam mischievously as I lead him even deeper into the forest.

"Only a bit farther," I tell him. I'm painfully aware of my shaking hands. Never before have I been afraid of Everett Nightgale. Finn must've shaken me up.

I have this strange feeling I'm being watched. I figure it's just me being paranoid. *Finn doesn't know where you are*, I assure myself. *He made that clear with his message.* His words ring in my ears: *"You are meant to be my wife. We will live together, have a future together, a family. Just tell me your location."*

I whip around. Everett stares at me strangely.

"Yes?" he says.

I gulp. "Must have been hearing things."

He nods. He probably doesn't care. He just wants a story. With a story comes money. And money, to someone as greedy as Everett Nightgale, is everything.

Our footsteps muffled by the muddy ground because of rain two nights before, we trudge on to the practicing range.

Most of the equipment has been pushed out of the way. The stuff that isn't is used as decorations or stabilizers for the huge set-up designed by Milo. A banner tied to two targets that are nailed to trees hangs over our heads. It reads: NEW STORY! In front of the wooden cabin where we keep extra swords and armor is a huge billboard, marked with all sorts of ways to make our story enticing, interesting, and read-worthy. The billboard also has layout ideas for the newspaper. I'd be lying to you if I said this isn't normal. Milo has great decorating skills. Therefore, our newspaper is one of the best-selling newspapers in the kingdom—and that's saying something.

Everett chuckles. I forgot he was there. It startles me a bit.

"Always shoots for ze stars, he does," he mutters.

I let out a breath. Wind blows through the treetops, tickling the tall branches that reach up to the sky, as if trying to touch it. I love our forests and greenery. All of it is so natural. So uneven. So full of mistakes. But that is why I love it.

We stand there for a moment while Everett surveys the scene, studying Milo's work. It's peaceful. I keep quiet and busy myself by letting my mind trail off.

The sun sparkles as dark clouds begin to surround it. Wait. *Dark clouds?*

What is happening with the weather?

Sounds of footsteps, marching in unison, fill the forest.

"Get behind me," I hiss at Everett, who quickly obeys and cowers behind me. I draw my sword and hold it high, trying not to think about what it could be marching into my forest.

Footsteps thunder in the forest. It sounds like multiple people, maybe an army.

What—

A group of teenagers emerges from the shadows, all wearing green T-shirts that read CAMP SERENITY and then their names.

A girl named Xelma steps forward.

"Leader Viggo wishes to speak with you," she says, her intimidating brown eyes looking down at me despite the fact that I'm taller than her.

My mouth turns down into an expression of disgust. "And why would I speak with her?"

Xelma sticks her sword into the muddy ground. "Leader's orders."

I run my tongue over my teeth, contemplating this.

Elysian has always hated me. She has good reason to, after all. But why would she want to speak with me unless …

"You have information on the missing prince," I say, realizing.

The boy to the left of Xelma nods solemnly. "Some say he is facing torture, the only fate worse than death."

I gulp. *I wouldn't put it past Finn.*

Everett steps out from behind me. "I am ze supervizor of zis camp, and if Ashlyn 'ere turns down the opportunity to speak with ze leader of your little group, I would be more zan 'appy to."

When the boy on the left of Xelma speaks, his words are covered in an accent I can't decipher. "Sorry, she specifically asked for 'Ashlyn Kave.'"

I sigh. What do I have to lose? Finn is back and trying to track me, he's stolen the prince, my enemy sworn has information on it, and if I don't go, I'll be prodded by Everett with questions on why I didn't (not to mention most of those questions will most likely include the words "ridiculous" or "incompetent").

"Fine," I say, crossing my arms. "But can I bring someone?"

Xelma sighs. She studies the sword in my hand before her eyes dart to the ground. "Very well," she says finally. "So long as it's not this fool." She raises her arm and points to Everett, who is too interested in scowling at the kids flanking Xelma to notice what she's said.

"Trust me." I glance back at Everett and lean down so only she can hear me. "I've got better friends than him."

CHAPTER 4

ELYSIAN

"Are you sure this is the best idea?" Sage asks me nervously, pacing the mess hall.

Sorin leans back in his chair and rests his feet on the table. "C'mon, Sagey, Ash won't hurt you."

She brings her hands down on one of the tables. "I told you to stop calling me Sagey!"

It's been a day or so since my incident, and Sorin has developed a new stupid nickname for Sage because of her maturity: Sagey. I think it's hilarious. Sagey—I mean, Sage, not so much.

Every time someone calls her that or laughs when Sorin makes fun of her while using that nickname, she'll send them an ice-cold glance with her emerald eyes that tells them to shut up or be tested even more during her class. (And, trust me, her class is hard when Sage *doesn't* hate you.)

Luckily, since I'm her best friend, it's different for me. I can call her whatever I want and get away with a warning—a pop of her knuckles that tells me just enough not to talk about her new nickname for the rest of the night.

"Sunshine's right," I say, referring to Sorin, and Sage's smile is distinguishable from behind a curtain of red. "How bad could she be?"

"You don't know her." Sage's smile vanishes. "At least, not anymore. Everything is chaos when it comes to that girl. Remind me why we're telling her stuff about something this important again?"

Sorin chuckles. "Because the boss said to. And you're just mad because you hate her."

"We all do!" Sage sends an apologetic look to me. "At least, we all *did.*"

It's important, a voice in the back of my still-throbbing head says. *The prince is in danger.*

"Trust me," I tell her. "You *do* trust me, don't you?"

She looks up at me through her eyelashes. "Of course I do. But … I don't understand you. She's our rival. You know this, right?"

I sit up straighter. Even Sorin looks slightly uncomfortable now. "Of course I do."

Sage starts to say something, maybe along the lines of "Why are you doing this then?" but a group of our campers, hauling a dark-haired, annoyed-looking girl, taller than all of them, interrupts her.

My breath stops in my throat. That girl …

She is the girl from my wacky dream. The same brown-haired, firebending, powerful little girl, except she isn't a little girl. She is older, yet she has the same face. The same face as her mother.

"Hey, Sagey, check if she's breathing, why don't you?" Sorin says with a smirk as he studies me.

Sage smacks my arm. "Focus," she hisses.

The campers shuffle forward and almost drop her into the seat. Her jaw flexes as she is plopped at one of the tables. Sorin's relaxed expression turns to a glare as his eyes settle on her, and Sage isn't much better. Her hands curl into fists as she stops her pacing.

"All right." The girl's eyes dart around the mess hall, no doubt thinking several things about our sense of decoration. Well, my sense of decoration. "What do you want, Viggo?"

A bad taste fills my mouth as I realize I haven't prepared. What to start with? "I've lost my memory and I can't remember my best friends, much less my sworn enemy," or, "The prince of our kingdom is missing and I've happened to get a message through a dagger randomly strapped to my thigh with information that's probably useless." Yeah, neither of those sounds good.

"Well?" she demands.

"Missing," I say finally. "The prince is missing. And I think I know where he might be."

Something flickers in her eyes, but it's gone in a matter of seconds, replaced with boredom. "And? I think I know where he is, too, and my information is probably much more accurate than yours."

The cracking of Sage's knuckles echoes in the empty mess hall. "You knew about this?"

The girl smirks, mirroring Sorin's usual expression. "Of course, Jobbs. What do you think the headline of the mortal newspaper is?"

Sage told me Camp Havoc manages the mortal newspapers, and uses that money to fund their camp. Honestly, it's a smart idea.

"Right," Sorin says, resting his elbows on the table. "So, give us your stuff if you know so much."

The girl sighs. "You called me here; you give yours to me first."

Sage rolls her eyes so hard that I'm afraid they are going to pop out of their sockets. "Stop being difficult, Ashlyn, and give us what you got."

Ashlyn.

"I told you, *Sagey*, it's Ash."

Ash, then.

"Can we just get this over with?" I say, breathless, still in awe that this girl is the *one*. Not *the one*, I mean, like, the one from my dream. Yeah.

Ash flicks her eyes over to me. Her scowl deepens. "Well, of course. You've never really been one to stay in one place, huh, Viggo?"

Sage puts one of her arms in front of me defensively. "Who the hell do you think you are, talking about that? You have no right—"

"It was a long time ago, Sagey. Calm down." But she smiles. Ash loves the circles she's making us run in.

I have a sudden urge to run my fingers through my hair.

Sage steps on my foot as if reading my mind, as if she knows I am about to lose it. Ash really makes me mad. So ... why is she so *interesting?*

"This has been such a friendly reunion," Sorin interrupts, his eyes moving from Sage to Ash, "but can we get to the subject at hand, the reason we called this annoying tree here?"

"I'm not a tree," Ash says, crossing her arms across her chest defiantly. "Just because I'm tall and you're short doesn't mean—"

"We get it already," Sage groans. "Did you bring your minion with you?"

"He got lost in your huge gift shop. Quite selfish to have a whole gift shop dedicated to your greatness, wouldn't you say?" She smiles bitterly and shouts something I can't understand into the quad. A second later, a tall guy with dark hair and light brown skin appears in the mess hall, sitting in a seat next to Ash. He catches my eye and smiles. Obviously, he's a nice guy. I have no memory of him.

"We're here because we know where Ameer is," the boy says. "He's-"

"In the castle dungeons." I look at him expectantly. "Is that what you were going to say?"

He opens his mouth, but Ash sends him a glare and he says quickly, "Yes, actually. He's in the dungeons."

"Okay, we don't need a test to know you're hiding something," Sorin says, raising his eyebrows, suspicious. "What were you really going to say, Belittle, before she harassed you?"

Ash's jaw clenches harder and her fists begin to curl at her sides. "I don't harass anybody, Torsney. You've got me mixed up with someone else."

"You mean a terrible person?" Sage narrows her eyes at Ash. "It's easy to get confused when comparing the two, you know."

"Stop!" Belittle cleared his throat. "Just stop. Nobody harassed me, and it's my decision if I want to share that with you."

"Well, technically, it's not," I say, shooting a glare in their direction. "You don't have a choice. Right now, at this very moment, the prince is being tortured in a cell with no food or water and no one to call for help. Do you really want to be the one responsible for his death if we don't do anything?"

"We're going to do something," Sage says, a smug look on her face, "but only if we have the correct information."

Belittle crosses his arms, just like half of the people in the room. "Why are you so bent out of shape over something I didn't even say? It's fine. He's in the dungeons. End of discussion."

"*I* say when it's the end of the discussion, Belittle," I snarl.

He frowns. He obviously isn't enjoying the way this talk is going.

"Right," Ash says sarcastically, "since you're a great big leader now. Milo is my junior leader, just like Sagey here for you. He has just as much a say as I do."

"So none at all?"

"What happened to the *serenity* in Camp Serenity?" Ash grits her teeth. "I thought you were all over peace and love and kindness and helping, are you not?"

"Great, so we know he's in the dungeons," Sorin cuts in, nervously looking at Ash and me. "But in which dungeons?"

Sage opens her mouth, but Milo Belittle begins to talk.

"In the dungeons of room 106, closest to the castle," he says matter-of-factly, and everyone in the room gasps.

"What?" I ask.

Ash stifles a laugh. "Gods, are you braindead? Everyone knows the story of room 106. Except for stuck-up 'leaders' who think they're too important to learn the story. That explains it."

Sage shoots daggers at Ash with her eyes before turning to me. "The story of room 106 is ancient. It starts back three thousand years ago, when Buit was founded. Jackson Ramirez Buit, the founder, stumbled across it after finding land for the castle. No one knows how it was built, or who was inside it when Buit went through the door and was slaughtered, but everyone who has lived in Buit all their lives knows it's haunted. Rumored to have spirits whispering in your ears, possessing innocent bystanders, killing and torturing tourists. It's been fabled as the biggest death spot in Buit. If you want to die, head there and hopefully your body will be found before you rot."

When she pauses, I say, "That doesn't sound too bad. They're just rumors."

"Oh, you don't know the half of it," she starts. "What's not a rumor's the fact that it moves. The building is carried everywhere by the spirits that haunt it, making it impossible to be found more than once. Most people who go inside and make it out alive find themselves halfway across the country."

"So … how are we supposed to find him?" Panic settles in my stomach. If we aren't able to find the prince in the given amount of time, exactly ten days from today, he will be dead.

"Exactly." Sorin brushes strands of his blond hair out of his face. "That's what makes it the worst place to hide someone, the moving part. If the prince survives, and we are able to make it to the house in time for the deadline, who's to say the building won't disappear or the spirits won't kill us the moment we step inside?"

"He wouldn't do that." Ash speaks quietly, but everyone in the mess hall can still hear her.

"What?" Sage lifts her head. "You know who captured him?"

"Of course," Ash snaps. "I know things."

"Well," I start pointedly, "who is it?"

She hesitates. She moves hair out of her face. "Why would I tell you that?"

I huff. "Stop being difficult and tell us who's behind all this, because we don't have time to fight! You realize if we don't save him before it's too late, he could die? He could be beaten until he's dead. He could be burned to death. He could have drowned. There are so many ways he could die or be tortured right now and yet you're leading us on then somehow being quiet again."

Something like fear swept over Ash's features, but it is quickly replaced with a scowl. "Finn Brocker. His name is Finn Brocker, and he wants to marry me."

We let that hang in the air. Only one word crosses my mind during this brief silence: *Huh?*

"Where have I heard that before?" Sorin is first to break the silence. "Isn't he in, like, a gang or something?"

Ash takes a deep breath. "Yes. He's a known fugitive, wanted for killing several innocent villagers."

"And … he wants to marry you?" Sage's voice is quiet when she speaks. I was sure all of us were thinking the same thing: *This is insane.*

"Yes." It is Milo who answers her this time. "It's strange, yes, but true. We want to take the prince from him, we really do. But Ash here is the only one who knows Finn's real potential. If you're going off on a rescue mission to save him, you'll need her to come along."

"Gross!" I shout without thinking. Sure, I sound like a whiny little girl, but I can barely stand Ash while she is several feet away from me at my own camp. How can I deal with her when she's right next to me in the wilderness?

59

"It really is," Sage agrees, and her face contorts into a disgusted look of her own. "But … we have to, Lys."

I suddenly notice how quiet Ash is. She hasn't complained at all about this arrangement. Instead, she is staring down at the floor while twirling her sword, most likely without noticing. I have only known her for a few minutes, but I have figured out how important the prince is to her. Either he is someone important in her past or a role model, I don't know. But her admiration is obvious.

"Fine," I grumble, remembering the other people in the room. "So long as the little gremlin stays in her own spot. And no one else is coming."

Both Milo and Sorin break out in strings of retorts and complaints about how it isn't fair we get to go and they don't.

"You need someone to support the humor in your group," Sorin says, looking at me and Sage reproachfully. "We know Sagey can't do it since she's … well, as dry as her name. Not to mention Little Miss Leader over here *never* makes jokes. You need me!"

"And you need someone to keep peace," Milo offers. He leans forward on the table. "That's my power. Keeping people calm. Plus, I'm Ash's best friend and her junior leader."

"Exactly," I say. "You need someone at *your* camp to keep order and peace."

"Yet you're bringing your junior leader," Sorin mumbles.

"That's because our campers can handle themselves," Sage

retorts, rather harshly. She turns to Ash. "Can yours?"

Ash's fists curl at her sides. *The zombie lives.* "Yeah, actually," she says. "I know you think we're all hooligans, but really, my campers are probably more civilized than yours. I mean, at least they don't force people in for a 'discussion.'"

"Are you *really* trying to start another fight?" Sorin asks, his face turning red.

"Your little girlfriend started it!" Ash shoots back.

Milo looks frantically from Ash to Sorin. He rests his hand on the table and says, "*Stop.*"

His voice is amplified through the mess hall as if he is talking through a megaphone. The vibrations in his voice seem to crawl up my skin and enter my brain slowly. I instantly begin to relax. I watch Ash, Sage, and Sorin do the same, but it is like they are doing so in slow motion. I feel completely calm.

Once Milo removes his hand from the table, things begin to move normally again. He looks around the room, triumphant.

Sage talks first. "What—what did you do?"

"I told you," he states calmly as if this happens every day. (With Ash there, it probably does.) "My power."

Wind whistles past my ear. Sage had informed me of my power: controlling the weather and wind. Sometimes, though, the wind would stray out of my control and become in tune with my emotions. It was hard to decipher the wind—and even harder to decipher my emotions—but, on occasion, it made sense. This was a calming wind. I barely know my emotions, but I know my wind. And that ... well, I have yet to determine if that was a good thing or a bad thing.

"Your power?" Sorin grins like a maniac. "And I thought I was cool with being able to control sunlight. Making people feel high— now that's a power."

Milo glowers at him.

"We don't have time for this," Sage reasons, and all of our heads whip toward her. "We need to get to the prince. Our deadline is in ten days, and we've spent the whole morning arguing about the correct information and the incorrect information. We have it now, so let's hit the road."

The boys lean forward eagerly in their seats.

I sigh. "Fine. You two can come."

I'm pretty sure Milo and Sorin's shouts of triumph can be heard on the other side of the forest.

CHAPTER 5

ELYSIAN

I can feel Ash's stare on me as I pack my bags.

We have been separated into groups for packing, since Ash and Milo needed to go back to their camp to get their things and all of us agreed it would be safer if we went together (I didn't trust Ash's comment about her campers not being hooligans and dangerous; sue me). Unfortunately, Sorin, Milo, and Sage also agree that the leaders go with each other and they stay in a group of three.

I believe Sage's exact words were: "Look, I don't want to be with the witch herself either, but this is Sorin and Milo's decision, not mine. Now, go, run along. You wouldn't want to show her you're scared, would you?"

And now, Ash stands in my doorway, leaning against the frame, studying me with those harsh gold-speckled hazel eyes that tell everything yet nothing about her at the same time.

"Can you hurry?" she asks me impatiently, tapping her foot on the wood floors.

"I *can*," I growl, "but what's the fun in that?"

Ash rolls her eyes and sighs. I grunt as I shove clothes into my suitcase. I am going as fast as I can. How silly of me to think she actually notices that while she is watching me attentively.

"You can occupy yourself in a way other than staring at me, you know," I say, and Ash shifts uncomfortably.

"In what way?" she retorts. "It's not like your angelic campers are going to appreciate me walking around everywhere, spreading my hooligan germs in their faces." I feel my cheeks turn red. It is obvious that she enjoys having power over me. I feel extremely stupid as I try to recall why we are enemies in the first place. Rivaling camps. But why?

"You look like something's causing you pain," Ash blurts, raising an eyebrow. "Like you're trying to think of something. Are you braindead, Viggo? Because that would explain it."

"I'm not braindead," I grumble, shoving the last piece of clothing I have into my tiny, cramped suitcase.

Ash looks down at me, her features contorting into confusion. I can practically see the gears turning in her brain through her eyes.

"You don't have to know everything about me, *Ashlyn*," I add harshly.

I pick up my suitcase and extend the handle so I can roll it instead. Gods, with almost all of the clothing I own squeezed into one suitcase, it is definitely hard to carry.

A hand pushes me to the wall. It catches me off guard. I drop my suitcase, which makes a loud thumping as the plastic wheels hit the wood floor.

"You will never," Ash hisses, her voice quiet, "call me Ashlyn. Do you understand that?"

With every word, the wall behind me grows hotter. Because I am worried about a fire hazard, I nod. But only grudgingly. Ash runs her tongue over her teeth, not believing me, but letting it go. She removes her hand from the wall, and I am free to go. Not that I need her permission. I could've gotten out perfectly fine by myself. Definitely.

She follows close behind me. So close, in fact, that I can feel her hot breath on my neck as we shuffle out of my cabin and trek through the woods to her camp.

"Where are you going?" she asks me after stopping suddenly. I keep going. It isn't my fault I have amnesia and can't remember where her camp is.

"The entrance is right here." Ash motions to a wooden sign that reads CAMP HAVOC.

"Oh, right," I say, like I still remembered where it was. "You really should put that sign in a better place."

"Why would I do that," Ash says with a mischievous glint in her eyes, "when we're not looking to be seen?"

As if on cue, the sunshine shines through the trees, like the entrance to heaven. I raise my eyebrows. *Impressive, but it'll probably be like hell.* I let Ash lead me through the entrance. And, honestly, I am surprised by what I see.

Cabins, all different sizes and shapes, line the edge of the camp. All are decorated differently and uniquely in their own way. Campers talk by the huge bonfire with jagged rocks to the left of us. Right in front of us, a wooden mess hall with several doors around the rectangular shape is filled with campers enjoying lunch. To our right is a string of buildings with different labels, written in a language I am not able to decipher.

Ash notices my confusion. "Our campers come from all around the globe, but most come from France. Therefore, we write most of our labels in French."

"And if you don't speak French?" I ask pointedly.

She rubs her arm guiltily. It occurs to me that she herself might not be able to speak French.

"Milo will translate if you need him to, but there are English labels right under the French ones."

My eyes shift to the mess hall. "It's lunchtime?"

"Yeah, I guess." She shrugs. "Although, sometimes when the campers get bored, they'll get a snack from the mess hall."

"And the cabins?"

Ash follows my gaze to the wooden structures, smiling at their imperfections. "I designed them. Great, aren't they?"

"Chaotic, more like," I mutter.

"That's what makes them great, Viggo."

She begins to make her way to the first cabin on the right. Her cabin. It is decorated strangely, not like the others. I guess that's what I should've expected while being here. Flames are painted along the bottom of her cabin, and the door has an inscription of her name: *Ash Kave.* The roof is painted black, and on the windowsill is a leather scabbard.

"Home sweet home," she sighs, and opens the door to an absolute pigsty.

Her bed is a mess, unmade and turned at a weird angle on her bed frame. Sheets are dropped on the floor as if they are meant to be there. A black couch sits in the corner, helplessly drowned by a mountain of clothes. Her nightstand holds a glasses case and a book titled *Kingdom of Buit: The Origins.* Two wooden doors to the left side of the room are open, showing off a destroyed closet.

And that smell.

"Gods, did you just eat beef in here for weeks or something?" I ask, plugging my nose. "It smells like a dead cow."

Ash puts her nose in the air and sniffs. "It does? Huh." She shrugs. "Never noticed."

She turns away from me and begins digging through the clothes in her closet. I can feel her smirk, even if I can't see her do it. Her long brown hair covers her face like a curtain, giving me the perfect opportunity to notice the tattoo on her back. A black-and-white fire.

Fuego y Luz.

Spanish.

Fire—Light.

I don't know how I understand it. Maybe I spoke Spanish before I lost my memory. Maybe it is just good intuition.

"You have a nice tattoo," I find myself saying.

Ash whips around. She pulls a ratty T-shirt over the black tank top she was wearing, hiding the tattoo.

"Don't talk about it." Her eyes harden. "Don't talk about it," she repeats.

I try my best to straighten things up while she digs for clothes probably lost forever in that disgusting pile, but it is no use. Every time I touch something, Ash scolds me not to without looking. I don't know how she does that. It's like she has eyes in the back of her head.

Finally, she finishes. She stuffs the last of her cow-smelling clothes into a suitcase with so many holes that it can be confused for Swiss cheese, and we exit her cabin. She takes long strides down the lawn, and the fact that her legs are long makes it hard for me to catch up.

"You're mad at me because of a tattoo?" I ask her, breathless, as we enter the forest. We—well—*she* turns at a clearing of trees.

"I never said I was mad at you," she shoots back, her voice cold but steady.

"Yeah, you didn't have to say it." I cross my arms.

She begins to walk faster.

"Where are they meeting us?"

"Right outside camp, on the main road," I answer.

She turns around. "There is no main road outside of your camp."

"Oops." I narrow my eyes at her. "What's with you and that tattoo?"

Ash's jaw clenches. "Why do you need to know?"

"Because," I reply stubbornly.

"You're just nosy, huh?"

"Yep. Now tell me."

"And why would I do that?"

"Fire. Light."

She gulps. "You speak Spanish?" she asks me.

"Sure," I respond casually. "I know more about you than you want me to, Ash. Whether you like it or not, that tattoo is important to you, which means it has something to do with something you're passionate about."

"What happened?" She says it so suddenly I almost lose my balance.

"What?"

"What happened? The Elysian Viggo I know would never say these things. She would never lie. She would never demand this from me." She tries to hide it, but her eyebrows knit together ever so slightly. "So what happened?"

69

"I hit my head," I say cautiously. "Went swimming, got disoriented, hit my head on a rock. Amnesia."

"Amnesia?"

I clear my throat. I am not liking the way this conversation is now pinned on me. "They're meeting us near the entrance," I tell her quietly.

I trudge on. Ash seems to be stuck, for the next time I see her, I am looking back at her as she stands in the woods, her emotions guarded. I motion for her to hurry before heading out the entrance of Camp Serenity.

Leaving my camp.

My campers.

My home.

* * *

"About time," Sorin says to me as I meet up with him, Milo, and Sage about three yards from the entrance. "We thought you got lost or something."

Milo cranes his neck over Sorin's shoulder, though he is already several inches taller than him.

"She's coming," I promise him. He smiles.

Sage raises an eyebrow as Sorin wraps one of his arms around my shoulders and drags me away from Milo. Sage follows, protesting.

"You got lost, Lyssy?" Sorin asks, a smirk plastered onto his pale face.

"Why do you say that?" I answer, trying my best to act as if I don't care.

"You can't get involved with her, Lys," Sage says, her eyebrows creasing. "Ash ... she's not a nice person. She's your enemy. She's our enemy. She's insane. Do you see the problem?"

"I get it," I say, removing Sorin's arm from my shoulders. "She's my enemy. But does she have to be?"

"If you have a death wish, then no," Sorin replies.

We all turn around when the sound of leaves crunching can be heard behind us. Ash has pulled her hair into a knot. Her suitcase is covered in leaves and mud. I wonder what she has done to look like this.

When her hazel eyes shift over to mine, I instantly look away. What is happening to me?

"Where are we headed?" Ash calls to Sage. Her eyes leave mine, and I am able to breathe again.

"Room 106," Sage responds hesitantly. "Unless you have a better idea?"

"Well, how are we supposed to get there when it shifts?" Milo asks. The two start to walk over to us.

"He's got a point," Sorin notes, glancing at Sage expectantly. Sage shoots a glare back.

"I know what I'm doing," she snaps, mostly at Sorin. The sun hits her red ponytail, turning it to fire. Sorin steps back, intimidated but grinning. "I've created a chart of the appearances and disappearances of room 106. So long as we stay on schedule, we'll be able to make it there in time."

"Of course you made a chart," Sorin mutters, laughing under his breath. I smack his arm, but I, too, am trying to contain my laughter.

"We only have ten days," Milo points out.

Ash nods her head in agreement. "What happens if we don't make it in time? I mean, room 106 is all the way across the kingdom."

"Trust me on this," Sage argues. "Milo's right; we don't have much time. But if we're able to stay on this path"—she takes out a yellowed map of the kingdom, scribbled on with a red pen, from her backpack—"we'll be able to make it."

"Yeah, that might not be that easy," Ash says. "The whole kingdom knows I'm a Magic, and they're out to get me. Not to mention the whole royal guard knows I'm a threat so they want to kill me, too—"

"You never told me this!" Milo protests. "When did that happen?"

"Now is not the time for questions," Sage says. "Just stick to the plan and you'll be fine, Ashlyn."

Ash moves some hair, stuck to her forehead because of the hot sun, out of her face. "Why does everyone keep calling me Ashlyn? It's

Ash!"

"Hate to ruin this pleasant conversation you've got going on, but you might want to hold that thought, Fire Girl," Sorin interrupts. "We've gotta go."

I follow his gaze to a few hundred feet from where we stand.

Guards.

Royal guards flank the main passage to get to the village part of the kingdom.

Sage curses under her breath. "I forgot. The royal guards always guard the village. If you're here with us and they're after you, we can forget about saving the prince."

One of the guards turns around. Sorin pushes me and Sage back against the brick wall that supports the entrance gates. Milo does the same to Ash.

Sorin raises a hand and waves. The guard glances at him suspiciously.

Sorin is about as tall as the guard, if not taller, and his shoulders are broader. Next to him, the guard looks like a kid.

"You boys headed to the village?" the guard asks, raising an eyebrow at Milo. I note how he doesn't do the same to Sorin. My fists clench at my sides.

My breathing is heavy as I try to stay as still as possible. Sage's chest rises and falls much slower than mine, and I can tell she is trying to calm herself.

"Yes, sir," Milo responds, dipping his head. Sage informs me that it is a common courtesy to bow to guards who work for the kingdom, out of respect.

The guard clenches his jaw. "Fine. Go ahead. But surely you won't mind if we check your pockets?"

The question … it isn't directed at Milo *and* Sorin. It was directed at only Milo.

"That seems rather unnecessary, doesn't it?" Sorin tries reasoning with the guard, but he just glances at him before pulling out his sword and starting toward Milo.

Ash steps forward. I notice this out of the corner of my eye. "Ash—"

Sage slaps her hand over my mouth. My interruption distracts the guard. He whips his head toward the brick wall, noticing me and Sage backed against it. He grunts, his lip curling. Before he can do anything, Ash swipes at his ankles with her sword.

The guard cries out in pain and drops to the floor.

Ash now stands in front of Milo, holding her sword level with her chest. Sorin unsheathes his own weapon and holds it at his side, ready to strike. The other guards turn around as if just noticing their fellow guard is missing. One of the guards notices Ash, Milo, and Sorin, and storms forward, raising his sword.

He makes the mistake of striking at Ash first.

She lights her hand on fire and heat begins to climb up the hilt, then the blade, turning it into a white-hot deadly weapon. The guard makes his first strike, but Ash ducks out the way. His blade clangs against the cement.

Sage unsheathes her dagger. She stops me before I can join the fight.

"You may have your fighting reflexes, but you can't fight. Not when you have no memory of what you should do."

So I stay against the wall, watching Sage join the party. Even Milo pulls out his weapon and steps from behind Ash. He begins fighting another guard, one-on-one.

I scan the fights.

Sorin snaps his fingers and sunlight follows the guard, trying to stay in his eyes. He runs around, trying to lose the sunlight, all thought of fighting Sorin lost. Sage stretches out her hand, and instantly, vines growing on the walls surrounding the guards spring to life and attack the guard she is fighting, making him use his energy to cut the vines away. Ash is using her sword instead of her power, slashing wherever skin shows. The guard she is fighting, somehow taller than her, screams in agony as he clutches his abdomen where his newest wound has appeared. Blood begins to stream onto the concrete. Ash just smiles and goes to help Milo with his guard.

I feel so useless. Sure, I have lost my memory, but I can still fight. The sword I have balanced correctly in my hand. It feels right when I use it. I understand Sage wants to protect me, but didn't I teach her everything she knew?

"Hey, Lyssy!" Sorin calls. "Could use a clean-up!"

I smile. Maybe I am useful.

I blow air out of my mouth and a huge gust of wind pushes the guards back, all the way to the other side of the village.

Ash wipes her hands on her shorts and sheathes her sword.

"What a nice way to start a quest," she mutters, flicking blood off her cheek.

"Isn't it?" Sage says, letting her hands relax at her sides so the vines become limp again.

Sorin snaps his fingers once more so the sunlight is directed toward us. Not directly on us, but providing enough light that we will be able to stay warm.

Milo closes his eyes as he calms himself. When he opens his eyes again, he looks completely at peace.

"Certainly a way to get us excited, huh?" Sorin offers. He motions for me to hurry up, and we head straight through the gates to the village without any trouble.

Leaving the first round of blood on the floor.

It won't be the last.

CHAPTER 6

SORIN

"Sorin, can you get the sun away from my eyes?" Elysian complains, covering her eyes with her hand.

After a few hours of walking, we sit under an awning that belongs to a little bakery in the village. The castle is out in the middle of nowhere—an extra precaution for intruders in the village. Room 106, unfortunately, is right next to the castle. Several miles away from any civilization. A lot of walking. And a lot of sunlight.

I sigh. "This is the third time today, Lyssy."

She just smiles sweetly. Next to her, Ash studies her face and grimaces. "Ugh, you two are too nice."

Ash stands and wipes her hands on her shorts. She has been doing so since when we fought the guards, as if she is scared something from the guards is stuck to her hands.

"I'm going inside to see if I can get some food," Ash decides.

I snap my fingers, and the sun seems to turn in a different direction. Most might think of this as cool, as amazing, as astonishing (I have gotten that one a lot), and it is, but after a while I get bored of it. So I can control sunlight. And? I don't have a *cool* power like Sage's, where she can control the literal earth. I can't breathe and start a tornado like Lyssy. I can't light someone on fire like Ash (well, technically, I *could if I really wanted to*), and I can't make people feel like they are high (shout-out to Milo).

Speaking of Milo—where is he? The baker hadn't allowed us to go inside, but Milo used his powers and the baker welcomed him with open arms. He has been in there for what feels like years, but I know it is only an hour depending on the direction of the sun. Or, what the direction used to be before I changed it.

"Thank you," Lyssy says pleasantly.

"Hey, Sagey, you alive?" I turn my body so I am facing Sage. Her face is buried in that map she made, her ponytail hanging over her shoulder. She wears a forest-green tank top that exposes her collarbone, and black shorts. She looks … well, as good as an uptight, earthbending nerd can.

"I'm fine, Sorin," she hisses back sharply. She lifts her head. "What do you need?"

While she is distracted, I take the opportunity to sneak a look at her map. It is really accurate. It even has all the fields and empty plains the royal family just use as a place to host their beauty pageants.

Sage jerks it back.

"What, scared I'll find a flaw?" I ask her, smirking without noticing.

"You can't even find your own flaws, much less mine," she

retorted. "So, no, I'm not *scared*."

Ash returns a minute later, looking annoyed.

"I swear, I'm going to—"

"Well, you're a little bundle of sunshine, aren't you?" I mutter. "I'm guessing it didn't go so well?"

"That little bakery owner thinks he knows everything," she says angrily, her hands curling into fists. I can practically see the heat radiating off of her. "'Oh, yeah, you're that little delinquent Magic who ki—'" She stops herself suddenly and stares ahead, at the horizon. Ash clears her throat. "Point is, Milo had to use his power again, and then that insignificant, rude *jerk* kicked me out again!"

"Oh, boo-hoo," Lyssy mumbles, messing with her hair.

I snort.

Ash turns to Lyssy. "Did you say something?"

Sensing a fight, I say, "Is there air-conditioning in there?"

"Yeah," Ash responds. She narrows her eyes at the bakery door. "You can try staying in there, but that ever-so-pleasant baker seems to be discriminatory toward Magics." She says it bitterly.

"Probably just hates you," I answer, and Sage stifles a laugh.

She rolls her eyes as I step into the bakery, but at least she isn't threatening anyone anymore.

* * *

Ash is right; it is air-conditioned in the bakery.

The cold hits me like a brick wall. I stumble back after stepping inside and use that moment of being off balance to quickly survey my surroundings.

Two wooden shelves sit in the left corner, stacked with different candies of all sorts of colors. Several stools are stacked next to those shelves. The actual check-out counter is just plain light wood, and under the counter, assortments of different kinds of bags of goodies sit on hanging shelves. To the right of me is a whole shelf of bread, and next to that is another shelf of cookies, cakes, and cupcakes. Behind the counter, Milo talks animatedly with the baker, an old man with saggy cheeks, gray and not much hair, dark skin, and a relaxed look on his face that tells me Milo had definitely used his power.

"Sorin!" Milo says, acknowledging the presence of another person in the room. "I thought you were Ash. Knowing her, she'd probably come back in here and try to—"

"Not that girl again." The old man's face twists into a disgusted expression. When he speaks, I notice a slight resemblance between his and Milo's voice.

"No, she's not here," Milo tells the baker, something like fear flashing over his features. "This is Sorin. He's also a Magic, but a peaceful one. He controls the sunlight."

Funny, says a voice in the back of my head. *No one's ever called me peaceful.*

The baker doesn't say anything, but he nods at me. I nod back. Milo motions for me to sit on the empty stool next to him. I raise one leg over the counter, and then the other until it is only a short distance to the stool. Not needing to move my legs much since I am taller, I plop down in the chair.

"I was just telling Mr. Dupont here about our plans to rescue the prince," Milo informs me.

I glance at him, one thought visible in my eyes: *Is he trustworthy?*

Milo nods.

"Yeah," I say, turning toward the baker, Mr. Dupont. "My friend, Lyssy—I mean, Elysian, is leading it. Along with Ash."

"You're telling me you're letting *that* girl lead this little trip of yours?" Mr. Dupont looks horrified.

"Well, she's"—the word *nice* lingers on my tongue for a minute—"not as bad as she seems."

Mr. Dupont raises a disbelieving eyebrow.

"Really," I argue.

He sighs. "Mr. Belittle was telling me you need a chaperone."

I look at Milo inquisitively. "He was?"

Milo looks back at me and smiles sheepishly.

"He was." Mr. Dupont looks bored as his eyes study me. "And I would be more than happy to chaperone your field trip, but I have my bakery to run. The villagers rarely come here anymore, but there is one lady who comes every week. Her name is Evelyn. A very sweet woman." His eyes soften as he talks about her. "I can't let Evelyn down."

"Oh, that's fine," I say quickly. I honestly don't want this old man on our trip. "We really aren't in need of a chaperone. We appreciate your hospitality, though."

Mr. Dupont opens his mouth to say something else, but screams sound from outside.

I stand from my stool, fast. Milo does the same. Mr. Dupont looks from Milo to me nervously.

I fling myself over the counter as the door flies open.

Ash's head pops inside. Her eyes are wide and her hands are shaking. "We have to go." Her words are rushed. This is serious.

I hurry out the door, Milo following close behind.

Several rows of guards stand only about ten feet from where we are. They have weapons, dozens of weapons strapped to their armor. It won't be long before they spot us: the group of Magics with a known fugitive. We have to move.

Before I know what I'm doing, I grab Sage's wrist and run. Ash, Milo, and Lyssy follow close behind. Sounds of shouts and guns being fired echo in the distance. I look back as one of the royal guards throws a bomb at the bakery, probably assuming there are more of us there. It goes off in a matter of seconds.

I turn back, tears stinging my vision. But I can't stop running now, not when the guards have realized what power they have.

Sage and I run in harmony. We both realize how important this is. We can't be caught. Not if we want to rescue the prince. Not if we want to make it out alive. Not if we want to make it home sooner or later.

Finally, the guards' shouts fade, and we're able to rest. Fields of grass surround us. Sage and I sit under the shade of an apple tree.

"Dammit," Sage mutters. "I forgot the royal guards do annual inspections of the village, just to make sure everything's all right."

I nod, pretending I'm listening.

I feel ready to throw up.

Mr. Dupont was in the bakery at the time of the explosion.

He died.

He died in his bakery.

He let Evelyn down.

CHAPTER 7

SAGE

I lean against the tree trunk, letting the smell of apples fill my nostrils. Even though most of them are dry and withering with no one here to pick them and keep them out of the sun, the fresh smell is still in the air.

I laugh, mostly out of hysteria. We've escaped the royal guard not once, but twice, and both times without a scratch.

I look down at my map, curled in my left hand. That is when I noticed Sorin's long, narrow fingers closed around my wrist. His fingers are warm, whether from the heat or the running, I don't know. And I shouldn't care.

His chest rises and falls. Remembering where I am, I wrench my hand back. It seems as if all my blood rushes to my head when I do. The feeling is quickly gone, replaced with one of terror.

Sorin stares over my shoulder at the map I quickly skim over. We are on Apple Tree Road. It isn't really called that, but everyone in the kingdom knows of this apple tree, so it is only fitting that they call it that.

"We're off course," I breathe. "Do you understand what this means? It—it was already going to take days to get to room 106.

Apple Tree Road is even farther from the castle, meaning even farther from room 106, meaning even farther from the prince, meaning we might not make it in time! Room 106 might be gone by the time we get there!"

"Woah, calm down," Sorin says, noticing my uneven breathing. "It's all right. We'll make it. I promise." He holds out his hand, and instead of waiting for me to shake it, he takes my hand and shakes it himself. "You know," he whispers in my ear, "you can rely on others sometimes, Sagey. We're a team."

He stands from his spot on the grass and walks to meet the others, to see if they are all right. I watch him carefully as he moves from person to person, lifting them if they need help up, wiping tears from their eyes if they slipped out, being a good person. Sorin Torsney is so annoying. So, so annoying. Aggravating. He makes me angry. But he is remarkable. Kind. Intelligent. Happy. It is oddly endearing.

I shake my head and remove my eyes from Sorin. What am I thinking? Gibberish. All of these thoughts running through my head, they are gibberish. They make no sense. I must be thinking them just to think of something, just to supply my mind and distract it from the train wreck we left behind. On this journey, there is nothing but thinking. If you don't think, you are dead. If you aren't fast, you are dead. Yet somehow Sorin seems to do neither.

I push that thought from my mind. Yes, it is bashing Sorin,

which I was all for, but it is thinking about Sorin, something I have decided not to do. Maybe if I don't think about him for a certain amount of time, he will disappear. But is that necessarily a good thing, or a bad thing?

Elysian notices me resting against the tree and comes to sit next to me. "What was that about?" she asks, glancing from me to Sorin.

"I have no idea what you're talking about." But I can feel heat rushing to my cheeks.

"Oh, I think you do." Elysian bumps my shoulder with hers. "Your enemy, huh?"

"I didn't say he was my enemy," I say quietly. "An innocent man died when we left the bakery. Can we focus on that?"

Her eyes harden.

"That wasn't your fault," she says gently.

"I never said it was." My tone is harsh. When I feel her recoil, I sigh.

"I—I'm sorry, really. It's just … a lot. What if something happens to the campers? What if we can't save the prince? What if this whole rescue mission is a death trap that ends up with our blood spilled?"

Elysian is quiet for a moment. Then, she says, "It won't be like that. I won't let it. We won't let it. Our campers will be fine. They know how to handle themselves. Even if something happens, the older ones will protect the younger ones, find shelter, fight to survive, just like how we taught them." She grins sheepishly when I glance at her. "I'm guessing that's how we taught them."

"That is," I agree in a hushed tone.

It seems as though Elysian never lost her memory now, as we sit against this apple tree, but at first, it was obvious. She knew nothing. Our routines, our schedules, our practices, our cabins, our dress code, our tendency to hug when greeting people—all of it was new to her, yet it wasn't. I was heartbroken when she didn't remember me, and by the way she looked at me when she told us the news, that look of pity and guilt, I wasn't doing so good at hiding it.

But now it is part of my daily routine. Oh, yeah, remind Elysian to take roll today, or, tell Elysian about our lesson on sword fighting at three. It was normal, it was natural, it was routine. And routine is everything.

Or, at least it is to me. That is probably why this map is so consoling to me. Knowing we have a routined way of getting to the castle, of saving the prince, of doing good, it keeps my mind at ease. But now my brain is running around in circles, trying to comprehend how this wonderful routine is messed up.

It is your fault.

No, it isn't my fault.

You are the one who created this plan, aren't you?

That doesn't mean it is my fault.

Doesn't it, though?

I push those thoughts from my mind. They don't do any good.

They only make me pity myself, and self-pity, especially when someone else is relying on you, is never good.

Sorin's words rang in my mind, bouncing from corner to corner: *You can rely on others sometimes, Sagey. We're a team.*

"Sage?"

Milo's voice yanks me out of my thoughts.

"Yeah?"

"You might want to see this." He leads me over to the dirt road. On the right of it, Sorin and Ash are muttering things and looking at the ground.

"What is it?" Elysian asks, and Ash and Sorin make way for us.

An old newspaper, torn and dirty, sways in the breeze. The only thing keeping it from flying off into the sunset is Sorin's foot, resting on the right corner of the newspaper.

"A newspaper?" I say, confused as to why they want me to see this. "Don't you guys write the newspapers?" My question is directed at Milo and Ash, but Sorin answers.

"I don't think they wrote this one," he says, pointing to the headline.

I crouch down so I can read it better.

ARE THE MAGICS THREATENING TO OVERTAKE BUIT?
A report by Thomas E. Dupont

"Dupont?" Elysian says, reading over my shoulder. "Wasn't that the name of the baker, the one who died?"

"Must've been his brother," Ash responds, a hint of bitterness in her words.

> Allegedly, two summer camps called Camp Serenity and Camp Havoc have been built by Magics, and used as an all-Magic society. I write "allegedly" because even the best of the Royal Guard has yet to discover these camps, hidden by the illegal magic used by one of these Magics. Some non-Magics say they have seen the camps in person, yet after leaving, the location has completely deserted their minds. Whether these camps are used for the better or for the worse, I cannot tell you. The name Havoc definitely does not sound trustworthy, but have you ever met a trustworthy Magic? The reason for the title of this article is one, and one only: The King of Buit's son, the Prince, has been discovered as a Magic. And not only that, but a water Magic, the most powerful of the Magics, alongside fire, earth, and air Magics. Does this mean the Prince, who has always rebelled against his father's wishes, will go against his own kingdom to join these ruffians, these outsiders, these traitors? Read on to find out.

I rise to my feet. The prince, a Magic? "Who would write that?"

"A man working for the kingdom," Milo answers solemnly. "Someone being paid well."

"I knew that bakery owner didn't like me!" Ash says. "This hatred toward Magics, found in the article written by someone with the same last name as him, would explain his hatred toward me! Not to mention I'm a known fugitive for the kingdom, for the king."

"I think there are more reasons than that," Elysian says with relish and a bitter look at Ash.

Ash glares at her but doesn't say anything.

Strange.

"I thought your camp was the only way the mortals got newspapers," Sorin says, his eyes looking as though he was contemplating his entire life.

"It *is*," Milo says, his voice even. "But this newspaper was clearly published two or three years ago. Our newspapers weren't our source of income several years ago. They surely had another way of selling newspapers, yet I'd never really learned what that way was. My father used to work in close quarters to the newspaper publishing office, but he never tried to explore it. It's too late now."

I look at my map. It doesn't show an abandoned newspaper publishing office on there, but I am trying to accept that maybe my map doesn't have everything.

"It used to be right there." Milo points to a portion of my map

I've labeled as "field," which is close to the bakery we'd visited. "They tore it down. Said the villagers were becoming depressed with it being so empty, and it was taking up valuable land. They never did anything with the actual land after they removed the building, so I guess that was short-lived. Not once did I ever hear anyone in the village complaining about it, but to each their own."

New thing to add to my "information that might be important" section of my brain: Milo used to live in the village. Not sure why that would be important, but why not add it? It might come in handy, having this knowledge about his past.

"I'm guessing this Thomas Dupont guy was really important to be talking about something that must have been very serious to the king," Elysian reasons.

"He must have," Milo agrees. "But I never heard of him. Either the publishing company was keeping him quiet until a case like this came along or … he wasn't actually with the publishing company. He published and sold it independently."

"You were good buddies with the baker," Ash interrupts, pointing at Milo. "Did he say anything about his work before being a baker?"

I take a closer look at the publishing date.

Five years ago.

Before people found out about the camps.

This is a fake newspaper.

A fake.

A trap.

I should've seen the damn plot holes.

I search for soldiers, frantic. Where are they hiding? How did they know we'd be here? So many questions swim around my mind.

I finally spot one. A soldier, wearing the royal logo, a raven, on his armor. Weapons are strapped to his belt and chest, but he holds a gun high, in front of his face. It doesn't look like a normal gun, but a tranquilizer gun, or something of the sort. And it is aimed at Sorin.

"Move!" I push him out of the way, which is a good thing, but feel a prickly sort of pain climbing up my leg, which is a bad thing. It is only going to be minutes before I pass out.

Luckily, now the others are on task. They search for the soldier. Either it is the fact that the bullet in my leg is messing with my brain or the fact that I am now sprawled on the floor, writhing in agony, but I seem to see more soldiers hiding in the tree itself.

Sorin crouches down next to me while the others draw their swords and deflect the bullets. His features are contorted in confusion, and something else I can't make out.

"You saved me," he breathes, looking down at my leg. He rips the bullet out, making me breathe in sharply.

The bullet is long and gray, with red blood sticking to the end of it. My blood. On the blood-soaked end are three pliers that expand once they reach human skin. The ultimate paralyzing device if it gets to the right nerve. And if the guard that shoots it could aim correctly.

He stares at the bullet for a moment, his bright blue eyes dark as they study it.

"I need to get you to safety," he says finally, yanking his sword out of its scabbard and turning around so he can deflect the oncoming bullets.

"Cover me!" he shouts, turning back around to pick me up.

I get a chance to look at my wound. It doesn't look good. The skin around it is starting to bruise and turn purple. There might have been a sort of poison in the bullet. The wound itself is circular, with tiny amounts of blood dripping every few seconds.

It isn't a big wound, but it could very well be deadly.

Sorin puts his left arm under my legs and his right under my torso. His breathing turns shallow as he realizes, possibly, how light I am, how sick I already am, how close to dying I am. My breathing slows. It is like my lungs are threatening to not work, to stop providing me oxygen, to stop letting me live. I gasp for breath; my chest rises and falls rapidly. Sorin's grip on me tightens.

"I'm going to kill him," he mutters, and I am too dazed to appreciate it.

He carries me far, as far away as he can from the fight. He looks down at me with pity before resting me against a huge, smooth boulder.

"I'll be fine," I say, my voice barely a whisper.

"Let's hope," he says back with that smirk, that smirk that was so familiar I can't help but mirror it, that smirk that tells me everything is normal, that Sorin is normal, that he believes things can go back to normal. That smirk makes me relax. It makes me calm.

"You're an important part of our team. The only slightly smart one, if you don't count Milo. Speaking of Milo, I'm going to go get him. Stay here."

I smile. "Well, it's not like I can run away, now can I?" With every word, I wince.

"Just … don't talk, okay?" His eyebrows knit together. "Though I am proud you made a joke." He winks before sprinting back to Apple Tree Road.

And I am alone.

I reach for my map, trying to use that as a distraction. My hands are shaking violently, but luckily, I have just tucked my map into my pocket, meaning it isn't hard for me to reach.

My hands shake so much I can barely read it. It isn't like I want to. I just want something familiar in my grasp.

My injury is starting to hurt more. The poison sends sharp pains up my leg that seem to echo through my body, making everything ache. I wince. Every time I move, more pain courses through me.

I busy myself by looking at my map. I wish I had a pen, so I could pencil in that old publishing company building. Even if that newspaper is a trap, and Thomas Dupont might have just been a random name, Milo wouldn't lie about something he thinks to be important.

Unless he would.

I don't know him that well. Ash does, but can I really trust Ash?

I decide not to waste the little time I have on all this negative thinking. I can trust Milo. I have no reason not to. He is my friend. Like Sorin says, we are a team. And what is the point of a team if the teammates don't trust one another?

"Sage!" The sound of hurried footsteps and Milo's voice disrupts the quiet. I let my map drop to the floor. Milo and Sorin are Healers. They can help me. I allow my eyes to close, hoping they would open again. It was a foolish thought, really, that I couldn't trust Milo.

Isn't it?

* * *

"When is she going to wake up?"

I recognize that voice, no matter how groggy or drowsy I might've been. It is Elysian's.

Someone sighs. "We're not sure. The poison in the bullet is uncomfortably close to her bloodstream. Luckily, Sorin and I caught it just in time, before it could do serious damage, but she still might not be able to stand on it for a few days." Milo.

My eyes flutter open.

95

I am sprawled on a bed, a heavy blanket covering my left leg, my right leg elevated on an old pillow. Several chairs surround my bed, accompanied by Elysian and Milo. For some reason, I feel slightly disappointed that Sorin isn't there. Where is he, and why doesn't he want to visit me?

On the other side of the room, the knob of the wooden door is twisted strangely, locked. Maybe Sorin does want to visit me, but they aren't allowing him to. But since when do I care if Sorin cares about me? He is never serious.

I can't like him. He can be my friend, I decide. My friend. He is my friend. Nothing more.

He should not even be my friend.

Bookshelves line the room, covering the walls with an assortment of dusty pages and ripped covers. Somehow old books like that make me feel comfortable. They are well loved, yet still there, meaning I can read them whenever I want and feel at home. On the right and left side of the bed are two nightstands buried in medications and towels bathed in blood that I assume are mine. I also notice a small painting of a sunrise hidden behind trees sitting next to my things, collecting dust. It looks like it hasn't been touched in years.

Where are we?

"Sage?" Elysian's eyes light up as she notices my consciousness.

"Sage?" Milo repeats, turning his head to look at me. "You're awake?"

"You're awake!" she says.

"Where ... are we?" I ask. It takes a while for me to get the words out because of the pains now in every single one of my joints. I guess that is part of the poison. It affects my whole body, not just the wound itself.

I stretch and reach for my pocket, when I realize I don't have the same clothes on as before. I am dressed in a pair of pocketless joggers and a plain T-shirt, meaning I don't have pockets, meaning I don't have my map, meaning ... it could be lost.

"It's fine," Elysian assures me. "We're at Sorin's mom's house. She lived in the village, so we just went back and we"—she stops when Milo raises one of his eyebrows at her—"I mean, Milo and Sorin, nursed you back to health." She pauses as I grimace. "Mostly."

"Your clothes were so blood-soaked, we had to put them in the washer," Milo says. "But your map is right here."

Even though it hurts, I breathe a sigh of relief. That problem is diverted. Now for the new problem.

"You went back to the village?" I look around the room frantically for some kind of window, some kind of proof that Elysian isn't just lying to me.

"Well, we kind of had to." She looks me up and down. "It's not like you were just ready to start moving again after the bullet incident."

"How far back does that put us?" I ask Milo urgently.

He places his hand on my shoulder and says calmly, knowing the way I am going to react, whether it be good news or bad, "You were out for about two days."

"Two days?"

The words feel sour in my mouth. If we weren't going to make it in time to room 106 before, now we definitely aren't going to. Two whole days of me just sleeping, lying in a bed while others surrounded me and wished I would get better.

I hate Milo's look of disapproval even before he gives it, before I ask my question.

"Why didn't you just continue with the mission?"

"Continue with the mission?" Elysian looks to Milo like, "Can you believe this girl?" "And leave you alone like this? You needed us, Sage, and we weren't willing to leave you. You would help one of us if the roles were reversed, so why not do the same for you?"

"But you might not be able to save the prince now!" I retort, biting my lip to keep from wincing. "He's more valuable than me, so why didn't you just … go?"

The doorknob jiggles, making me direct my attention toward that.

"Is she awake?" says a muffled voice.

Sorin.

I look at my fingers when I realize it's him. He cares. But why does he care? Why do any of them care about me at all? I haven't done anything for them, yet they saved my life. My fingers tremble as tears blur my vision. I can't cry. Not now. I have already slowed them down enough by trying to be heroic. I will slow them down with my tears. I will make them think I am not entirely okay. And I'm not. But why bring attention to that when I am already in the spotlight more than I want to be, and for reasons I don't want to be?

Milo stands from his wooden chair to unlock the door. My stomach churns. I shouldn't be nervous. This is Sorin. My friend. But I am.

He breathes a sigh of relief when he notices my open and alert eyes, my slouched position, my twiddling thumbs.

"Thought you were dead, Sagey," he says, and a pang of anger hits me hard when he says that nickname. I hate that nickname. Doesn't he know—doesn't he care—about what I had told him, my journey to get to Camp Serenity, the things I had to do, the people I had to leave behind, the people I had to *kill*? No, of course not. Of course he doesn't care. He never sees the importance of anything, never recognizes that maybe some things he says can hurt people. He never cares about other people. He never cares about anything. I have no idea why I decided to be his friend at that moment. Why I have let my guard down, why I have let him get through the barriers I had set up for several years, why I let him wreck that, why I let him wreck me. Even if it was only for a few days, I am ashamed of myself. Just a nickname. That is all it takes to get me back to feeling the same way I have always felt about Sorin. He is incompetent, and dumb, and careless. He is reckless. And that is not endearing.

"Um, Sage, you okay?"

I lift my head. I haven't realized I have put it down. I glare at Sorin, and say, as sharply as I can without wincing too much or making it feel like someone is electrocuting me, "I'm fine."

"Oh, okay," Sorin says, his Adam's apple bobbing. I surprise him. So what? I don't care. He is the one who got me into this mess in the first place. If I hadn't tried to save him … "Mom says lunch is ready, if you want me to get you something."

Elysian studies me and Sorin, and noticing the rising tension, she offers quickly, "I can. It's fine, Sunshine."

"I'll go, too," Milo agrees, his eyebrows meeting. His voice has a hint of question to it, but I ignore it.

I glance at him, shaking my head, frantically. No way can I stay in here with Sorin. I will probably smash something.

Milo just smiles sadly and stands from his chair, as if telling me this is for the best. I don't think it is. I think this is for the worst. Can you blame me?

"So we're at your mom's house right now?" I ask, my face stone, my words clipped and tight.

"Yep." He leans against the doorframe, his long legs visible at the cuffs of his jeans. He follows my gaze to his calves. "Yeah, these are old pants. Mom just put me in them. They're from high school. Not like I'm gonna wear them out."

He is so relaxed. I don't understand how we can be. He hates me. Ever since I got the job he so wished for, he has hated me. He has been nice to me before, but he is infuriating. I don't associate with people who make me mad, who make me feel powerless and full of hate. After all, the main fuel for hate is powerlessness and fear.

Yet he trusts me. It is obvious. He feels comfortable when he's around me. I make this assumption because of his relaxed stance, his slurred words, his calm facial features. I am intelligent enough to know these are all signs of being comfortable. Or anger, depending on the person. Or …

Love.

But that can't be possible. It will never be. I hate him, and he hates me.

Yes, that is it.

A question nags at the back of my brain.

"Why didn't you leave me behind?" I voice it out loud.

Those previous answers aren't enough. I need to know why *he* didn't leave me.

"You saved me." His voice is just as quiet as mine. "I couldn't leave you. Not after that act of selflessness."

He raises his head, his bright eyes so blue they almost hurt. We stare at each other like that, not breaking eye contact. After a few moments, I narrow my eyes and he looks away quickly.

Sorin clears his throat. "Besides, you would have done the same for me. Right?"

A tiny voice in the back of my head says I would, but the bigger voice that speaks for the reasonable part of my brain makes me say, "I would honestly think saving the prince would be more important. Plus, no one I know lives in the village, much less my mother. She died when I was young."

It comes out more harshly than I mean it to.

His eyes turn sad. I turn away. I can't stand to see him that way, but I am angry. I tried to save him, and now my leg is filled with poison that could kill me, yet he is acting like everything is fine, which is the thing that makes me dislike him in the first place.

"So ..." He turns to walk away. His back is to me when he rests his hand on the doorframe. "You wouldn't stay with me when I needed it?"

I bite back my honest response and let my anger take over.

"No."

CHAPTER 8

ASH

I let out a breath, smoke taking up the air in front of me.

"You really shouldn't smoke if you don't want lung disease." I recognize this voice. Elysian.

"What do you want?" I ask, taking another drag, just to annoy her.

"I'm bored," she says, tracing patterns in the cement with her finger, "and you're the best shot at entertainment I have. So, go on. Tell me a story."

We are sitting on the porch outside of Sorin's mom's house. It is decorated with flowers and different inscriptions with cheesy sayings on them. It makes me wonder who thought that was a good way to decorate the place that people see when they're running from royal guards (that is the only reason why villagers leave their houses anymore).

"I don't have any stories to tell." The sun shines brightly, so brightly it makes me wonder if Sorin is messing with it. Clouds streak across the pale blue sky. I focus my attention on that instead of focusing on the glare Elysian is boring into my skin.

"Sure you do," she retorts. "Like about that tattoo on your

shoulder."

I hunch my back as though she can see it, but it is covered by a T-shirt of Sorin's sisters that she left when she went to work for the king. The T-shirt itself is stained with paint, creating the assumption of Sorin's sister being artsy. I wouldn't be surprised if she is.

I remove my cigarette from my mouth. "I don't want to talk about it."

"You never do," she says, and I turn my head to study her. "Now's the time to do it. Get it off your chest."

Fire. Light.

My mother.

What I did.

How I ...

"I'll pass," I say, feeling uncomfortable but hiding it well.

"Well, there's got to be *something* you can tell me," she complains.

I sigh. It is obvious she isn't leaving any time soon, meaning I have to entertain her, unless I want her to bother me consistently while I just try to take a smoke. Don't I deserve to have just one moment of tranquility, one moment where nothing matters except for the fact I have made it this far?

"My dad," I start, dropping my cigarette and stomping on it so the ashes fade into the concrete, "was a very nice man. Before you say anything, yes, this is important to the story. And he married my mom. My mom looked almost exactly like me."

I fight off the tears that start to gather in my eyes. I can't cry; I can't be weak. Not in front of this girl, not in front of anyone. Mother taught me that.

"My dad invited his brother to their wedding reception. My uncle never really spoke to my dad. The only time he did was during formal gatherings or holidays, and it was because he viewed my dad as weird for the nice things he did and said. My dad came from a very wealthy family that valued work and determination over love and kindness."

"Does this story even have a point?" Elysian's tone is bored, but she has moved to one of the large, fluffy chairs set up on the porch, eagerly sitting on the edge of her seat, waiting for more of my story. I smile slightly. Mother was never interested in my stories. All she cared about was money and power. An odd mix for my dad.

"Those wealthy families were considered the Plenty," I continue. "These were important people, the Plenty, because they were the people who had all the best jobs. They worked in offices, for the king, as police officers and guards for the royals, and business owners. My dad owned a business that was extremely special to the royal family, and my uncle was jealous. That was another reason why they didn't really talk. Miraculously, the invitation got through to my uncle and he appeared at their wedding. He marched up to my dad and smacked him across the face before leaving."

Elysian's face contorts into one of confusion. "But why would he do that?"

"I'm telling you that," I respond calmly.

I guess this storytelling thing helps both me and her.

"Apparently, my dad had sold the business to someone else, a person not in their family, and a plain villager. Not one of the Plenty."

"And that was a bad thing?" she asks, practically falling off her chair.

"Well, yes." I put my hands in front of me. "Selling anything when you are a Plenty to a villager is considered traitorous. And my dad was deeply disappointed. His own brother, whom he had taken the time to write a detailed, amazing invitation for, slapped him at his wedding."

I honestly think I am just piling on, but Elysian's gaze on me doesn't waver for a minute.

"So my mom grabbed his face like this." I reach forward and place my hand on the side of her face, trying not to show my distaste in what I have done. "And she said, 'He isn't worth it. You are amazing, and I know that it seems like the end of the world right now because everyone has abandoned you, but I haven't. I will always be here.' That put him in a happy mood, and they continued their wedding, without my uncle, driven to greed by the prospect of power, to interrupt them. The end."

I remove my hand from her cheek and back away from her, trying to hide the fact that I am wiping my hands on my shorts. I don't know what brings me to do it; I just feel like giving a visual representation of what that moment looked like. Doesn't that boost the storytelling process and make it better?

A strand of her shiny brown hair falls in front of her face. I have the urge to move it. Maybe that is just my cleaning instincts or something more. I don't really care enough to figure it out.

"Well ..." She clears her throat and flicks the hair away from her eyes. I relax. I don't know why that strand of hair bothers me so much. "That was a *really* good story."

I smirk, almost unwillingly. "Of course it was. I was telling it."

Elysian rolls her eyes. "Just"—she picks up the butt of my cigarette and drops it in my palm—"smoke your cigs."

I drop the butt again and follow her inside.

✷ ✷ ✷

Marian Torsney's house is strange.

There are dozens of bookshelves, lining every room we can walk in. Signs are hung upside down or crooked on the mint walls, most of them saying stuff you find at a convenience store known for selling "Live, Laugh, Love" and "You Go Girl" signs. The shape of the house is a big L, with the bedrooms off to one side and the living room and kitchen on the other side. And another thing about this place Sorin calls home: There are windchimes on the doorknob of every room. Whenever you walk in one, they start jangling. Supposedly they are meant for alerting Marian if royal guards or dangerous people sneak into her house, but I am not buying it. Who is dangerous in the village, and why would royal guards want Marian Torsney?

Sunlight streams through an open window, birds chirping loudly as if to remind us it is time for them to be out. Too bad if we venture out there, Sage will probably lose her injured leg (would that really be so bad?) and the guards will be after us. I do not want any trouble, not while we are staying here.

I guess I just answer my own question. The royal guards might try to find Marian Torsney because of us.

"Mighty fine morning, isn't it, dears?"

Marian appears, blond curls and all, carrying a laundry basket that is stacked with clothes. She speaks in a high, singsong voice that reminds me of one of the birds outside her window. Draped around her waist is a flour-coated apron, though I don't understand how she got flour on her when she hasn't been cooking anything that has to do with flour (she's been heating up pork chops). Under that are a baggy blue-and-white striped T-shirt, cuffed at the sleeves, and beige khakis.

Elysian's voice is soft when she corrects Sorin's mom. "Mrs. Torsney, it's lunchtime."

She takes the laundry basket from Marian so there won't be any chance of an accident. So considerate, so kind, so *peaceful*. It makes me wonder how she can stand herself.

Marian whips her head toward the large, somehow square clock on the wall and sighs thoughtfully.

"Is it? I could've sworn that friend of yours just woke up, so I figured it must have been morning time. I thought yesterday went by fast. Well, technically, yesterday is today, so does that make today yesterday? And what about tomorrow? Will tomorrow be yesterday, too, or will it be today?"

"Mom."

Sorin walks into the room, stifling a yawn with his hand, though his stance says it all. Something has happened in that room with Sage, yet he doesn't want to admit it. All the better if I don't have to hear it, I guess.

He rakes a hand through his hair, messing it up.

"You're confusing them. Stop it, please."

When Sorin offered this place of refuge, none of us had any idea what his mom would be like. We just knew, or *they* knew, that they had to get Sage to safety before something else happens. Luckily, his mom was in the village, so we just backtracked a bit and moved in here. Only for a little bit, of course. My point is, none of us had any idea of their relationship, much less that it would be so *bad*.

Marian's face turns sad. The corners of her mouth bend down

into a frown. "Sorry, dear, I didn't mean to. How is your little friend doing?"

She sends a knowing glance to Elysian. They think Sage and Sorin will eventually date. I don't disagree, and honestly, if I am being especially nice, they look actually kind of cute together. But I don't meddle in other people's affairs, and not romantic ones, so I haven't said anything.

"She's … fine." He walks past his mother, Elysian, and me without another glance in our direction. I am glad. Sorin is annoying, and I don't really think much of him. The only reason he was allowed to come is that he is funny, and he isn't even that funny.

Elysian clasps her hands together politely. "Did she get the lunch I gave you?"

Sorin looks back and waves a hand dismissively. "It, uh, it didn't come up. Sorry. I probably left it outside her door."

Before Elysian leaves the room, Marian grabs her arm. "Please, let me know if she likes it."

Her bright blue eyes, which would be exactly like Sorin's if they were not streaked with green, hold so much desperation that I almost feel badly. I mean, this lady lost her daughter to the Royal Guard, the people we are running from, and now, not even her own son wants to talk to her, to acknowledge her, to thank her, even. She just needs someone to say they are proud, just like all of us at times. Or for some of us, we need it all the time.

"Sure." Elysian smiles warmly and Marian loosens her grip on her arm, relaxing. Elysian exits the living room and heads toward Sage's bedroom.

Sorin plucks an apple from Marian's apple tree. She has placed an apple tree in the middle of her living room, so tall even the shortest branches brush the ceiling, and so filled with apples that the aroma will probably never leave this house, not after she moves out or after she is dead. We all have to die eventually, and with this prince-being-captured thing, the royal guards and the king are probably hungry for blood, Finn's blood, and since they can't have that, they will kill everyone else.

But that is just an assumption.

Marian ignores me and trudges toward her son. That is when I notice her pale feet, shoved into red heels that are extremely shiny and tall, so tall she is almost taller than Sorin when she stands next to him and uses his shoulder for balance. I wonder how I didn't notice them before. There are hard to miss.

"Sorin, please." Marian's words are hushed but her demeanor is not, meaning I can tell exactly what they are talking about just by the way she stands, the way her mouth moves, the way her eyebrows crease, the way she shifts nervously from foot to foot, the way her hands move frantically, all signifying nervousness. I have always been good at reading people. Time to put that skill to use.

"I know you're mad at me after what happened"—a raise of the shoulder and exposing her neck, she is telling the truth—"and I know I've done many wrong things in your life and in mine"—fluttering her eyelids, she is uncomfortable with the topic at hand—"but please, forgive me."

"I can never forgive what you did," Sorin mutters, glaring at the woman beside him. Marian whimpers like a hurt dog. I find myself becoming increasingly curious. What happened in Sorin's past, and why is it so important?

I tell myself to forget it, when—

A shriek sounds from the bedrooms. I practically sprint to that side of the house, Sorin following close behind me, and Marian close behind him.

When we enter the bedroom, Sage is on the floor, gasping and clutching her leg. Elysian is reaching for something outside the window, screaming. Sorin rushes over to Sage, whispering words of encouragement. A scowl appears on her face.

Elysian's head whips back around toward where Marian and I stand. Her face is deathly pale, her blue eyes wide, her brown hair tousled and messy, as if it has been moved around during a fight. She says something so quiet I can't hear it, but it seems as though she can't say it again.

Not until seconds later when she breathes:

"They have Milo."

* * *

I feel myself stumble back into Marian. It feels like I have run into a brick wall.

Elysian's eyes well with tears.

"I know," she whispers. "We-we were just sitting there, talking and-and then the people, the-the royal guards came for him." She hiccups between words. "They said that he-he was perfect for drawing you in, for luring you in, for getting us to go there." She ends with a final hiccup.

Sorin wraps Sage's bullet wound in bandages carefully, avoiding her eyes. Whatever happened before Milo was taken, I don't know, and I don't care. He is gone. Milo … is gone. Marian gasps, noticing how serious the situation is. She moves from behind me and helps me to the wall so I can stabilize myself.

"I'm going to make tea," she says nervously, glancing around at us, these random teenagers in her guest room, crying over someone we've lost. Sorin is the only one she recognizes. She has barely met me or Elysian or Milo or Sage, yet she understands how important this is and has a selfless need to satisfy our worries as well as her own by distracting herself.

Sometimes I wish my brain didn't want that in a mother so much.

I nod, letting Marian go off on her own to make tea. I would be lying if I said this whole situation doesn't chill me to the bone. How have the guards figured out where we are, and why is Elysian the one who is by his side when he is captured? Why couldn't I have been there? Then maybe he wouldn't've been taken, and we'd still have our Milo. I'd still have my Milo.

"I"—another hiccup—"I'm sorry."

A sour voice in my head tells me to say sorry isn't enough. I keep my mouth shut instead, thinking if I talk the tears will spill, and Mother always taught me never to be vulnerable in front of other people. If I cry, I will put all of her training and teaching to waste. Her training and teaching are all I have left of her, the only part that I haven't killed. I can't let go of that, too.

"I know," is all I managed to say.

Sage glowers at the floor while Sorin quickly stands from the floor and takes a step back from her. I hear Elysian gulping air and trying to keep in her tears, but I honestly don't care. I don't care. Milo is my friend, not hers. If I don't get to cry, she doesn't. That is what I normally would've thought, if it was any other of my friends. But Milo … I don't care what anyone else does anymore.

"I'm back!" Marian's singsong voice sounds from outside the door. Vomit leaps up my throat so I sit down on the edge of the bed. Marian flings the door open and sets a tray of tea next to me. Sorin sighs, relieved to have a distraction, and makes his way toward me. He picks up a cup of tea and holds it delicately in his fingers.

"Do you want any tea, sweetheart?" Marian asks, craning her neck so she can see Sage.

Sage, instead of answering, closes her eyes and gasps. I notice her badly wrapped leg. The wound is still partially visible, and even more blood than before, now tinted with green, is flowing out of it.

I clench my jaw and bend down to fix it.

"What the hell did you do, Sorin?" Elysian asks behind me, wiping tears from her face.

"I—" Sorin stops when he notices what we are talking about. "She snapped at me so I couldn't do it correctly."

Sure, says a bitter voice in my head. *And I just lost my best friend, but I'm not complaining or becoming a baby over a girl snapping at me.*

I take the wrap off and get a good look at the wound. Since her accident, I have really stayed away from Sage, so I haven't paid attention to the wound or the amount of discomfort it gives me. I try my best to shield it from Sage in fear she'll start moving if she sees the state it is in, but really, I want to shield it from myself as well. The skin around it is peeling and stained with blood and bruised. The wound isn't circular like the bullet anymore, but more like a distorted square. The bullet has really dug deep into her skin.

I carefully put the bandages to the side and turn back to ask Elysian for more, but she is already gone. Marian and Sorin watch from across the room, Sorin fascinated and Marian nervous.

Elysian returns moments later with gauze. I lift her leg and put it on the back of her calf first, then wrap it around her leg. She winces in pain while I do so, despite the fact that I am trying to be gentle.

Soon, the blood stops, blocked by the gauze. Sage doesn't relax, but her face of pain isn't as twisted.

"Have you wrapped a wound before?" she asks me, looking down at her tightly bandaged leg.

I am about to answer honestly by saying Milo taught me, when I catch myself and remember where I am. Milo is gone. He isn't here to be proud of me. He isn't here at all. He is gone.

"Uh," I say instead, wiping tears from my eyes before they spill, "you wouldn't believe how many kids can get hurt during training. Milo"—I trust myself enough to say this—"Milo was normally the one who healed them, but sometimes, when the infirmary got full, he would call me in and tell me what to do." I choke on my last words, then breathe, "Sorry."

Elysian stares at me curiously. I glare at her so she will look away, but she doesn't. She holds my gaze as her eyes fill with pity. I look away instead. I don't need anyone's pity, especially not *hers*.

"We should start looking for him," Sorin says gently. "Did you hear where they were taking them?"

"They didn't say," Elysian responds, removing her eyes from me. "They were royal guards, so I would assume the castle."

"But—" Sage winces when she tries to talk. "But that'll take days."

I think about what Milo would say if he were there. He would point out a secret passage that isn't marked on Sage's map. He would … he would solve the problem.

"So?" I cross my arms over my chest, suddenly angry with her. Does she not believe in Milo? Does she think we can just leave him behind?

"He's as important to this team as you are. If you aren't willing to go get him, I am, and I will."

Sage's lips part slightly as Elysian pulls her off the ground. She grimaces when Elysian leads her over to the bed. When that train wreck is done, she looks back at me.

"You're seriously saying I don't care about Milo? Of course I care about Milo! I agree with you, he's an important asset. I was just pointing out the fact that we would never make it in time if we lost more days searching for him. The map is very specific. If we go off course, who knows what could happen? The prince could—"

I lose it. I decide I am leaving. I can't put up with them anymore. Before storming out of the room, out of the house, out of the village to look for Milo, I say, deathly quiet, "If any of you want to be good people and follow me to look for him, you can. If you want to be morons and rely on that stupid map, be my guest. I'm sure Sage would appreciate it."

CHAPTER 9

MILO

I lean back calmly against the wall of my cell.

Even if Sorin calls my powers drugs, they still work. I feel completely and totally at peace.

"What do you know?" a guard screams at me, his face contorted in rage, the blade of his sword pointed directly at my Adam's apple.

"I know," I say with a pointed, cross-eyed look at the blade, "that you could poke someone's eye out with that. It's unsafe."

"It seems like that's the whole point," the guard snarls. "Now, tell me what you know about room 106."

I wave my hand lazily, noticing my words are slightly slurred the next time I speak. (Okay, maybe my powers do make people high.) "That little detail? I already told you, I barely know anything about that place."

The other guard standing outside of my cell calls back to the first guard in front of me. "McHale, you good back there?"

I can only see her dark-as-night hair and traditional black armor, and I can only hear her voice, muffled under her helmet, but I know she is perfect. She has to be, with a voice like that. Smooth and clear, like wind.

"I'm fine, Calahan!" McHale's hand tightens around the hilt of his sword. "I know you know things, Milo Belittle. And we will get those things out of you, no matter what it takes."

He stares at me for a second, his face turning alarmingly red, like he's expecting something. Then he sighs, mutters, and drops his sword, letting it clang against the cement of my cell.

"I quit," he says to the guard at the front. "You take him."

Calahan nods before stepping into my cell. Slowly, and once McHale and the other guards are gone, she closes and locks the door to the cell so only faint light from the half-hidden window at the top of the room streams in.

"W—what are you doing?" I ask, all calm fading away. Panic settles in my stomach as she walks toward me, scowling under her helmet. The sound of her metal armor rings in my ears.

"I am going to ask you one question," she says quietly, crouching down so she is level with me, "and you have to answer honestly, or I will give you to another guard. Trust me, you don't want that."

"What's the question?" She has a question for me, and I will answer it honestly, whether it be about our mission or not. She is just so beautiful, I can't even remember why I am here in the first place.

I am not expecting it to be the question it is at all.

"Where is Sorin?"

I stare at her blankly. "What?"

"I know he was on your mission, Belittle, don't play dumb," Calahan snaps. "So where is he? Did he come in with you?"

"How do you know about him?"

Calahan's eyes narrow. "I've read about him. Now, answer the question."

"He …" I pause. Mrs. Torsney never shared the address with us, and Sorin wasn't any more willing to share it either, whether in fear we'd find her place again or for secrecy reasons, I don't know. "I'm not sure."

"So he didn't come to the dungeons?" Her menacing gray eyes are hopeful. "That means he didn't do anything stupid for once. Where is he?"

"I already told you." I try to keep my voice as steady as possible, but I am confused. Where has she read about Sorin? All the newspapers and books never once mentioned him, because he is a Magic and Ash just doesn't like him. And why would books, which are published by the king or people close to the king, talk about Magics?

"I'm not sure. I don't know the exact address."

"Address." She turns away from me and taps her chin with a long, pale finger. "So he's in the village. But where …?"

Calahan begins to pace my cell, muttering things under her breath. I sit quietly where I am. *She's kind of cute when she thinks,* says a voice in my head.

I pinch myself. *That's not what I mean. I mean, she thinks all the time, but right now.*

Okay, that's also not what I mean. She always looks cute.

I mean—

Calahan whips around. "We're leaving. Get your stuff."

I stand so quickly that I almost fall backward. Luckily, Calahan reaches forward and grabs my wrist before I do.

"Are you always this clumsy?" she asks me, a smirk on her face.

The same smirk Sorin always has on *his* face.

I ignore it and let her keep holding my wrist as she unlocks the cell door and almost sprints through the long corridor of jail cells.

One man near the end of the hallway calls, "Nice day, isn't it, sweetheart?"

I clench my jaw, ready to punch that guy, when—

"I wouldn't expect you to know, since you're locked in that jail cell," Calahan says with a sweet yet sarcastic smile. She flutters her fingers at him and leads me to the very end.

"All right," she whispers to me. "There are going to be hundreds of guards in there. Keep your head down, and try not to make a noise. You are one of the best-known fugitives in the whole kingdom because of that friend of yours. Almost everyone in there will be bragging about your capture, so—"

"Look." I point behind her, next to the huge doors leading to the hundreds of guards that want to kill Ash. The tiny door is labeled ARMORY.

She turns her head quickly, probably expecting a guard, but she relaxes slightly when she notices the door.

"Of course!" Calahan pushes me toward the door. "There's armor in there. Change and meet me in that room." She motions with her head to the huge doors. "I'll be to the right of the entrance. Talk to no one, do you understand me?"

I nod and duck inside the armor room.

* * *

"You look different."

A tall guard with his helmet tucked under his arm stops me when I try to find Calahan in the room behind the big doors. The room is huge and circular, with white tables and chairs stacked in the corners. It seems to be either a meeting room or a party room. I can just barely make out two more large doors at the other side of the room, cracked open to let in the slight breeze. If you ask me what time it is, I couldn't tell you. Being in the dungeons really sucks the life out of you, apparently.

I don't respond to the guard.

"Are you new?" he says, trying to study me as much as he can with one of the royal helmets stuck on my head.

I shake my head.

"Don't talk much, do you?" The guard laughs. "I remember this one time, we had a new guy who *never* talked. He just nodded and shook his head." He stares at me curiously. "Your name isn't Peter McGwire, is it?"

I turn away from the guard and shuffle quickly past the other guards. None of the others say anything but give me strange looks as I walk past them. I try not to draw much attention, but I am pretty tall, something that is always considered strange in my family since my dad is the tallest in my family and only five feet nine inches.

To the right of the entrance. That is what Calahan told me. It should be easy to find her, with her tendency to draw attention, but I can't find her. It seems as though she has disappeared in the sea of guards, lost in a maze of the king's loyal followers.

Something tells me that if she is in close relation with Sorin, she can't be as loyal as the others. Sorin is the epitome of rebellious and obnoxious, like Ash, and, as it turns out, Calahan.

But how *did* she find out about Sorin in the first place? The whole kingdom hates him, and they would never put "his kind" in books, or newspapers that the king or the castle reads. In fact, I am willing to bet the castle doesn't even have newspapers delivered, because the only newspaper company is currently our camp. If the mortals want newspapers, they have to read ours, which includes Magic news, and is written by Magics, so the king has a good reason for not allowing his followers or his workers to read them. Which brings me back to my first question: How has Calahan found out about Sorin if she read about him? What book includes Sorin Torsney? And how do I get one? If Sorin found out about there being a piece of paper with his name on it, he'd probably want to sign it.

My eyes search the large room frantically. If I can't find Calahan before someone figures out who I am, I will probably be dead.

Which way is my right anymore? I can't see the entrance doors because of the number of people gathering around me like a swarm of mosquitoes, covering my line of sight and disabling me from moving.

Suddenly, someone places their hand on my shoulder. Thinking it is a guard ready to arrest me, I whip around so my loose armor hits them in the face.

Calahan clutches her now-bleeding nose. "Gods, you have good aim, especially for someone so innocent seeming."

I quickly apologize.

"No time for that," she says quickly, letting her hand drop at her side with a loud clang. "We've gotta get out of here and find my— Sorin." She points to another set of large doors on the wall right in front of us, on the side of the room. "That is a secret way to get out of the dungeons."

"Is it really much of a secret?" I observe, and she scowls.

"Well, normally, guards aren't trying to escape with a known fugitive," she says, "so, no, those doors aren't. But be my guest. Walk through the main doors, and see how many guards try to stop you."

I shrug.

She stands straighter, satisfied at the fact that I don't say anything. "Right. So, we go through those doors. Outside, there'll be an assortment of different carriages, most holding supplies."

"Carriages for just supplies?" I ask, my eyebrows coming together.

"Well ..." Calahan pauses. "They used to be for the prince to ride in, but ever since he was captured, the workers just use them for supplies for the castle." She sighs and looks up at me through her beautiful, long eyelashes. I think my legs are going to give way and I am going to fall, but that never happens. "It's different now that he's gone, you know. He always treated everyone else like the royalty that he was."

"He's not dead," I say gently and quietly. "I think I know where he is."

She looks away from me and clears her throat. "Sure you do. We've got a mission to complete. Find Sorin with no way of knowing we'll get there alive and unnoticed, and with no directions because you don't know the address. Perfect." She walks away from me, leaving me to trail behind her.

Even though we are only a few feet apart, I am still afraid I'll lose her. This room is wall-to-wall with guards, and most of them want to kill me, so I am not exactly eager to stray far from her. She is the only sort of comfort I have. At least I know not everyone (I mean, not the pretty ones) want to kill me. And she knows Sorin, and she doesn't hate me, and she is just … trustworthy. Calahan seems strangely familiar, as if I have met her before somewhere. I just can't remember where.

I feel like a dog following its owner at a park—lost, curious, and somehow blending in.

We stop right in front of the side doors. Calahan puts an arm out to stop me from walking straight into the doors. I'm surprised by how strong she is.

But it's not like I expect her to be weak and fragile.

She's stronger than Ash, I think, the voice that says it so loud that I almost miss what Calahan says.

"We're going to go out these doors and then straight past the carts," she whispers to me. "The guards are mostly the ones who make sure the carts are in good shape, when they're off duty. But don't think that means they'll let you slide by."

She raises an eyebrow, then laughs under her breath. It is barely a laugh, more like a skeleton of what used to be a laugh, but has been turned into something else after working at the castle. I am not surprised; the castle is run by the (as Ash says) "blood-sucking, Magic-hating, always-shunning-people" King.

"I would rather it be me than Ash," I say, and I mean it. I would rather be tortured to death, choked, and shot before I let anyone kill

Ash. She is my best friend.

Calahan studies me. "That courage, that love you feel for your friend, that need to be the hero—it will destroy you, just as it destroyed everyone else." She blinks at me. That is all I can see because of the helmet covering most of her head, but I have a feeling she isn't wearing her familiar scowl when she says her next sentence. "And you know, I'm really starting to like you."

I feel myself smiling.

"Okay," I say, "so we go out these doors, somehow sneak past the guards manning the carts without me being noticed, and then run to the village."

Calahan nods. "Right." She is quiet for a minute before she says, "Quickly," and motions for me to go first, but I hold my ground.

"I really think you going first would be better."

She nods and pushes on the doors so they open, and she walks through them.

* * *

Sunlight shines hot on my face. I have been in the dungeons for only about three hours, but I already missed sunlight. It felt like three years being trapped in that tight cell with barely any room to breathe, and only one window partially available for use.

Several carts line the cobblestone road, built for carriages. Most of the roads in the village are made of dirt or aren't roads at all, just grass with tracks. But, of course, the best has to be made for the king. Cobblestone is very expensive, sold only by the richest people in the kingdom, for a great amount of money. It is no wonder why the villagers can't afford to get cobblestone on their roads.

Calahan wasn't kidding when she said guards protected the carriages. There are at least three for each carriage, staring at the horizon, guns and swords at their sides. Normally, the kingdom doesn't use guns. That is what my father told me. Then Ash killed her mother and ran, so the Royal Guard is required to have guns everywhere, no matter where they go, in case they run into her.

Gold is packed into one carriage, and food in another. Clothes and glass and tubs of who knows what fill the others. I have no idea why you would put gold and food, the two most desired items for thieves, in the same place, guarded by people overcome by five teenagers, but people's brains work differently.

"See?" Calahan says, pointing to the different carriages. When one of the guards turns his head in our direction, Calahan drags me behind more barrels of supplies. "They're very protective of those substances."

"They're trained to be," I say matter-of-factly. "Right?"

Calahan nods stiffly. "The king trains his new recruits day and night. When I first signed up, I was worn to the bone. He's very thorough in training. Prepares you for everything."

"Even being sliced in half with a sword?" I ask, partly out of curiosity, partly out of trying to be funny.

"Keep that up and I'll show you what that feels like," she replies, raising an eyebrow in challenge.

I raise my hands to show her I don't want a fight.

She just focuses her attention back on the guards.

"When should we walk past them?" I ask her, all attempts at humor lost.

Her eyes turn a darker gray. "Just follow my lead," she answers without looking at me.

She grabs my hand, still focusing on the guard, and pulls me forward. We are in a rush, and it makes sense why she's moving fast, but I wish she wouldn't. The clanging of our armor alerts the guards at the carts, who instantly spring to action, unsheathing their swords and holding them high—and at us.

"State your name and your purpose," says the guard at the front. I squint to see a shiny metal name tag around his neck (he must have been new). Apparently, his name is Erwin Alexander.

"We're not here to cause trouble," Calahan assures Alexander. "We just have an important meeting."

"About *what*, exactly?" another guard behind Alexander, manning the gold cart, asks.

"I honestly don't think it's necessary you know that, intern," she snaps.

"Oh, I think it is."

Our heads whip toward the new voice. Or, for me, the old voice. The guard I bumped into just minutes ago stands in front of the big doors, studying the scene.

He has a smirk of pride on his pale face, obviously basking in the triumph of who knows what.

"I just figured out why you never talk," he says, his smirk widening when his eyes shift to me. The guard begins to circle around me and Calahan like a snake sizing up its prey. "You see, two guards were assigned to Milo Belittle, an incredibly powerful Magic on the run with Ashlyn Kave, whom the king has wanted to execute ever since before she became a murderer."

I gulp. This will *not* end well.

"Those two guards were Joey McHale and Zora Calahan." He leans forward so his mouth is right next to Calahan's—or I guess Zora's—ear. "You wouldn't be familiar with those people, would you?" he hisses.

The guard backs away from Zora when her jaw clenches and her hands turn to fists.

"When McHale stepped away to take a break from this criminal, Zora had the job of looking after Milo. Unfortunately, he seemed to escape." The guard's gaze flicks over to me. "And apparently, he disguised himself in armor and swore not to speak, not unless he wanted his identity to be revealed."

The intern narrows his eyes at me. Alexander tightens the hand around his sword.

The guard, in half of a second, raises his gun and points it at a gap in my armor. Those guns are filled with poisoned darts that will latch on to nerves and paralyze you. Why do I know this? Well, I have dealt with one head-on and watched it almost kill my friend, and I am not exactly eager to be the dying friend in that situation.

"Take one more step and I swear I will shoot," he threatens.

I raise my hands. Zora does not. Instead, she keeps her eyes on the guard. It is a wonder that he holds his ground, even when he knows she is looking straight through him.

"I wouldn't do that if I were you," Zora mutters, her voice low, eyes now trained on the gun. "Believe me, I've been working here longer than you have and I'm betting every piece of knowledge about that weapon you've obtained is either wrong, or I can best it."

Very slowly and carefully, she reaches for her gun while talking so that the guard doesn't notice.

"Like what?" the guard asks, raising an eyebrow in expectancy.

"That it can do this."

In one final and swift motion, she holds her gun high and shoots it straight at the guard's head.

He slumps to the floor, red blood tinted with green decorating the concrete.

I stare at the body in shock, just like many of the other guards. Perhaps they are not expecting her to shoot, or they have no idea that she took her gun out. I am just surprised that the bullet killed someone so quickly.

Zora walks over to the body, whistling and cracking her knuckles. She stops just above it and kicks. And so quiet I can barely hear her, she laughs that ghost-laugh, and it sends a chill through me.

Alexander seems to remember he has a job to do. He lunges forward at Zora, but I can't let that happen. I pick up the gun from next to the guard's dead body and shoot it at his neck where there's a gap in his armor. He drops to the floor, his eyes rolling up into his head, his limbs limp as his sword clatters on the cement.

I slap a hand over my mouth, horrified. Have I really done that? Have I killed someone, especially a royal guard?

Zora holds out her hand, and I give her the gun. As quick as lightning, she shoots every single one of the guards manning the carts until they are all dead, their blood soaking the floor.

She wipes her hands on her armor and grabs the sword from Alexander's dead body, putting it in her old sheath. "We won't need this," she says, either to me or to herself, I can't be sure. She places her current sword in the trash can and starts circling the carts, shoving things into a bag she'd stolen from another cart.

"It gets easier, you know," Zora says suddenly. "Killing people."

"You're saying I have to do that again?"

She turns around. Discomfort must be visible on my face because sympathy fills her eyes. It is soon replaced with the same stone-cold look she gives everyone most of the time. "Not necessarily."

"Then how will it get easier?" I ask, feeling my hands shaking at my sides. *You killed someone. You are a murderer, a traitor of peace.*

"You learn to deal with the guilt." She leans against a cart, piling food into her bag.

"That voice telling you you're a monster; it eventually fades into nothing but a whisper of what was, not what is. A skeleton of a saying, a muffled version of your deepest regrets. You remember that you only kill for survival, and a little bit of spite. And then ... well, it goes away. You find yourself living normally again, not thinking about the person you killed or the things they might have done if they were alive right then, and you finally have serenity with yourself."

She smiles, as if remembering a time she had serenity with herself.

"It's peaceful, and you feel like your mind has cleared. You feel as though those thoughts that chained you to the belief that you were horrible have finally cut the chains, have let you free. And it's awesome."

I smile slightly, looking down at my feet. "Thank you, Zora."

"Please." She slings her bag over her shoulder and motions for me to follow her down the road.

"Call me Selena."

CHAPTER 10

MILO

My legs are starting to become tired.

We have been walking for who knows how long, just wishing we can find our way back to Mrs. Torsney's house. It barely makes sense to me how Selena knows where that house is (or said she knew) because I never told her the address. Has she been stalking us or something?

But why would she? It isn't like we are big celebrities or anything; we are just trying to get the prince to safety. And Sorin is especially not a celebrity. Before this mission, I didn't even know his name.

"There's going to be a convenience store just a few miles from here," Selena says suddenly, making me come back to reality. "We can take a rest there."

"But where is *here?*" I ask, looking around at the vast, empty fields surrounding us. Cattle graze the brown grass, chewing slowly. A barn is to one side of us, yet the lights are out and it looks like it has been abandoned for years. Definitely not the best place to take refuge in.

"I remember this road." She taps her chin thoughtfully. "Just not what it's called. That is Mr. Chen's barn. He's worked in that barn for twenty years. Or, he *did*, until the guards came after him. Apparently, they were angry that he was teaching the villagers and the people who passed by to be independent and stray from the kingdom's rulership."

"Just by farming?"

"Yes." Selena looks ahead, her long black hair swaying in the breeze. She's taken off her helmet a few miles back. Since we are in no immediate danger, I have done the same, and it feels awesome not to be trapped in that tight space, to be able to talk without concern, to feel a sort of freedom that being hidden under a helmet could never satisfy. "He was a dear, sweet man. I think you would like him."

I stiffen. "Really?"

"Really." She looks up at me through her eyelashes, a gesture that makes me blush, and say, "I tend to know people just after meeting them. I wish you would trust me. Just because I'm a royal guard that doesn't mean I'm insane, or untrustworthy, or just plain traitorous."

"I never said it did," I say quietly.

Her thundercloud-gray eyes burn holes into my skull. "Then why are you so nervous around me?"

I clear my throat. I just met her, so I can't tell her I have a bit of a crush on her. She would think I am weird, or stupid, or something.

And, she'd reject me.

"How many miles until the convenience store?" I ask her awkwardly. She removes her eyes from me and continues walking, staring straight in front of her.

"Three."

And that is the end of our conversation.

* * *

I would be lying if I said I wasn't expecting something nicer when Selena says "convenience store."

Perhaps I'd envisioned a five-star restaurant, filled with lavish foods and fancy seats. Maybe a karaoke stage.

But not a run-down old apartment building with a tattered sign reading BERTY J'S: WE'LL MAKE SURE YOU HAVE YOUR CONVENIENCE.

"Holy," I say, studying the building. "What the heck is this?"

Selena smiles. "You don't normally swear, I see. This is the convenience store I was telling you about. It's not fancy at all, but my parents used to take us to this place all the time when we were hungry."

Us?

"Really?" I feel my mouth twisting up into a look of disgust. There are much better stores in the village, so why her parents didn't just take her to one of those is beyond me. "Why?"

"My uncle ran it."

"Your uncle's name is Berty J?"

She laughs that skeleton laugh, and even though the breeze is only light, I shiver. "That's a nickname, silly. His real name is Daniel, but he thought Berty J would be more fitting for a convenience store."

"Oh, yeah." I think about what Sorin would say, and find myself saying the words aloud. "I totally want to go to a place run by, I'm sure, an intelligent man, Berty J."

She laughs again but stops herself when a random gust of wind tickles us.

"It's going to get cold," she says, starting toward Berty J's. It amazes me how fast this girl can switch gears. But I have yet to find out if that is a good thing or a bad thing. When I don't walk with her, Selena looks back and motions for me to follow. I sigh, breathing in the sweet smell of pine and fresh air, and then I start to walk toward Berty J's as well, hoping the name doesn't fully represent the place.

* * *

Selena pushes open the door.

The aroma of several-day-old bread hits my face like a brick wall.

Numerous pastries and candies fill the white organizers, taking up every aisle. Freezers filled with drinks and frozen treats only the royal family is allowed to have sit against the back wall. In the very center of the room is a counter painted black, displaying more candies. A burly man wearing a lime-green apron and a smile is positioned behind it.

Hello, Berty J.

Berty J has dark hair, like Selena's, cut short. He honestly looks like a lumberjack, with tan skin and muscular arms. His red plaid T-shirt is not helping.

As soon as he notices Selena, Berty's face cracks into a huge smile. He opens his arms to hug Selena, but she stays where she is and folds her arms across her chest.

"Seal!" Berty says, hopping over the counter, walking briskly over to Selena and wrapping her in a tight hug. She stays limp in his arms, and when he finally releases her, her jaw unclenches. I haven't even noticed she'd clenched it.

Berty focuses his attention on me. He cocks an eyebrow up in confusion and tilts his head, studying me. "Who's your little friend here?" His eyes focus on my armor. "Surely you didn't bring a guard here to arrest me, Seal."

"No," she tells him stiffly, her eyes flicking everywhere. "If I wanted someone to arrest you, I'd do it myself. I really think you'd be safer with me."

Berty's smile fades slightly. "Of course." It returns quickly. "I trust you, Seal."

There is silence.

Only a few moments later, I say, "I'm Milo. My name is Milo Belittle. And, I'm not a guard, so you don't worry."

I hold out my hand for him to shake it, but Berty smiles wider and wraps me in a hug just as tight as the one he gave Selena.

"Well, Milo, I'm glad you're here." He pulls away from me and glances at Selena. "But ... why are you here?"

"If I told you, Uncle," Selena says, walking away from Berty to study the store, "you would be in danger. And honestly, you're my favorite uncle."

"Is this another one of your stunts, Seal?" Berty doesn't look surprised at all. "I remember when you said you wanted to be a guard."

He turns to me, talking casually, as if sharing a memory. I am careful not to share that I have never met Selena before today, not even knowing her first name until a few hours ago.

"Her mother threw a hissy fit, screamin' about all sorts of things: this is the thanks she gets for raising her kids right; how can she work for someone against her own brother, that sort of hellish stuff."

Selena stops dead.

"Selena has a brother?" Gears begin to turn in my head, gears I didn't even know existed.

She has the same smirk as Sorin, is looking for Sorin, and seems to have an obsession with him. And she knows where Sorin's mom lives.

"No," she says suddenly, so harshly the words feel like knives plunging into my stomach. Gods, how does she do that? "I don't. He's … gone, anyway. It wouldn't matter."

It is quiet for a little while. The silence is unsettling. I have always loved quiet. Most of the time, quiet means peace. But this kind of quiet … this is nervous quiet, tension quiet, anxiety quiet.

"Guards are after you, aren't they, Seal?" Berty asks quietly, his smile gone. It is also unsettling to see his ghosts of smile marks unfilled by happiness. The light in his eyes hasn't died, though. Maybe that is why silence—uncomfortable, stuffy silence—doesn't last long around Berty J.

"Yes." Selena stays where she is, frozen in the aisle. "I might have killed a few."

"I figured as much," he says, going around to all the windows and doors, locking doors and closing blinds. "That's why you have swords." He motions, without looking, at the swords shoved into scabbards hanging from Selena's armor.

"Well," I start, but Selena finishes for me.

"It's mandatory for guards to wear swords at all times."

Berty chuckles lightly, though the situation we are in had barely any light to it. "So proper. Should I call you Sealy of the Royal Guard now?"

A gust of wind hits me. Hard. There are no windows open in the store, though.

Selena must feel it too, because she shivers and says, "They're coming. I'm sorry, Uncle. I shouldn't have gotten you involved."

"I taught you everything you know about sword fighting, kid," says Berty, walking, surprisingly relaxed, over to a chest on the right side of the store.

I wonder how I haven't noticed that chest before. Berty messes with a lock and the chest clicks open, showing off a display of silver-bladed weapons. He leans down and picks up the sharpest one, pricking his finger on it to test it. A dot of blood appears on the fingertip of his index finger.

"Don't worry about me."

Okay, so everyone, even the convenience store owner, knows how to fight, I think. *Great. I really need to catch up.*

Another gust of wind spreads through the store. Selena breathes it in and sighs it out.

"They are getting closer."

"Is there a reason why the Royal Guard uses wind to announce their entrance?" I ask.

"Yes," she replies quickly. "And I will tell you when I believe you're ready to know. It would be horrible for me, but it would help you."

"Why would it be horrible?"

"They would kill me."

With a bang, the door slams open. The guards that file in have their guns raised. I notice they are protecting their faces. On their sides are swords and assortments of other things that could kill us in seconds. Or, rather, can kill me in seconds. Selena and Berty will find ways to protect themselves.

"There you are," says a guard at the very front. Another one I've seen in the large room, before we escaped. He has a long, faded scar from one side of his face to the other.

"I've been looking for you." He smiles mischievously.

"Everyone has," Selena says, raising her chin high, her hands hovering over her swords. "What makes you special?"

The guard turns to look at her, lowering his gun. "Ah. Zora."

I thought her name was Selena.

"I told you if you went out with me, things would be easier," the guard continues. "Yet you've settled for helping this scum."

He motions to me.

Rude.

"I haven't settled for this," Selena—or Zora—says. "I had to. You know full well I had to find him. I have to help him."

Also rude.

"Yes," he breathes. "I do remember that. You're a traitor, Zora. I promised to help you, but ... goes to show you can't exactly trust

142

everyone, huh?"

"I am not a traitor," she shoots back, deathly quiet. I know this isn't going to go well. "And I am not a coward. You are."

"I'm sorry, but I don't remember betraying my kingdom." He gives her a wicked grin. "That was all you."

"You didn't betray your *kingdom*."

"Then how am I a traitor?"

"You betrayed *me*."

The guard stares at her for a moment. I clench my jaw. I don't condone violence normally, but this guard makes me angry. He hurt Selena, and hasn't she suffered enough already, with being dragged away from her family, trained and tired every day, forced to fight for something she didn't believe in?

"You're still hung up on that?" The guard's face twists into a snarl. "You're more sensitive than I thought. I bet you believe 'what we had was real,' and that I'd 'never leave you for anyone.' Am I right?"

"No," Selena responds, her face cold. Even though the man is taller than her, it still feels like she is looking down at him. "I always knew you were power hungry, only using me to get what you wanted. But guess what? So am I. And I was, too."

In a quick move, Selena wraps her hands around the butt of his gun and pulls the trigger, shooting at his foot, so a stream of blood flows and a strangled cry sounds from the guard.

Go time.

Berty and I move forward in unison, picking two guards each to fight. I have no idea how I will come out of this fight unscathed, and maybe I won't, but I still have to try. I am not going to sit back and let someone innocent (Berty) and someone I have grown fond of (take a guess) die just to protect me. That is the only reason they are fighting in the first place.

I raise my sword, my hands shaking violently. One guard strikes to my left while the other heads to my right. Okay, so maybe this isn't such a good idea.

One of the guards jabs at me with his sword. I duck out of the way just in time. The other guard slices his sword in the air, as if trying to convince me to surrender by intimidating me.

I raise my eyebrow at him, challenging him to do more.

I probably shouldn't.

The guard advances and plunges his sword in the air next to me, just missing my stomach. I block his next moves with my blade, uncomfortably aware of my moving feet, almost dancing in an effort to not get killed by the second guard who is trying to knock me off of them.

The guards eventually switch as I anger them. I am just too quick for them to hit. Now, I am facing Selena, who is pointing her gun at the guard, now limping, raising his sword and coming toward her. The barrel is pointed directly in between his eyebrows, but that doesn't stop him from trying to kill her.

I look around, trying to form an idea while also fighting for my life. A close strike to my knee brings me back to reality. Why are they chasing me again? Because I am friends with Ash. But why are they chasing Ash? Because she is a Magic …

Slowly but surely, an idea appears in my mind.

I subtly lead the guards over to the counter. Still fighting and jumping every few seconds so I am huffing in "out of shape," I remove one hand from the hilt of my sword and place it on the counter. I have to have strength to use my power, which is a problem. Most of my strength has been taken during the fight.

But I glance at Selena, hesitation stopping her from pulling the trigger as the guard backs her into a corner while laughing wickedly, and I glance at Berty battling two grown men by himself, struggling, blood flowing freely out of an open wound in his calf, sweat running down his determined face, and I make my decision. If I don't do this, they will die. I will die, and that will be the end. They will die for nothing, and I will die trying to use my power but failing and letting a fatal blow hit me, and I won't be able to help my friends. I won't be able to help the prince out of his prison, the one thing we all agreed we wanted to do when we prepared for this mission.

With utter force, I command, "Stop."

Everyone freezes. Even I feel the slight effects of my own power. While they are frozen, I run to Selena and take her gun from her. And without a second thought, I shoot every guard, including the one in front of me, the one who Selena has previously had some kind of relationship with, the one who hurt her, in the head.

Then I come back to my senses. The adrenaline leaves me, and Berty and Selena become normal again.

She looks around at the bodies covering the floor. She smiles briefly. That is, until she notices my face.

I am shocked. I have single-handedly killed five royal soldiers with their own gun, and I did it with pleasure. What kind of murderer, what kind of psychopath, am I turning into?

"You did this?" she asks me, and I can hear how impressed she is in her voice.

I drop the gun, unable to comprehend what just has happened. "Oh, gods. Oh my gods. I killed people, Selena, I killed them."

"All's fair in love and war," she says, quoting the king's adopted motto from an old proverb. "And your intention was to save, not kill. But you did a pretty good job of it."

"Not helping!"

Selena glances at me guiltily. "Sorry."

A groan sounds from the other side of the room, the side Berty is on. He has collapsed as blood streams from his wound by the second.

Selena rushes over to him. I trail close behind.

His face is deathly pale, and he's lost so much blood I am afraid.

Sage hadn't lost this much blood when she was shot in the leg with that poisonous bullet.

"Uncle?" Selena says to him, crouching down to be next to him.

"Seal?" Berty manages. He doesn't sound good. "Are they dead?"

"Save him!" she shouts at me, her voice shrill and demanding. "Do it, please. We won't be able to take him on our mission, but at least he'll be safe here."

"I can't," I tell her solemnly.

"What?" Selena's face falls. "What do you mean?"

"His injuries are severe. I've only been trained to heal teenagers, and he would take two Healers to survive."

"But—but I can become one."

"It takes several years of training to become a Healer," I say. "Just like in your training to become a guard."

"He's right, Seal," Berty says to Selena. "I'm not gonna make it, but that's all right. You know I'll see you again someday."

Tears begin to fall from Selena's eyes. "Please, Uncle. I can't lose you. Not after I've lost everyone else."

"You've got Milo."

She ignores him.

"You need to be saved." Selena looks at me, her cheeks red, her black hair completely still and not swaying like it normally did. "Please, is there any way—"

"If I could save him," I say softly, "I would've already been trying to."

A sob sounds from Selena, and I notice that it is strange to see her so vulnerable. She looks back at her uncle. "I am so sorry."

"Don't be, Seal," Berty tells her, a smile on his face. A smile that is familiar. The smile of all dying people, knowing they are about to die. "It's not your fault."

"I love you, my favorite uncle."

"Seal, I—"

Berty's eyes close immediately. His speech stops, and his limbs are limp at his sides.

"No!"

Selena's scream is piercing, hurts my ears, and my heart.

I help her up and whisper, "The hardest part about any job is learning how to say goodbye."

I let her sob on my armored shoulder as I lead her out of the convenience store. I find the dirt road and continue as we did before, one of us scared, the other cold.

Just now, it is hard to tell which is which.

CHAPTER 11

SORIN

"Great. What are we supposed to do now?"

Lyssy crosses her arms as the door slams behind Ash. Sage just stares at the door, her mouth open.

It's not like I don't understand. Ash loves Milo. He is her best friend. I would go after Lyssy or Sage if they went missing, wouldn't I? But why does she have to leave now?

"This is great," I grumble sarcastically. "We've lost our fighter and half of our brains, and we're just supposed to stay here until they get back."

"No," Sage says sharply. "We're not leaving them out there."

"You're injured," Lyssy points out.

"If I may," says my mother cautiously, looking from me to Sage to Lyssy, "there is a serum I gave to Sorin whenever he was hurt. Now I would never use it, because it was developed years and years ago—who knows what the side effects are—but it worked."

"Why didn't you tell us about this earlier, Mom?" I ask her, still a hint of menace in my voice. I have no memory of ever taking this serum, but if it worked for me, it might work for Sage.

"Well, I had just met the girl," she responds, sending an

apologetic look my way. "I had no idea how bad her injuries were. However, now I know, and it does list severe pains on the bottle, and I'm assuming she's feeling some severe pains."

Sage nods. I wince. My mother's excuses always come in handy when she needs them. I have experienced her lying to my face, her making excuses, her acting the victim, and I am tired of it.

"Mom, if this is just a way to manipulate her into liking you, you can forget it," I say sharply. "Sage is too smart to be fooled by you, and I wasn't. So don't expect the same results with her."

Lyssy looks from me to my mom curiously. Slowly, she says, "Where's the medicine?"

Mom's mouth twists into a smile. "Finally, someone believes me." She glances at me, her smile widening momentarily, before leaving the room, motioning for us to follow.

I stop Lyssy as she is leaving, hauling Sage in her arms.

"You're really going through with this?" I ask.

"Of course," Lyssy says, her face becoming concerned. "What happened to you, Sorin? Normally, you're so happy-go-lucky, and here, you look like you're terrified of everything your mom does."

I glance at Sage for support, but am disappointed at the fact that she is staring at her wound, the blood still blocked by Ash's awesome wrap. Maybe she worked in the food-truck business, making burritos. I wouldn't be surprised. Maybe Sage's leg could be called Bullet Blood Bite.

I chuckle at the thought before coming back to my senses. "What?"

"She's a pathological liar, Elysian," I say, so sharply I am almost taken aback by my own statement. I have barely used her full name before. "She hurt me with her lies. She—she made me go against my own ways of life. So, yeah, I am scared around her. Scared she's going to take me away from the people I love."

Sage raises her head at those words.

It is quiet for a moment.

Then, "Are you kids coming?" My mom rounds the corner and bumps into Sage, causing her leg to turn a bright red. Sage cries out in pain. Mom stares at it in sympathy, but I know it is fake. "Let's get you fixed up, huh?"

* * *

"Thank you, Mrs. Torsney, really," Lyssy says. Her legs dangle off the edge of the counter in the bathroom that I used to lock myself in to get away from my mother. I blink at the image of my red face as I stare at myself in the mirror, hot tears running down my face, and it fades away.

She is waiting to catch Sage in case she falls backward while Mom helps Sage walk. I decide not to help. I don't want to encourage my mom any further.

"Of course, dears," my mom responds, her blond curls flying

everywhere. "You're Sorin's friends. Of course I would help you."

Sage smiles to herself.

I clench my jaw and ball my hands into fists. Great, now she is manipulating my friends, just like she manipulated me.

Sage stumbles, trying her best not to put too much weight on her leg. "This medicine really works," she says, smiling at my mom.

My mom grins back.

Ringing fills my ears.

"Right?" Lyssy says, picking up the pill bottle and reading the ingredients. Something is wrong, though, because her face twists into one of confusion. "Huh."

"What?" I ask, storming over to her. If my mom did something—

"Nothing."

And that is it. Nothing. No ingredients, no name, nothing. Not even the amount people are supposed to take.

Mom sets Sage on the edge of the bathtub and quickly walks over to us and steals the bottle from Lyssy's hands.

"Oh, an old printing mistake," she says as her eyes widen, staring intensely at the bottle. "It's either that or Sorin ripped it off when he was a little baby." She reaches up to stroke my cheek, but I smack her hand away.

"Oh," Lyssy says quietly.

"What did you do with the packaging, Mom?" I ask carefully,

dangerously quiet. I am almost never quiet. As plenty of people tell me, I can never shut up. But this is serious. If she gave Sage something that could harm her, I will harm my own mother.

"I did nothing, I swear." My mom's eyebrows crease. "Are you feeling alright, Sorin? Do you need some medicine, too?"

"I'm fine." I glare at her. "But are you? You're going to be caught eventually."

"Doing what, Sorin?" she asks me as a clock in the living room, one of her many ones, chimes. "I'm trying to fix what we've destroyed."

"No, Mom." I gulp, trying to hold back tears. "You're trying to fix what you've destroyed, and it's not working. I'm taking my friends and I'm getting the hell out of here, because you are not trustworthy enough to keep us here. And, in case you haven't noticed, we have a mission to complete and friends to find."

I snatch the bottle from her hands and leave the bathroom to start packing our things. Maybe if we hurry, we'll be able to find Ash, then Milo, and make it to room 106 before time runs out.

Lyssy follows behind me. Slowly, so does Sage.

"What are you doing, Sorin?" Lyssy asks me as I frantically search for our things around the house. "She's just trying to help."

"I don't want her help!" I shout. "She's tried to help me for years after she made my life a living hell, and how did that turn out? I left her, Elysian! I left her to go to Camp Serenity because I knew I'd find some sense at that place, some sort of calm and normal, like other kids felt with their moms! You don't know her like I do, and trust me, Elysian, she's not trying to help. She's trying to get you to stay with her forever by bribing you with treats and trinkets and drugs!"

"Oh, please," Sage says from behind Lyssy. "This isn't a fairy tale. Your mom isn't the witch with the candy house. She's not bribing us. She's just being nice."

"*Why does no one listen to me?*" I say, shoving things into one of the plastic bags on the counter.

Lyssy sighs. "This is important to you, huh? Well, I'll go pack."

I am too mad to even care about her generosity.

The sound of footsteps fades. I think I am alone.

Until, "What did she do to you?"

I pause. Sage. I thought she hated me. Doesn't she hate me? "Why do you care?"

She hobbles over to me. Raising my chin with her thumb, she says, "I asked, what did she do to you?"

I don't mean to start crying. I really don't. But everything just overwhelms me, and before I know it, hot tears are falling down my face. Sobs leave my mouth before I can stop them and Sage wraps her arms around me.

"Sorin," she whispers in my ear, "do you really think I'd be bribed with drugs?"

I chuckle a broken chuckle. "No," I say, and my voice is raspy.

She hugs me tighter before letting go and limping away.

I smile at her back, but stop myself. Now my feelings for her are even more conflicted. I like her, but not in *that* way. And she likes me sometimes, but not in *that* way. Other times I dislike her strongly. She hates me sometimes. I have no idea what to do. Do I buy her flowers and apologize for every mistake I've ever made, or do I trip her as she is walking past and leave her at my mom's to fend for herself? There is no in between.

I shake my head to bring myself back to reality and begin to pack again, this time less angrily and with wet cheeks.

* * *

"So, this is fun," I say to the silence. We, meaning Lyssy, Sage, and me, trudge past several clusters of oaks that seem to be taller than the sky itself, past buildings the villagers must forget about, past wildlife that are taller than me and wildlife the size of my pinkie finger.

"Oh, yeah," says Lyssy, a nasty expression on her face. "I've always loved walking in circles with no idea where I'm going, what I'm looking for, or how I'm going to survive." She fans herself, even though she is dressed in the least amount of clothes of all of us, with her short-shorts and white crop-top, both from my sister's closet.

Sage says nothing. Her wound isn't as bad. The skin around it is peeling, which means it is healing (or trying to), and the sickly green tint has been reduced to a darker yellow.

155

I have made the smart decision to opt for a hat, which eventually makes my scalp itchy, so I leave it at a pond. Maybe not the smartest decision.

I stretch. The sun is just starting to slowly inch toward the horizon, teasing the kingdom with the last hours of sunlight, of warmth, of daytime. I am sick of daytime.

Daytime is time to think. And thinking always makes me uncomfortable, smarter, or more serious. Who says that does anybody any good?

Sage shivers. Her pale skin has goosebumps that I almost mistake for more freckles. "Couldn't we have left earlier?"

Yeah, the wind is strong, but it isn't that strong. Maybe I am just tough, but I barely feel anything.

"Apparently we couldn't've left soon enough," Lyssy says, scowling at the ground.

I decide to distract myself. "Hey, Sagey."

Sage groans. "What do you want?" Exasperation is evident in her voice.

"Nothing," I say. "Just your kidney."

"Why in *the gods' names* would you need my kidney, Sunshine?"

"Three is always better than two. I mean"—I motion around at the three of us—"we, including you, my little ray of happiness, are living proof of that."

"I hate you," she announces with a short sigh. "I really, truly hate you."

"Now, I know it's probably dry because of how much blood you lost—"

"Stop talking."

"But I'll take it nonetheless."

Sage claps a hand over my mouth and pulls me down to the ground, behind a bush. My shirt catches on one of the branches and the fabric clings to the leaves for dear life. I try not to be too disappointed. Lyssy stops in her tracks. Rustling comes from far away, but still in the forest.

"Spies," Sage mouths.

"Spies?" I mouth back, creasing my eyebrows for emphasis.

Lyssy sends a terrified, wide-eyed look in our direction.

A scream cuts through the silence. Laughter after that.

The spies are torturing someone.

And by the next string of curses, I am pretty sure I know who it is.

Panic settles in my stomach. Who knows what kind of power they have, especially if they are torturing Ash, one of the strongest people in our group? And making her scream?

"Stop!" Ash demands before shouting in agony again. "Stop it!" Her words are drowned in sorrow. I can tell she is in immense pain.

I can't think of anything to lighten the mood, not when I am so focused on making a plan to get Ash out of this wretched situation.

Sage suddenly perks up. Her eyes widen and she raises her head. She smacks my arm repeatedly, rather hard, so I rub the spot on my arm after she is done. Lyssy sends us (well, I should say, me) a confused glance. I shrug.

"You'll never believe this," Sage whispers. She takes her map from her pocket and flips it over, so the backside is facing up. "Do you have a marker?"

"Oh, yeah," I say, "of course. I always carry writing utensils with me in case you ever need to scribble on a map." I raise my eyebrow at her. Okay, maybe I can still find a way to make it funny.

She raises an eyebrow right back.

Sighing, I search for a pen or pencil in my pockets. And what do you know? When I remove my hand from the left pocket of my shorts, I pull out a black pen.

"Thanks," Sage says, her attempt at being sweet making me want to laugh.

"Yeah, you're welcome."

She takes it from me and begins jotting down a strategy.

"Should I just label this Sage's pen?"

"No, thanks."

"Why not?"

"There are *teeth marks*, Sorin. Teeth marks. It's disgusting."

"Will you two stop flirting and hurry up already?" Lyssy whisper-shouts from behind me.

I feel myself blush furiously as I face forward.

We fall silent, waiting for Sage to finish her project.

Are we flirting? It doesn't seem like it. It just seems like friendly banter. Or, not-so-friendly banter. I don't like Sage, not like that. Or maybe I do. I have no idea what to think anymore. Do I or do I not like Sage?

Luckily, Sage thrusts the paper into my chest, sending me tumbling backward into a tall oak. I am happy for the distraction but not happy for the pain I feel in my chest now.

"Here," she whispers to me. "Check it over. You are the thicker lines. Elysian's the thinner lines."

"Are you calling me fat, Jobbs?"

Sage passes me a glare that tells me to shut up or she'll probably make that tree fall on me, so I do. I skim it over, not really paying attention. If I do something wrong, Sage will either yell at me for it or we will start arguing. One or the other.

I hand the paper to Lyssy.

She takes it hastily, obviously in a rush.

Another one of Ash's shrieks reminds me why we are even doing this in the first place.

I am distracted when Sage stands up quickly. So quickly, in fact, that she winces and almost falls backward. Luckily, I stand too, just so I can catch her.

She just uses me to stabilize herself before trudging forward, around the bushes, almost directly into the soldiers. She stops, though.

"Remember the plan?" Sage asks me and Lyssy.

Lyssy nods.

I just try to think of what would happen after we rescue Ash, not the fighting and saving part.

Why is there so much rescuing in this trip?

"Sorin." Lyssy's harsh whisper makes me come back to my senses, and I nod.

So we continue forward. In silence.

The confidence I feel is short-lived when someone—or rather something—slams into me from behind. I run into Sage, who falls on her leg and begins to cry out in pain.

The thing that ran into me is pinning me to the ground with its knee, all of its weight focused on my back.

Talk about back problems, I think to myself.

The thing is a man. A very tall, very muscular man. I will discover this being dragged into a short brick building, situated behind the woods we are trekking in. A building made for spies. Meaning they have been able to see, and hear, us the whole time.

The man's name is Fernando. I will discover this while being locked in a jail cell, breathing heavily, scared for my life after I notice the guns hanging on the wall of the cell.

And I will also discover we have failed, I have failed, when another one of Ash's screams fills the silence, this time followed by an echo.

The echo of a gunshot.

CHAPTER 12

SORIN

The first thing I notice is that there is nothing in the cell.

No food, no entertainment, no way to communicate with other people, no nothing. There are two small windows, both at the top of the room, one on each side of the cell. Neither let any light in. A small bucket of water sits to my left, but it is full of mud and dirt and bugs. I'll probably be poisoned if I try to drink it.

Stone walls surround me. Almost everything is stone. I am even sitting on a stone bench, situated in the middle of the cell. Even with the windows, it is cold and dark. So, so dark.

I shiver.

Every minute that passes feels like a decade. If I am locked in this prison for any longer, I think I am going to lose it. My jaw clenches automatically and my fingers begin to twitch, begging to see someone, to touch the human race. I haven't been locked up for long, but all my life people have surrounded me, bathing me in love. My sister almost always went forgotten, even by my own mother. Everyone fixated on me. I wasn't surprised when she decided to be a guard for the king, even when my mom reminded her she was going against me. I understood her, in a sense. I went against my mom, and she went against me. We aren't that different.

She is a Magic herself.

I don't remember much after she left. My sister was the artistic one, always, and I was the adventurous one. This was also a reason why everyone was surprised when she left to work for the king. That level of bravery is almost unreachable, especially now that the prince is gone, especially for my sister.

I always had known she had an adventurous side, just lying in wait for the moment it was unveiled, and I had always tried to pull it out of her somehow, but it had never worked before. I miss my sister. I haven't seen her in years. I sit in that jail cell, reflecting on our past memories, and the feeling of helplessness that is so strong I can almost taste it only grows.

My favorite memory with my sister is late one night. I was sitting on the couch, watching the daily news that featured the king's announcement. He always had new announcements. I believe this one was for a new security called Z.O.R.A that never made it too far. Zen's Organization Resolving the Apparatus, if I remember correctly.

My sister looked up from her board game. She loved games and puzzles and things that worked her brain like that. She always had.

"Z.O.R.A.?" she asked me. "That sounds like a dance studio." She smiled. My sister always had the best jokes. I learned everything from her. She began to dance around the coffee table in our living room while I laughed.

"Maybe I should call you that from now on," I had muttered, a big grin on my face.

My sister giggled. "Maybe you should."

I smirked at her.

I wish that moment could have lasted forever.

From then on, I called her Zora. She was referred to as Zora by my parents, and close family members. Almost everyone I knew had called her that.

Until the day she left.

My sister had always wanted to be a guard for the king. My relatives had shamed her for it, but I didn't care enough about dying to hate my own sister. She wasn't bad; she was just wanting to serve the kingdom.

My mom had stood stiffly behind me, next to my father. My father was a muscular man with a drinking problem. I wasn't surprised a year later when he just didn't show up one day.

"Goodbye, Selena," my mom had said, her voice so flat yet so sharp it could've cut through steel.

My sister shifted nervously on her feet, the bag on her shoulder swaying in the doorway.

"Don't come back!" my dad slurred. He said drinking always helped him cope with harder things. Not surprisingly, he had been drunk during this event.

I had just looked down at my older sister. My mom was short

and my dad was tall. I got the tall gene and she was stuck with the short gene. So even though I was only fourteen and she was eighteen, she had to look up to me every time she wanted to talk to me. "I love you, Zora."

She had smiled a sad smile. "I love you, too, Sorin." She reached up to ruffle my hair. "Always."

I smiled back, feeling tears begin to well in my eyes. "Always."

She shut the door behind her. I watched the door for minutes after that like a lost puppy, wishing, hoping, *praying* she left something at home so she'd come back.

But even now, as I sit in that cell, I haven't seen her. Not in five years.

Your own sister, they used to tell me.

She betrayed you.

How can you stand it?

I would've kicked her out if I were your mom.

Now, normally, I wouldn't condone violence, but ...

There was no good reason for her to leave.

Working for him, *too? Is she insane?*

You must be feeling horrible.

Eventually, their words they thought were helping have gotten easier to ignore. I never especially liked those villagers. Those who had sympathy instead of empathy. Those who try to make the best of the situation by making others feel worse. My sister, even if she did leave to work for the king, was never one of those people. She was my best friend.

She is my best friend.

I wonder randomly if my sister knows I am locked up. If the spies have already reported to the king and his soldiers that they found some Magics trying to save a dead one.

Will she try to save me? Or are her duties so important she won't risk saving her own brother?

I think and think and think and think until I can't think anymore, and the thoughts cloud my brain, making everything foggy and disoriented, and tears somehow appear on my cheeks and roll down my face to my chin, and depressed sobs break the lonely silence of the cell, and I can't tell if the sobs come from me or someone else, hiding in the shadows of the gloomy space. I think until it feels like my brain is broken and malfunctioning slowly, not loading enough, not recognizing things quickly enough.

I think so hard I think I am delirious when someone who looks exactly like Ash opens the door to my cell in one swift motion, keys in her hand, a mischievous smirk and reckless glint in her eyes, and says, "Let's get the hell out of here."

CHAPTER 13

ASH

"How in the gods' names did you do that, again?" Elysian asks me for, like, the fourth time.

I sigh. Honestly, I am growing tired of giving her the story.

"The first gunshot was just a warning," I say, thinking back to the spies' headquarters. "That's what the spy told me. He said if I messed up again he would actually fire at my head. What he didn't know was that I was distracted because I was trying to make a plan using the keys dangling from his pocket.

"So, when he wasn't looking, I stole his gun and aimed it at his head. It was quite simple. I just threw flames at the tree behind him that were quickly extinguished, obviously, and it got his attention." I think for a moment. "At least, I think they were extinguished. Actually, now that I'm thinking about it—"

"Back to the point," Sage says, her voice flat. Can you believe she hasn't even said thank you for my rescue mission? Ungrateful, if I do say so myself.

"Right. I threatened to shoot him if he didn't give me the keys, and of course he did. Then I used the keys to unlock the main doors, snuck into the cells, and unlocked them. Every guard who got in my way—well, let's just say there was a lot of blood after I was done with them."

"But how did you know where to find us?" Elysian asks.

"I … don't know," I admit bluntly. "It just felt like I was getting closer to something important, and I followed my instinct, and then I found you guys. It was pretty easy."

Sorin snorts. "Glad to know we give you instincts."

I glare at the ground as I walk, thinking. Honestly, I don't know how I found them so easily. It just seemed natural, like following a trail of breadcrumbs.

"Spies," Sage mutters. "Why are there spies in the middle of the forest?"

I shake my head.

"I was searching for Milo when I found them. Or, rather, they found me. When I didn't give them information, they tortured me. So, yeah, I have no idea. What, is it not on your little map?"

I'm disappointed by the amount of relish in my voice. I don't want to be mean to Sage, not really. I'm just starting to realize that maybe we won't find Milo, and I'm exhausted, and I have no idea where we're going. We could be walking in circles right now and I wouldn't know.

Elysian huffs from next to me. She's a lot shorter than I am, and I find it hilarious. The high and mighty Elysian Viggo, bested by me, just because I'm taller than her. She really makes a title for herself, but she's not as good as she thinks she is.

I glance at one of the trees as we pass. Words are engraved there.

All's fair in love and war.

The words are familiar, yet I can't remember why. Then it hits me, and *hard.* The slogan for the kingdom. The slogan all guards go by in their daily lives. I only know this because of how many times I've almost been caught by them as a child, how many times I've been so close to the people willing to become murderers to get me captured, that I can read the slogan printed on their armor, right on their sword arm. It differs with each person but is always on the forearm, reminding you that *you* got yourself into this mess, that if you choose to use your sword for something bad, you will not be shamed for it.

I am a terrible person.

And I have been since I was seven.

I always will be. Nothing will make me feel good about that, not even a printed saying. Not even the feeling of holding a sword and knowing that if I kill these guards, it will get me closer to the boy who saved me from dying when I was fifteen. Not even the fact that somehow, someday, I will find him and save him and the favor will be repaid.

And not even the fact that what I'm doing is utterly amazing and only something a person with good in their heart would do.

You see, there are two kinds of people. The good people, who do everything just to be viewed as nice, and they really could be evil on the inside, and the people with good in their hearts, who really do want to help and want to do things and only have good intentions.

We walk until I can't feel my feet. I'm numb, a shadow of other people, as we stop in front of a large clearing, looking around for more spies, and it's so quiet, so, so quiet that I can hear my own heart beat.

"Where are we?" Sorin asks, confusion in his voice, and I agree with him for once.

I glance around at the tall trees. "A forest."

"An ocean?" Elysian is on the other side of the clearing, staring down.

We've reached a dead end.

"Well, that's just perfect," Sorin mutters. "I don't think any of us have the power of water manipulation, right?" He looks around at the group of us, his eyebrow raised expectantly. "Perfect."

I go to see the ocean.

The cliff stops abruptly and if Elysian hadn't put her arm out to stop me, I would've fallen off it. Beneath us is water crashing against sandy rocks. The water is dark and polluted: probably another one of the king's brilliant plans. The sound is so loud I have to cover my ears from going deaf. Elysian looks perfectly fine. In fact, she's smiling.

"This water is familiar," she says, and that's it. A gust of wind brushes past us, meaning she's using her power, but she says nothing else.

This would be fine, if I didn't have the same thought.

This water is the water where my mother and I fought.

But how would she know that?

"Well, that's amazing." I can almost *feel* Sorin's sarcasm. "Let's just all jump in and go for a swim, shall we?"

Elysian stares at the water curiously.

She plops down at the edge of the water, letting her legs dangle above the loud waves.

I sit next to her and try my best not to recoil when I do. Lately, it's like my body has been acting on its own.

You know this isn't one of those times, says a tiny voice in my mind.

Hush.

"Do you …" She hesitates, then changes her question. "Got any more stories for me?"

I sigh, closing my eyes and letting the sound of the water overwhelm my ears. It's calming to hear something so unaffected by the problems that seem to consume everyone's entire lives. The ocean doesn't interfere; it just sits and waits and waits and waits. It watches, too. Watches and waits and sits back and watches and watches and watches.

I wish I could just watch instead of being in the action.

I've always been the instigator. I didn't necessarily *start* the fights, but fights revolved around me and my powers and who I was. Who I am. The fights started *with* me. It would be nice to watch people fight about other things, like which pets one another liked, which drinks were better, which restaurants had better food.

The normal things.

"None," I say, opening my eyes and looking past the water, into the horizon. The sun is low and covered by tree branches hanging overhead, so the sun isn't as blinding. "Gods. This whole thing has fallen apart."

"I know." She chuckles. "It's kind of funny when you think about it. We started this trip with such good intentions, but now we've been captured by spies and guards several times, Milo's disappeared, we've met Sorin's mom, Sage has been shot, and I *still* haven't discovered what that tattoo means."

I freeze. Then I relax.

"You're good, you know." I raise an eyebrow at her. She's not smiling but she's not serious. The corners of her mouth are upturned into a tiny, tiny smirk. "Maybe even better than me."

"Maybe." Her words are whispers. She's now facing me. Elysian tries to touch my tattoo, but I shrug out of reach. "Why don't you trust me?" she asks, and there's a hint of disappointment in her voice.

"I do," I argue, but she cocks her head, studying me, unbelieving.

"It's just … you don't want to know why I got this."

"Haven't I made it clear that I do?"

I wait for words to fill my mouth, but I say nothing. It's too quiet, and I'm strangely uncomfortable. *Just watch*, I tell myself. I turn to see Sorin and Sage, now arguing again in the shadows of the tall oaks. Sage is standing on one leg, the bandages around her leg soaked in dark red blood. Sorin has his eyebrows furrowed and an expression of disbelief on his face, completed with annoyance. Sage is talking so loudly and angrily that spit is coming out of her mouth. The scene isn't flattering.

"What do you think they're fighting about now?" I say to Elysian, who's staring at me. I know this because I can feel her icy blue eyes glaring holes into the side of my skull. My question distracts her for a moment as she turns to study Sorin and Sage.

"Anything," she states simply. "They fight about anything."

I watch as they suddenly stop, Sage breathing heavily, Sorin's lips parted ever so slightly. And I watch as Sage hobbles forward and suddenly grabs Sorin's face, putting her lips to his. My mouth drops open.

Sorin looks just as surprised. His hands fly up, his eyes open wide. But he soon relaxes into the kiss, bringing his hands to her hips.

I watch in awe. Elysian looks just as surprised next to me. "Oh my gods," she whispers next to me. "Oh. My. Gods."

"Did you know about this?" I hiss to her.

Her wide eyes and her light, surprised chuckle gives away that she knew nothing. By the way they look when they pull away from each other, Sage and Sorin didn't know anything either. Sage's cheeks are flushed and Sorin has a lopsided grin on his face.

Elysian whoops from beside me. I just raise my eyebrows at the two of them. They look over to us as if noticing us for the first time. Sorin waves and Sage buries her head in her hands.

Sage storms over to us and sits down slowly. She's mostly talking to Elysian when she says, "Please tell me you didn't see that."

"All of it." Elysian smiles, mirroring Sorin.

"Even the fact that you initiated it," I add.

"And enjoyed it." Elysian wiggles her eyebrows at Sage.

Sage licks her lips, then laughs. "Yeah, I guess I did. But this is all so confusing. I mean, I thought I hated him."

"Don't be discouraged," I say. "Maybe you still do." I cross my fingers and earn a snort from Elysian.

As they begin to talk about Sorin and love and feelings, I zone out. I notice Sorin sitting behind Sage, watching with a curious expression, his head cocked. He says nothing, just watches.

Just watch.

* * *

I don't remember walking somewhere else. All I remember is Sorin saying nothing while Sage and Elysian talk and talk and talk. That grin is still on his face, yet smaller and less noticeable. There are glowing lights, but I'm too exhausted to say anything about them. All I remember is stopping in front of that glowing light, and an old woman, graying hair and all.

She brings us inside her house that smells like cats and gingerbread cookies—a strange combination, but I'm so tired I barely even think of it—and leads each one of us to separate bedrooms, promising she'll give Sage new bandages in the morning when she notices her wound. She says her husband left her his parents' house and that's why it has so many bedrooms. I don't care. All I care about is the moment when I tuck myself into bed and let my head fall back onto the pillow, forgetting everything, including my own brain.

I sleep a dreamless sleep.

* * *

When I wake up, sunlight is streaming through the windows. Sorin must not be awake or else he would've directed the sun somewhere else. I'm frantic, searching for my sword, and my *clothes*, once I realize I'm wearing something that I don't remember wearing before arriving here. The door is closed and locked, no sound coming through the house.

For a second I think I'm completely alone, and I start to panic.

Until the door creaks open, and in pops the face of Elysian

Viggo.

When I relax, it must be evident, because she relaxes too.

"I thought I was alone," she admits, sliding into my room and closing the door behind her. She finds a seat on the edge of my bed. "I checked everywhere. Sage and Sorin aren't in their beds. And Mrs. S, the old lady, isn't anywhere either."

"Strange," I say.

"Thank you," she says, surprising me.

"For what?" *It's not like you've done anything to help her.*

"For *this*. All of it. We wouldn't have been able to find it without you. Without you, we'd probably still be trapped in those stupid cells."

"It was me that got you in the cells in the first place."

"Yes, and it was also you who got us out. It doesn't matter how many mistakes one makes, only how one chooses to fix them." She smiles. "Maybe someone told me that before. It sounds familiar."

I pause at her words. *I was the one who told you that.*

"Maybe." I shrug.

Suddenly, as we sit there, quiet, Mrs. S pushes the door open. "Oh, thank the gods!" she says, putting a hand over her heart and breathing a sigh of relief. "I thought you two had disappeared or something!"

I recoil, but Elysian smiles. "After the comfort you've given us, Mrs. S, we would never run away."

Mrs. S smiles back. "It makes me happy to hear that, Elysian."

They both turn to me expectantly.

"Uh," I stammer, "thank you?"

"You're welcome." Mrs. S's smile returns and she's leading us out of my bedroom and to the small kitchen. The green tiles hold a bunch of inspirational quotes, most from authors. Sage and Sorin are sitting at the island, unspeaking, unmoving, staring down at the marble.

"Well, this is nice," Elysian says, surveying the kitchen.

"Nice" is definitely not a word I would use when describing her kitchen. More like cluttered, or maybe tiny, possibly "inspirational."

"Thank you, dear."

When Mrs. S says this, Sorin tenses, looking around frantically. His eyes land on Mrs. S, who is staring at him strangely, and he relaxes and goes back to staring at the marble. He thinks no one but Mrs. S noticed, but I did.

"Let's make breakfast, shall we?" Mrs. S suggests, and Elysian quickly steps forward to help her. Maybe she saw his strange reaction, too. Or maybe she's just trying to be a good person. I don't really care enough to think about it for too long.

I sit next to Sage. Her wound looks better. It's wrapped more tightly now, and she has fresh clothes on, like the rest of us. She's wearing loose pants, but the bandages are still visible somehow. I notice that she's not bleeding anymore. That's a good sign.

In a matter of minutes, three plates of breakfast are served in front of us. Elysian flashes a smile before giving all of them to us, but her smile seems to linger when she gets to me.

I tilt my head slightly in confusion, but then her smile's gone and she's turning away from me, talking animatedly with Mrs. S. I shake it off and eat. Maybe it was just a trick of the light.

The breakfast is so good I almost forget the ball of stress that's settled at the pit of my stomach. It comes back when I finally choke it all down.

I realize where I am. Where I should be. Why I even left in the first place. Our deadline. Holy—

"What time is it?" I ask, standing without realizing it. "What day?"

Everyone turns toward me. Mrs. S checks her watch. "I believe it's August first," she says, and I try to relax, but the last time I checked, it was July 29.

"*How* long have we been sleeping, exactly?" Sage asks, raising her head from her breakfast, suspicious.

"Well, you were so exhausted when you got here, I just thought you needed some rest." Mrs. S rubs her arm nervously. "I might have let you sleep for about, say, three days."

"*Three days?*" I storm forward but Elysian puts out an arm so I can't get to Mrs. S. "What do you mean we've needed rest for three days? We actually have somewhere to go."

178

"It'll be fine," Elysian assures me.

"No, it won't!" I retort, fighting her grip. "We only have three days. Three days to find and rescue the prince without getting killed."

"Oh, I'm sorry," Mrs. S says sympathetically, and I almost forget my anger. She just has the ways of an old lady that will make you feel instantly sorry for her. It even works on *me*. "If I had known, I would have woken you up, but you—all of you—were just so tired. I couldn't help it."

"I don't have time for this." I begin to pace. "We're already missing Milo. Who knows where *he* is. We're on the run from bloodthirsty guards for the castle when we're practically heading right into the source of them to find a place that might be gone by the time we get there. The prince is dying as we speak and if we don't save him, then there won't be a Prince of Buit. We will have failed and we'll eventually be killed by the guards and live for the rest of eternity in the fiery pits of hell because we didn't save him." I turn back to face Mrs. S. "So, yes, you could've helped it."

But no one is looking at me. They're all staring behind me, at the door. Sage's mouth is open and a wide smile is on Elysian's face. Sorin looks on the verge of bursting out into laughter, and Mrs. S looks incredibly confused.

"Fiery pits of hell, huh?" says a smooth voice I instantly recognize. "Well, that doesn't sound too pleasant."

"Oh my gods," Sage laughs.

"Oh my gods," I repeat, and whip around, looking straight into the eyes of none other than Milo Belittle.

CHAPTER 14

MILO

Mrs. S places a cup of tea in front of me. I'm sitting at the kitchen counter, squeezed in between Ash and Sage.

Selena is standing by the front door. She didn't want to come in, but Sorin went to meet her.

They're talking quietly yet animatedly, Sorin looking at her in disbelief and Selena feeling guilty based on her creased eyebrows and twisted expression.

Ash grabs my face and turns it toward her. "Why do you keep looking back there?"

Then she realizes and gasps. "You have a crush on that girl!"

"I don't," I grumble, "and can you not talk so loudly?"

"You totally do." She smirks, but it suddenly fades when she says, "Doesn't she work for the king?"

"Used to." My face is stone when I reply. "Does it matter?"

"*Yes*! She's the enemy."

"Do you really think I would have brought her here if she was the enemy?"

"Milo—"

"Ash—"

"*Calahan?*" Sorin says, spitting out the word like it's a slur. "Are you kidding me? Why didn't you just use your *real* name?"

"Sorin, please," Selena tries, but Sorin cuts her off.

"You're really that ashamed of me, huh? You don't want the king to know that you're related to a Magic, the very kind of person you've worked so hard to fight against?"

"You don't understand—"

"I understand plenty well, Selena." He crosses his arms. "I just—I miss the old you. The one who didn't leave me for five years. What else aren't you telling the king? Have you forgotten that you, yourself, are a Magic? Did that slip your mind when you were writing your resume or something?"

"You have every right to be mad, but not here."

"Why not?" Sorin asks. He shakes his head. He looks disgusted. "Don't want to embarrass yourself in front of your little boyfriend?"

I stand from the table and storm toward them. "She's not my girlfriend, and I am most definitely not her boyfriend."

Selena's cheeks redden. "Belittle, now is *not* the right time—"

"Yeah, stay out of this," Sorin says, shielding Selena defensively, "and *stay away from my sister.*"

"You don't own her!"

"Why do you even care? You've been gone for, what, four days, maybe, and you've had a sudden attraction to my sister?"

I feel my own face grow hot and open my mouth to retort, but I can't say anything. I've just embarrassed myself by coming over here and trying to resolve things by arguing. I don't do that. Ash does that, and she's insanely good at it. I feel stupid.

"Sorin," Selena says quietly and carefully, and her voice sounds dangerous, "just listen to me. And leave him alone." She takes a deep breath and starts talking. "I had to leave. They were short on soldiers, and you were so supportive, so I figured it wouldn't be that big of a deal."

"And it *wasn't* until you left me for five years!"

"I had to. The king's son, Ameer, has been missing for longer than you know, all of you."

At that point, Ash comes over to us. She crosses her arms over her chest. Sage and Elysian are sitting back, watching us from their seats. "What do you mean? How long has he been missing for?"

"At least ..." Selena sighs. "At least a year. You guys are somehow the first to figure it out, other than the guards of the king. The original plan was to go back two years ago, but then the masquerade ball happened and Ameer was arranged to marry this beautiful princess from another kingdom, so we had to prepare. My return was postponed. Then, Ameer was captured, and the king sent us out to look for him. So I couldn't come home again. I didn't want to leave you for five years, but the king needed me. And it's not like he was in the state to do anything himself—"

"Is he ever?" Ash interrupts, snorting.

Selena glares at her before continuing. "—considering he was dealing with the guilt of losing his son right after the excitement of having him marry. He barely comes out of the castle anymore."

"Sounds suspicious if you ask me," Ash says. She crinkles her nose. "Why wouldn't you be personally searching for someone you love if they'd gone missing, especially if you're the king of a kingdom and that missing person is the prince? It doesn't make sense."

Selena turns toward Ash, studying her. "You're Ashlyn Kave, right?"

Ash's jaw clenches. "Yes. Is there a problem?"

"Well, I understand that you have bad history with the king, but you have to cut him some slack. I mean, he's lost his son."

"Which is exactly my point. But I guess that doesn't matter to you since you're buddy-buddy with him, does it?"

"Ash, stay away from my sister," Sorin snarls, and Ash literally laughs out loud.

"Please, you can keep her."

"Stop," Elysian says from behind Ash, making her jump.

How did she get here? Ash mouths to me, and I shrug.

"This is exactly the reason why we're so delayed," Elysian continues. "We keep arguing with one another when we're supposed to be working together to save him. I'm sure Selena wants to rescue Prince Ameer just as much as we do, so we have to include her in our group now. She's not a danger to us. She's proved that. So can

184

we just let it go and start looking before things get out of hand?"

"We don't even know where we are, Lyssy," Sorin argues. "How are we supposed to look for him if we don't even know where to go?"

"Yeah, how did you two find us anyway?" Ash asks, raising an eyebrow at me.

"There may or may not be a tracking device on the sword I gave you," I mutter, rubbing the back of my neck.

"What the hell, man?"

"Seems like you need it," Selena interjects, "since you act like such a dog."

"That's it," Ash announces, trying to pounce on Selena, but I push her back and Elysian grabs her arms to stop her, and Sorin steps in front of Selena to protect her.

"You just keep proving my point!" Elysian hisses. "We need to leave, now, or we'll never find him in time. Stop trying to make each other mad and focus on the main point: rescuing the prince!"

"Exactly," I agree. "We only have a limited amount of time. Three days. It's not much. We need to do this, or the prince will die and his blood will be on our hands."

"Oh, dear," Mrs. S says from the kitchen. "You're leaving already? I feel like we've only just met. I have a whole lunch planned. Please, stay just a while longer. My daughter—she never visits me anymore. She's about your age, and I—I just need someone. Please?"

She gives those old lady pleading eyes and I collapse.

I say, "Of course," at the same time Ash says, "Absolutely not."

I say, "Why not?" at the very same time Ash says, "Why?"

"Because," I argue, "she only has us. Doesn't she, after all she's given to us, deserve just a little bit of company?"

"I'm sorry, were you or were you not the person just saying 'we only have a little bit of time, so we should use it wisely?'" she mocks.

Sage snorts from the kitchen table. When I pass her a glance, she shrugs and says, "What? It was a good impression of you."

Ash tips her head toward Sage before continuing. "Aren't you going to honor your word? Don't you say that's the most important thing a person can do? To keep their promises?"

"Don't try to turn this on me."

"Oh my gods, just shut up and drink some tea!" Selena urges, pushing me forward toward Mrs. S's counter where my untouched tea sits, bubbling. Sorin and Ash gape at us from where they're standing.

"What are you doing?" I hiss to her. "You sound like a teenage girl at a party."

"I'm trying to save you from Ash," she whispers back in her normal, monotone voice. From the way she and Sorin were talking earlier, it seems like this wasn't her voice before going off to work for the king. "It doesn't seem like she's the one you want to be around when she's angry."

She sits me down by the shoulders.

"Promise we'll talk later?" I ask hopefully, grabbing on to her arm.

A slight smile appears on her stone-like face when she says, "Right." She then trots right back over to Sorin, Ash, and Elysian, putting on her schoolgirl-like smile. Ugh, I hate that smile.

I sip my tea reluctantly. Sage stares at me strangely.

"Is something wrong, Milo?" she asks me. "You look … off."

"It's nothing," I lie. My eyes trail down to her injury. It looks noticeably better. I tried to help as much as I could, but Sorin was so defensive when we were healing her. I could barely even touch her. He kept muttering that it was his fault, and I just let him be. That's why her wound isn't healed yet. I should've helped, but he probably would've bitten my hand off. "Your leg looks better."

"Yeah." She smiles. "Mrs. S fixed it up. Ash did a good job, but after the spies captured us it got a little messy. I swear, that woman's a witch." Sage laughs lightly and I stare at her blankly.

"You guys got captured by spies and *Ash* tied your bandages?" I chuckle under my breath. "That girl tells me nothing."

"Long story," she responds with a shrug. "You missed a lot." She glances over at Selena.

"I still can't believe they're related," I say, staring at the two of them. "They look nothing alike." With Selena's dark hair, pale skin, and gray eyes and Sorin's blond hair, tan skin, and light blue eyes, they're different in so many ways. I'm still processing her first name and the death of her uncle and now she's related to Sorin? I feel like everything's going by so fast. Now I understand how she knew where to find Sorin's mom's—or I guess *her* mom's—house. Why she was looking for Sorin. It makes sense now.

But when I heard it, it hit me like a freight train. I'm still recovering from shock.

"I'm still surprised that you found us," Sage says. "In fact, I'm still surprised that you even survived being away from the necessities, like food and water, for so long."

"What do you mean?" I ask her. It feels like no time has passed.

"Did you stop at a warehouse or something? It's been four days." Sage raises an eyebrow. "I mean, you had to have food and water to live without us. Being with other people distracts you from needing those nutrients, but it doesn't seem like Little Miss Guard is much of a talker."

"Did you just make a joke, Sage Jobbs?" I snort. "Sorin would be proud."

"Don't change the subject," she scolds. "This is serious." *She's back.* "How in the gods' names did you survive with no food and water?"

"I … don't know." And I really don't. Whenever I woke up in the morning after Berty J's death (which I didn't have much sleep because of), Selena was awake. She looked drained, so I just assumed

188

she hadn't slept at all. But now that I think about it, how did we survive? I always felt refreshed in the mornings and kept having to support Selena on our way toward Mrs. S's house, but I hadn't thought much of it. Now ...

"You don't know?" Sage says. "Well." She pauses. "You should drink your tea. I'm sure you're thirsty."

Just then, my stomach growls.

"And hungry." She smiles and calls for Mrs. S. Instantly, a plate of food is in front of me. I start scarfing it down so quickly I almost forget to say thank you, but I do.

The sound of arguing slowly fades as I eat everything on my plate. It's so delicious, and I'm so hungry. I wonder how she makes such delicious food, but then the thought is gone as she places more breakfast in front of me and I eat it, too. I'm starving, yet I wasn't while we were walking. Now I know that there's something Selena is hiding from me.

"Woah," Ash says, appearing out of nowhere. "Someone's hungry."

"Sorry, did you want some?" I ask her through a mouthful.

She sits down next to me and laughs. "I'm so happy you're back. We—well, I—missed you a lot while you were gone, crushing on Sorin's petty sister."

"She's not petty, Ash," I mutter, deserting my now empty plate. "We're just friends. I don't know why you hate her so much."

"I have reasons," she argues. "Like, for example, she's a spy and a soldier for the very person we're working against. You don't suspect her at all, do you?"

"No." I cross my arms defiantly. "Why would she tell us that information if she was working against us?"

"She wants to get under your skin. She knows the effect she has on you, and she wants to use it to her advantage." Ash pauses. "I don't want you to get hurt, Milo. You and the campers—you're my family. You're all I have. And if she hurts my family, I hurt her. Now, we should go if we want to make it in time to the prince."

She stands, but I grab her arm to stop her. "At least try some of this breakfast before we go."

"I already did. I—"

Mrs. S places a plate in front of Ash.

I take a piece of bacon from her plate and shove it into her mouth. She's surprised at first but starts eating it and her eyes widen. When she swallows the bacon, she says, "Wow. I never really noticed how good your cooking is the second time around, Mrs. S."

Mrs. S laughs. "Thank you, my dear."

Naturally, Ash eats the rest of the food at the speed of light.

"You're right," she mumbles through a mouthful. "This is delicious."

Sorin, Selena, and Elysian come over to the island. Selena introduces herself to Mrs. S, but I know she knows something, because her eyebrows are creased like she's thinking.

"Would you like to try some breakfast, Selena?" There is a hint of malice in Mrs. S's voice, but I quickly forget about it when she smiles her old lady smile.

"No, thank you." Selena smiles back. She flexes her jaw, and I know something's off.

"What?" I whisper to her.

"Not now," she murmurs. "Not in front of everyone."

"Have I met you before?" Now she's turning away from me, talking to Mrs. S.

"That's ridiculous, dear." Mrs. S smiles. "I never leave my house. I find it hazardous. After my dear Robert died, I ..." Tears begin to well in her eyes, which are somehow tinted orange. Like they're on fire. "Excuse me." She wipes her tears. "I decided it would be better, with no one to protect me, to stay inside. I'm sorry if you believe we have, because it's just a crazy assumption."

"Right. Crazy." Selena narrows her eyes but relaxes her stance. "I'm sorry."

Mrs. S smiles politely. "You're forgiven."

All of us look from Mrs. S to Selena, waiting to see what they'll do.

She runs her tongue over her teeth. "Although ..."

"Yes?"

"If you're so serious about keeping yourself safe, why did you let strangers into your house? Especially when some of them," Selena tips her head toward Ash, "have weapons like daggers and swords?"

Mrs. S gapes at her like a fish. I'm pretty sure everyone else is doing the same. Everyone else besides Ash, who is now glaring at Mrs. S.

"Yeah, why did you? I mean, you gave me clothes, had to have changed me. My sword was strapped to my belt. Why didn't you kick me out?"

"Wow, this is delicious," says Sorin's voice suddenly, shoving some of Ash's breakfast into his mouth. Ash slaps his hand and he retreats quietly. Then he looks around at us, all looking at him like he's gone insane. "What? I'm hungry. And mine is already cold."

Selena rolls her eyes. "We're actually trying to get something done here," she hisses.

"Okay, that's *rude*—"

"How am I being rude when you're the one eating at a time like this?"

"I feel like I'm being hate crimed—"

Sage rests her hand on Sorin's arm and looks up at him. She whispers something to him and he goes silent.

Strange.

"Now, as we were *saying*," Selena says with a glare in Sorin's direction, "you have a motive that you entirely ignore when kids show up at your—"

"We're not *kids!*"

Well, my surprise at Sorin being quiet was short-lived.

"Door," she continues, as if Sorin never spoke. "Why?"

For once, Mrs. S is at a loss for words. "Well, I—I mean, they were just so tired—I couldn't leave them—"

"Now I know why your food is so good," Selena interrupts, realization dawning on her face. "You're a cook for the king. Probably a spy, no doubt. And now you're going to go tell him that you found the guard he's looking for, aren't you, *Maria?*"

"*Maria?*" we say in unison, everyone's heads turning to Mrs. S (or Maria, I guess), who is smiling proudly.

"You've always been a little too smart, huh, Zora? Or should I say Selena?" Maria asks. She swipes the plate from Ash. "Too smart to be working for Cirillo. Too brave. Too loyal. From the moment they stepped in here, I knew it was them. The Magics. The ones Cirillo wanted. The ones he wanted to execute."

"So you were going to help him kill us?" Elysian asks. She's up from her chair, Sage leaning against Elysian's shoulder to support herself. "You wanted us executed, after everything you'd done for us?"

"Of course she was," Ash barks. She forces a laugh. It's so pathetic, so sad, that I want to hug her. I know only too well about Ash's experience with execution. "You can never trust anyone. Gods, I can't believe I let myself get *tricked* like this." The last part seems

193

more to herself, but I hear it.

We're all standing now. Sorin has drawn his sword and Selena's hand is hovering over her belt. She still hasn't taken her armor off.

"You're despicable," I breathe.

"Thank you." Maria smiles, obviously unfazed. "You haven't been sleeping for three days because you were tired, my dears. You were sleeping for three days because I drugged you."

Selena tenses, and all of the blood rushes out of Sorin's face. He looks as though he's seen a ghost.

"I got the evidence I needed," Maria continues. "When I was done, I gave each of you a few sleeping pills so you wouldn't remember when you woke up. It worked perfectly. I know where your camps are, and I can't wait to give that information to the king."

"How, if we kill you first?" Selena says. A muscle in her jaw flexes.

"Everyone knows a good 'villain character,' as you would say, never reveals their plan *that* early," Maria responds with an evil smirk. I can't believe I ever thought she was just a sweet old lady. "Let's just state it simply: You will not kill me. And if you have the stupidity to try or succeed anyway, the king already knows about where you are. And he is disappointed in you."

She turns to Selena. "You are a good guard, yet you are guarding the wrong people."

"Can we just kill her already?" Ash growls. She doesn't have her sword, but Sage, Sorin, and Selena came prepared. Sage's dagger is intimidating—a hilt made of jagged emerald rocks and a blade at least a foot and a half long—and so is she. She's normally a genius girl helping with her geography skills but now? Her green eyes are narrowed at Maria, turning a darker shade than usual so they look like a shadow is cast onto them, but Maria's kitchen is mostly light. Her red hair looks like it's been lit on fire.

Sorin's sword is blinding, almost like it's been made out of real sunlight—which it probably has. The blade is about three feet long and the hilt is white and made of rubber. Something tells me it had to be made of rubber so the person holding it wouldn't overheat.

And as always, Selena looks like a ravenous hunting dog. Bloodthirsty. Murderous. And, of course, gorgeous.

Sorin catches me looking at her and sends a glare toward me. I ignore him and turn back to Maria, who is studying Selena, Sorin, and Sage as if she's surprised they have the nerve to stand up to her.

"Foolish kids make foolish mistakes," she mutters before drawing a butcher knife from under the counter, like she's prepared for this. "But tasty dinner," she adds, holding up her pointer finger.

"Gross." Sorin gags.

"Yeah, I agree," Elysian says.

"Silence!" Maria commands, and the room goes quiet. She holds her butcher knife threateningly, tightly. Something tells me she deeply relies on that butcher knife. Then a light bulb goes off in my mind.

If I just get the knife away from her, we'll have a shot to win.

Should be easy.

Then I remember.

Oh gods, I think, *it's a knife.*

My stomach twists.

Okay. You can do this, Milo. Don't discourage yourself. You're stronger than you know.

"If you had brains," Maria growls, "you would realize that I am older, more experienced than all of you. I was a guard for the king once as well, Selena, smarter than the others, smarter than him. And you know what Cirillo did? He placed me in the kitchens. He hated that he wasn't feared as much because of my intelligence, so I wasn't allowed to speak to anyone. I tell you this because you do not want to end up in the kitchens, any of you, no matter how … unfortunate your IQ level may be. It is a wretched place, especially when it is Cirillo's kitchen."

"There are more of us, old lady," Ash utters menacingly. "Meaning you're going to lose."

"Tell Cirillo I say hi when you meet him." Maria's face is expressionless. If I had to mark it, I'd say almost hopeful. She wants us to kill her? But she said she needed to get this information to the king. Nothing makes sense anymore. "I guess I should specify," she adds. "If you meet him."

Sorin's mouth is open when I study everyone. Ash's face is determined, set, angry. Elysian's is disbelieving, bewildered. Sage's is thoughtful, studying Maria, studying the room, probably looking for a way out of this mess. Selena's is recklessness, a victorious smirk. And Sorin's is disgust and shock.

"Let's fight," Selena breathes, her voice just above a whisper, but it's so quiet that I'm sure only we heard her.

We charge forward and Maria's hand tightens even more around the handle of the butcher knife, ready.

Not for long.

CHAPTER 15

SAGE

I'll spare the details.

Nothing much happened. Milo got the knife away from Maria, which I never would've thought of in that little amount of time, and then she was defenseless.

She is dead. Selena shot her. There was a microphone strapped to her apron that we broke into pieces before we left, leaving behind no Magics and no proof. We hope.

That experience was a nightmare, but I'd do anything to be back there, in the comfort of a house with beds and sleep and *comfort.* We've started walking again, gallivanting past sideways trees that the harsh wind is blowing (I love Elysian, but she has *got* to learn how to use her power or she'll blow us away), and Sorin is yelling. Again.

This time, he's yelling at me, and not his long-lost sister who is most likely against us but seems nice enough.

"When you kissed me, did that mean nothing to you?" he says.

Sure, he's not yelling *that* loudly or else the others would hear, but we're farther behind and they're walking fast.

I want to tell him I don't know. I want to tell him that I have no idea what is happening anymore because everything is upside down and if I had just stayed at Camp Serenity instead of playing the hero, I would've been so much happier. And I want to ask him how that kiss could have meant nothing to me when I was the one who initiated it. I want to, I want to, I want to, but I keep quiet, and he gets angrier by the second at my unresponsive grunts, his face turning an unflattering shade of crimson.

"Seriously?" he demands, his tone getting louder and louder. "You're seriously going to ignore me after all we've been through? I am so confused and you're not helping by just nodding or shaking your head, Sage."

I'm confused too, Sunshine. You're not the only one struggling.

"I can't believe you."

It takes a moment to realize those words are mine.

"What?" He stops in his tracks. "*You* can't believe *me?*"

I freeze, too. I can't bring myself to look at him. "No, Sorin, I can't." I take a breath before continuing. "You don't understand how hard this has been for me. It's taken me forever to figure out what I feel for you, whether it's just a crush or you're my enemy or what, but you're not making this decision any easier. And not to mention the fact that we're, you know, basically *walking to our deaths*. This hasn't been fun, and I do not need this pressure right now, so yes. To answer your question, *I* can't believe *you.*"

He's silent for a moment. "You're kidding."

"No, I'm not."

"You seriously don't know if I'm your enemy or not?" There's hurt in his voice, but I really don't care. "After everything you've done, after everything I've done, after everything *we've* done, you still don't know?"

"Can we not do this right now?" I murmur. I'm honestly slightly embarrassed, and I shouldn't be. This is *his* fault for bringing it up, *his* fault for making me think we could ever be more than friends, more than enemies. It's *all his fault.*

"Of course, Sage. Let's just sit and enjoy the view, shall we?"

I whip around. I am getting so tired of him. I still avoid his eyes. "I get you're mad at me, but we have something to do."

"You think I *want* to have this conversation?"

"Why else would you be acting like this?"

"Gods, Sage, maybe because I've been feeling the same way?" he yells, so loudly that the others stop.

He stares at me like I've shattered him. But he isn't being fair. He doesn't understand how hard I fought to keep him, how many battles I had with myself because *maybe* the possibility of being with him existed. *Maybe*, after all of this was over, we could be a couple and have a nice house somewhere and live with each other. Maybe he likes me back. And he doesn't get to tell me he's been feeling the exact same way because he truly doesn't understand what I've gone through.

"How?" I can barely hear myself.

"What?"

"How?" I repeat. "How could you *ever* be feeling the same as me? I am falling apart every day, waiting and waiting and waiting for this to be over because I want to be with you. I am fighting myself because I can't be with you. Because this might never end and I might never get to tell you."

He swallows hard. "Tell me what?"

"I might never get to tell you ..." I pause, taking a deep breath, trying so hard not to notice the fact that now our friends have stopped behind us, watching us, waiting for us to say something. "I might never get to tell you that I think I love you."

There's a long silence. Someone gasps and tries to laugh but someone else shushes them. Sorin stares at me, his expression unreadable. His bright blue eyes are cloudy and I feel so stupid. I'm so, so stupid for saying that. What if he doesn't like me? What if I just embarrassed myself by doing this?

I do the only thing I can.

I gasp, covering my mouth, shocked that I've actually said it, and I run. I run past our surprised friends, staring after me. I run and almost trip over large tree roots in the ground. I run and run, trying to get away. I almost forget that I'm supposed to be somewhere. That running from your problems never solves anything.

I stop in the middle of the forest, breathing heavily. It's completely silent. There are only faint sounds of birds chirping above me. I lean back against a tree, mentally hitting myself. Why did I *do* that?

I know Sorin. I don't know why I ran. He's slightly sensible. Maybe we could've worked it out? Maybe I could've told him I didn't mean what I said? Maybe he would've liked me back ...

No, it's a ridiculous fantasy. Sure, when I kissed him, he didn't pull away like he was disgusted with me, but it was the heat of the moment, and he was probably too shocked to do anything. And he cared for me when I got hurt, almost looking worried for me. But Milo did too. And back at camp, once he stopped sulking and regained his senses, it was like he looked at me a whole different way, and he wasn't angry. But all rational people calm down at some point, especially over something as silly as a position at a camp.

Rustling of tree branches startles me out of my thoughts. There is no way anyone could've found me unless they followed me, and none of my friends really looked in a rush to go after me.

It must be an intruder.

I pull out my dagger slowly, trying not to make any sudden movements. I've always been good with woodland creatures, since I am sort of connected to their home, and that is the number one rule when it comes to them: never make any sudden movements.

If anyone's dumb enough to intrude on someone with a visible dagger handle in their pocket, they should be treated as a wild animal.

As the sound gets closer, I tiptoe toward it. Then I spot a figure, unidentifiable under the shadows of the trees, and I trust my instincts. I cut their face with the blade of my dagger.

It's a small cut, but it's deep, and it will do damage.

The intruder shouts in pain, and I recognize the tone as a boy's. His hands fly up to the cut, cradling it like a newborn.

"Holy hell, Sage!"

Oh gods, what did I do?

I drop my dagger. Sorin's blood drips from it.

"Sorin?" I ask breathlessly. "What are you doing here?"

"I wanted to make sure you were okay," he retorts, an edge to his voice, "but I see now that that wasn't a good idea."

"Sorry," I mutter. "Really, I am."

He touches his face and the wound closes instantly, an effect of his Healing magic. All that's left now is a scar and dried blood.

"Why did you run?" he asks me.

I stop myself before I answer. I think about it, then I say, "Because it's the truth."

"And running from the truth is a good thing?"

"At times."

"You can be so difficult, Sage. I just wish you'd open up to me, to others. We're here to help." I hate that his words are the truth.

"Falling in love wasn't my plan," I whisper. "It wasn't part of the plan. Neither is opening up."

"Those rules have already been broken, haven't they?" He steps forward, finding me in the dark, and he tucks a piece of my hair behind my ear. "Why do you shield yourself from everyone who has ever tried to help you?"

I close my eyes. His touch gives me butterflies. I don't want to tell him, but it seems I have no other choice. "My mother was a Magic hater." That is the only information I give him, but it seems to be enough, because he pulls me to his chest.

"I don't hate you, Sage," he murmurs into my hair. "I never have. Not even when you got the position over me. Honestly, I was impressed."

"You were?"

"Who wouldn't be? You're amazing, Sage; you have always been amazing. First it was Elysian, then it was you, and your arrival definitely hit me harder. Since we're being honest here ..." He pauses and laughs lightly. "I think I've liked you, maybe even loved you since you got the job."

The butterflies in my stomach turn to helicopters as I replay his words in my mind. "You're serious?"

"Of course I'm serious, Sagey," he whispers. "I love you. I'm in love with you. I was just surprised you had the nerve to actually say it. And that you loved me back."

"So what you're telling me is ..." I chuckle under my breath. "You're a big fat chicken?"

His smile is grand. "Pretty much. I was too scared to make a move. But then you literally took a bullet for me, and I got an idea of how you liked me."

"So that's why you interrogated me."

"Yeah, and you *completely* lied."

"I did not lie!"

"You totally did."

"Okay, just because you have a god complex—"

"What? I do not have a god complex—"

"Doesn't mean that everyone *worships*—"

Before I can say anything else, Sorin lifts my chin and kisses me, soft and slow. My hand reaches up to cup his face, and I feel him smiling into the kiss. My stomach twists and turns, and my heart does backflips and cartwheels.

"Sorin? Sage?"

Elysian.

We scramble away from each other and it's instantly awkward. We just stand there until Elysian appears. Her brown hair is messy and if I'm being totally honest, she looks annoyed.

"There you are," she says, exasperation evident in her tone. "We were all looking for you after you both ran off and—" She notices Sorin's scar and my bloody dagger, sitting on the floor. "What the hell happened?"

Sorin clears his throat. "Where are the others?"

"They're waiting for us to get back," Elysian mumbles, trying to connect the dots. "I'm sorry, did you cut him?" Her eyes meet mine and I smile sheepishly.

I open my mouth to answer when she holds up her hand and says, "I don't even want to know. It's almost lunchtime and I didn't eat anything for breakfast, so I'm starving. Add in a love declaration and a bloody dagger and you've got yourself an appetite."

Sorin snorts. I feel my face turn red.

"Would you not also cut him if he was being a—"

"Don't finish that sentence," Elysian warns, and she motions for us to follow her. "We don't have time for your arguing."

Sorin smiles next to me. "You're happy we're together, aren't you, Lyssy?"

"Didn't I already tell you now is not the time?"

"I think you're mad because you'll never find anyone as great as I am for Sage."

She snorts. "Yeah, I'm always wondering when I'll meet a mini-Sorin who will torment my life and make just waking up in the morning a living hell."

I stifle my laugh. Sorin has the nerve to look offended.

"Well, *excuse me*," he murmurs. "I'll bet the others are happy for us."

"Yeah, they're so happy that you delayed their trip with a love declaration." She glances back at the two of us. "I'm glad you guys are happy, seriously. But can it wait until after we get past the whole mission thing?"

I nod quickly as we approach the others, and I realize I didn't actually run that far. My wound must've slowed me down. My cheeks glow red. *Oh gods, this is embarrassing.*

Ash looks me up and down. "Ugh, you guys are disgusting."

"Mad that you can't get a date?" Sorin taunts.

"No, I'm surprised that *you* could," Selena says, walking over to Sorin. She stands on her toes to ruffle his hair. Their height difference is really impressive. "But running off like that?" she whispers to him. "Not the smartest thing to do."

He grins. "I guess she's just too *irresistible.*"

I cringe. From behind the others, Ash screams, "If either one of you start calling each other 'boo bear,' I am throwing myself off a cliff!"

I laugh, enjoying the nice moment. The way things are going now, I'm sure it won't last for long. But it's nice to have it.

I find it unbelievable that Sorin *Torsney*, of all people, has liked me for such a long time. I got the position when I was sixteen. Three years. For three years I thought he hated me. I thought he was bitter because I got the job over him. I thought he left because I got the job over him. But he really left because he loved me?

He really knows nothing about women.

The election was when the camp had just started. Obviously,

since Elysian created the camp, she was the leader of it. Then she needed a junior leader, in case she left or got sick or died. She needed someone to inherit the camp.

I wanted power. I thought it would make people respect me. So I quickly signed up. So did Sorin. He wanted the same thing I did: He wanted to be known. Sorin and I had been childhood friends but grew apart as we got older. When I found out he enrolled, I was so angry that I stormed into his cabin.

"What in the gods' names do you think you're doing, stealing the one and only position you *know* I want?" I asked him.

He put his hands up in a surrender. "I didn't know you were applying."

"Oh, sure you didn't," I argued. "We've been friends since we were five. You should know this about me. But yet, you still signed up anyway. I can't believe you."

"Sage," he defended, "I swear, if I'd've known you were applying, I wouldn't have. But I really need this job. Are you going to ruin that for me by making a big deal of nothing?"

"No, *I* should be asking you if you're going to ruin this opportunity for me, telling *you* I really need that job. You don't get to act like this when you have never shown interest in anything that involves leading, other than being the line leader in when we were children."

"Speaking of which, you're acting childish," he told me, and my jaw clenched. My fists closed and I felt the need to punch him in the face, but instead, I just spun on my heel and left his cabin.

Then, for weeks, I didn't talk to him. While the votes were being counted for best leader, I avoided his gaze. At breakfast, lunch, and dinner, I walked right past him like I didn't care about him at all. And honestly, it hurt having to act that way around a friend who I'd had for ages. Eleven years, all down the drain because of an election.

The day finally came. I sat in the crowd, waiting for someone else's name to be said, and I was so surprised when my name was called, I almost fell out of my chair.

I slowly walked up to the front, and Sorin's eyes caught mine. His gaze was murderous, his normally cheerful eyes hidden behind a curtain of ice-cold hate. But then something else flashed in them, and he relaxed, even tried to smile at me. I didn't understand it at the time, but now, I do. He was reminding himself that he loved me.

I collected the badge that said my name. Under it was "Junior Leader of Camp Serenity." I was so happy I almost cried. Elysian noticed my feelings and hugged me. I think that's when our friendship sparked.

Two days later, Sorin ran away. All of his stuff was gone from his cabin. The mess hall had removed his name tag from the tables. Every trace of Sorin Torsney was gone, forgotten, and I felt absolutely horrible.

I remember the horrible feeling as I watch Sorin, smiling at his sister and the others, smiling at just the world, and I notice that it's evaporated, just like his anger. It melted because of his smile.

Pierced by those icy blue eyes, this time filled with admiration, not hate.

* * *

I pull out my map. It's dirty, wrinkled, and stained with all kinds of things. The words are barely distinguishable, but I manage to spot a passage to room 106, luckily. Unluckily, I have no way to mark it down and we'll easily get caught if we go there, since it's near the spy headquarters we were at earlier. Not to mention I have no idea where we are currently. All around us, it's just forest. I never knew how many forests Buit had.

Sorin's looking over my shoulder. He's trying to help, but it's not going well. His idea of a plan is climbing through trees until we find a big brick building surrounded by guards: the castle.

Which brings us to another problem. *If* we make it to room 106 in time (which is starting to look impossible considering we only have three days left before August fourth), who's to say we won't be caught and executed by the king or his forces?

"This trip is just a journey of rainbows and unicorns," Sorin murmurs from next to me, his breath hot on my neck. I shudder, then stop myself hastily.

I nod my agreement. "I wish I could just hop off into the

sunset," I joke and Sorin freezes.

"Babe," he says, and I stop dead, "did you just make a joke? I'm proud of you."

I blink. "Uh, *babe?*"

He clears his throat. "Um, is—is that okay? I mean, I don't want to make you uncomfortable or anything."

"No, no, you didn't." I feel a blush creeping up my neck. "It's just, you know, don't you think we're going a little fast? I mean, we've only kissed twice and we just said that we liked each other, so … uh, I don't know."

Sorin rubs the back of his neck. "Uh, yeah, I guess. Sorry."

"Uh, no, you're good."

Someone makes a retching noise behind us. "Gods, you two are so awkward it makes me want to bash my head against a wall."

"You love us, Ash." Sorin glances behind us and I crane my neck to see her.

"Plus," I add, "it's not like there are any walls anywhere close."

Ash shrugs. Her hair is in a bun with a hair tie I didn't know she had. She's wearing ratty clothes from several days ago. We lost our suitcases somewhere, and there are not any showers or laundromats anywhere in the forest. "Where are we headed?" She leans against a nearby tree.

Selena follows her, her arms crossed. She's taken off her helmet but refused to take off the rest of the armor, and the clang causes a lot of noise, so we can always tell when she's approaching. "Where even are we?"

"That's what I'm trying to figure out," I tell them, turning back to my map.

Sorin's stomach rumbles. "I'm starving," he says. "I actually miss that scary old lady. She made good food."

"Well, it's not like we can make a five-star restaurant or someone's mom appear out of nowhere," Ash argues, and I resist the urge to laugh.

He sighs, then looks around. "Where's Lyssy?"

"And Milo," Selena adds, glancing around at the woodsy landscape around us. She shoots Sorin a glare.

"Yeah, him too." He rolls his eyes.

"Watch it, Sunshine," Ash warns, a level gaze burning into him. "I could set you on fire."

"Then why don't you?"

"Because your little girlfriend would probably kill me."

I swallow and watch Sorin's Adam's apple bob. "Girlfriend" is more of a sensitive term now.

My map still makes no sense, and with them bickering behind me and two people possibly missing, I'm not going to get anything done. I decide I'll figure out a route later and shove the map back into the pocket of my sweatpants. They're actually quite comfortable and don't irritate my wound that much. Even if Maria was planning to hand us over to the king, she still had some decency in her, and some skill when it comes to cooking and healing.

"What?" Ash demands. She's confused by our sudden mood change, I realize, and I quickly try to draw no suspicion.

"Nothing." I whip around so I'm facing Selena and Ash. Sorin's shirt is tight and I can make out his muscles beneath the fabric tensing. I *seriously* hope Ash doesn't see that.

I walk briskly from the cluster (well, as briskly as one can when wounded) and search around for Elysian and Milo. They can't have gone far. They're both sensible, and they know enough to be able to tell when they're about to get lost. I mean, Milo has the power of peace, and the forest is always peaceful, especially today, with wind blowing through the trees and birds chirping softly and the sun hidden behind a few patches of clouds. Elysian has the power of controlling the weather, and since the forest is outside, then she won't have a problem. But I'm still worried.

Sorin follows me. He stares at me for a second, his bright blue eyes making my insides become butterflies. Ever since I learned he liked me back, my feelings have intensified. And rather quickly, considering he only just told me he liked me a few hours ago.

"We'll find them," he says to me, reading my expression. "We will."

"I know," I reply. I don't want to snap at him, but it's all so confusing and I'm exhausted like I haven't just woken up from a three-day-long nap and I'm being pressured to do so many things that I don't have the time for. Everything feels undeserved and everything is going downhill and I feel like the weight of the world is on my shoulders because if we don't save the prince then—

Sorin touches my shoulder. His skin is warm. I guess I should expect that from a sun-related Magic. His touch makes me shudder as a jolt runs through me. "Don't."

"What?" I face him.

"Don't overthink this," he says, his eyebrows crinkling. "We will find them, we will save the prince, we will make it to room 106 on time. You always get this concentrated look on your face whenever you're overthinking."

I blink at him. I didn't think anyone knew that. "I worry," I admit.

"I can tell." He chuckles lightly, and the sound makes those butterflies turn to birds. "We can start looking if you'd like."

"I—" I'm about to say I'd like that, when a gust of hot air tickles the back of my neck. It's in too much of a refined space for it to be the breeze, and goosebumps appear on my skin. I turn around, squinting at the bushes.

"What?" Sorin asks, standing next to me. "Did you see something?"

"Someone is in there," I say. It comes out as an accusation. "I know it."

"Let's not jump to conclusions—" He is reaching out to touch me when the bush rattles, and I jump backward, surprised.

"There's someone in there."

"It's probably just an animal," he mutters. "It's fine, Sage."

I wait for a moment, joining him at his side.

And then—

"I'm not an animal!"

The high-pitched voice of a child comes from behind us. We both whip around. Sorin raises his sword threateningly. His eyes are narrowed, and he looks ready to pounce on the voice.

Then someone ripples to life out of nothing but air.

A girl with hair the color of a deer's coat and pale skin stands a few feet ahead of us. She's barefoot, and there are twigs stuck in her hair. Most likely from the bush. She's wearing just a plain white dress, and it has grass stains on it. Freckles coat the bridge of her nose and just under her eyes.

She can't be older than twelve.

She's adorable.

I relax.

"No, you most definitely are not. What's your name?" Sorin asks.

"I'm Autumn," says the girl, with a quick smile. Then her face falls. "You guys aren't guards for the king, are you? My mom says the king sends his guards out to check the forests every other day. She says they find the animals and use them for feasts."

"We're not guards," I reply. "And that's horrible. Trust me, we're not here to hurt you."

"We're looking for a way to get to the castle," Sorin says. "Do you know any secret passages or anything?"

"Why do you want to go to the castle?" asks Autumn. She scrutinizes us. "You're sure you aren't guards for the king?"

"You're a Magic, aren't you?" I smile. She reminds me of me when I was little. My mom taught me well to never trust strangers, just as Autumn's mom did her.

Autumn nods. "Yeah. Why?"

I spread out my arm. I think of what I want to happen. I imagine lilies growing up the trunk of a tree, somewhere off to my left, and then it happens. The flowers rise from the ground and wrap themselves around the trunk, twisting and holding on tightly.

Autumn gapes at my handy work. "You did that? Cool!"

Sorin chuckles. "She's amazing, isn't she?"

Autumn nods eagerly. "You're like me. My mom would love to meet you."

I smile. Autumn is an earthbender. Fitting name. "I'd be delighted to meet her, but I have some things to take care of." The thought of Elysian and Milo fills my head. "Some people to take care of."

Her expression turns from awe to nervousness. "You're not

going to … *kill* … anyone, right?"

I tilt my head to one side. The poor girl has been so exposed to the kingdom's horrible actions that she expects them from just random passersby. *Again, she reminds me of myself.* "Of course not. I'm just missing some friends. They've wandered off."

Her warm brown eyes widen. "Does one of them have a tendency to be too nice and does the other one have weather powers?"

"Uh, yeah," says Sorin. "How did you know that?"

"Follow me," Autumn orders, and we motion for Ash and Selena to follow us before wandering into the dark abyss of the trees.

* * *

I never thought you could make a living in the forest.

This was before I saw where Autumn lived.

It's a clearing that's bigger in size. There are several houses made of wood logs. It looks like a little village. In the middle of the circle of houses, there's a fire. A cauldron hangs over it, steam coming from the top. They're cooking something, and it smells delicious. Positioned around the fire are more logs, these ones with deep indents in them, made for sitting.

Autumn leads us over to the house right in the middle: a short, stalky building made of wood entirely, a fire glowing through the open window. The window is just a square-shaped hole to the right of the door. I imagine they cover it up while they sleep at night to avoid bugs and noises that creep them out. That's what I would do.

"Come in," Autumn says, opening the door. She steps in and wipes her bare feet on the floor. It doesn't do much to get rid of the dirt, but the leaves are gone in a matter of seconds.

The house is pretty comfortable, for being made of wood. There's a wooden dining table to the right and wooden bed frames to the left. A few mattresses and blankets made of just leaves sit on top of them. In front of us is another fire for keeping the house warm, and beyond that is what I'm assuming to be the kitchen. The utensils are made of wood, like everything else. The countertops are made of wood. The counters themselves are made of wood. A cauldron, hot from the fire, sits on one of them. A woman stands in front of the cauldron, humming to herself. She stirs the stew with one of the wooden utensils.

She turns her head when she hears us. The woman has the same warm brown eyes as Autumn and her freckles are in the same places: along the bridge of her nose and under her eyes. She must be Autumn's mom.

Autumn's mom tenses. "Who are you, and what are you doing in my home?" Her eyes move from me to Sorin to Ash and finally to Selena. I remember that Selena still has her armor on when Autumn's mom's eyes widen.

"Mom, it's okay," Autumn assures her mom. "They're Magics."

218

"All of them?"

"Well, I don't know, but—"

"That one, there." She points at Selena with her wooden spoon. It drips stew onto the floor. "Wearing the king's guards' armor. You brought her here? You brought *them* here?"

"Mom, I'm trying to tell you—"

"Get out of my house!" Autumn's mom shrieks at us. "Now! We will not be punished just for living! *Go!*"

Sorin holds up his hands. "Woah, lady, we're not here to hurt you. We're looking for people."

"Yes!" She nods frantically. "Magics whom you are going to kill!"

"No," I say. "Our friends. We're all Magics. Do you really think we'd want to hurt our kind?"

Autumn's mother sighs. Her jaw is still clenched, and she waves the spoon threateningly. "Fine. But if you try *anything*, anything at all, you have to leave."

We all nod in understanding.

"And that one," she adds, pointing to Selena, "is staying outside."

"Hey, lady, that's my sister!" Sorin protests, and Autumn's mom just shrugs.

Autumn has to plead with her mom for a few moments before she agrees, and even then, it's reluctantly. "She's changing out of that armor then," her mom huffs.

Then, Autumn smiles widely. "It's time for you to meet my family," she says, leaving us standing in her house.

I have a feeling this is going to take a while.

CHAPTER 16

ELYSIAN

"Sage?"

I rub my eyes, wondering if I'm dreaming. How did they find this place? It's hidden well, behind several rows of trees, one after the other. I wouldn't have found it without Milo's sharp eyes. I didn't want to leave them alone, but Autumn's family whisked us away before I could think twice.

Now, Sorin, Sage, Selena, and Ash stand in front of me. Sage looks sweaty, muddier. Sorin is beaming. Selena looks uncomfortable. I'm guessing she's been forced to take her armor off, because she's wearing a plain white shirt and green camouflage pants. It fits her better than I'd expected. Her dark hair is a nice contrast from her light shirt. And Ash. Ash's face is streaked with dirt. Her sword is hanging at her side. She's tense, the muscles in her forearms flexing, and her eyes, flecked with less gold than when we started but gold nonetheless, are dark. Her hair is tied into a loose bun.

She's pretty.

Like, really pretty.

She meets my eye and stares at me. I stare back, registering that now it's a staring match, a fight for power. Sometimes Ash reminds me of a wild animal.

Her stare is so intense that I have to look away first. My gaze drops down to the floor. I can *feel* her smirking at me.

A body slams into me. The person smells like pine and old pages. *Sage.*

I hug her back. "I was only gone for a few hours," I laugh.

Her nails dig into my shoulder. "And you didn't think to come back?"

"Even if I did," I argue, parting from her, "I wouldn't know *how* to come back."

An old lady passes us, gray hair messy. She smiles at me and glares at the rest of them, like they're intruders.

Selena sends her a nasty look. Even without her armor, she sure is still intimidating. "Who the hell is that?"

I sigh. "I'm assuming you've met Autumn Tully?"

"And Mrs. Tully," Sage murmurs with a quick glance at the house that occupies Autumn and her parents.

"Well, that was Mrs. Tully, too."

They all stare at me strangely.

"Didn't you learn *anything* from the tour, guys?" says a familiar voice.

"Milo," Ash says with a sigh of relief. "I'm glad you're okay."

He smiles warmly. "We have *got* to stop meeting like this."

"Autumn's grandma, Mrs. Tully?" Sage asks, and I nod.

"Why are there so many?" Sorin says. "I mean, Tully isn't even a good last name."

"Why, I 'otta smack you across the face for that," a low voice interrupts. It's coated in a heavy Southern accent. Mr. Tully, Autumn's grandfather.

Sorin whips around. He holds up his hands. "Uh, sorry, sir."

"You're the one Miss Viggo was talkin' about, are ya?" Mr. Tully asks. He raises an eyebrow. "Soarin' Tore His Knee?"

"*Sorin Torsney*, sir," Sorin corrects.

Mr. Tully rolls his eyes. He removes a cigarette from the folds of his brown, mud-caked jacket and uses a stick that's burning in the campfire to light it. "Same thing." He motions for us to follow him, so we do.

He leads us to a tree. It's just a tree, but the trunk is covered in offerings and presents. "A little birdy told me y'all are headin' somewhere dangerous," he says. "The king's castle. You need luck. This here is the luck tree."

We stand there, staring at the luck tree.

"Uh," Ash says, "can I ask why it's called the *luck tree*?"

"'Cause it brings luck," Mr. Tully spits. "Why else?"

"But why this specific tree?"

"It's held for years and years and years." Mr. Tully takes a long drag of his cigarette. "Tallest of its kind, too. Been here since I was a kid, and it's as stable as I am old." He snuffs out the cigarette with his fingers and places it back into his jacket. Not a fan of littering, I guess. "The way it works is, you go to the tree, give it something, and then ask for luck on a trip or sum'n'," he murmurs.

"Like an offering?" Sage asks.

Mr. Tully nods. "Youse a smart one, missy. Like an offerin'. You give it sum'n', it gives ya luck in change."

"Well," Selena starts, crossing her arms, "how are we sure this isn't just a tree, and this story you're telling isn't just a story?"

Mr. Tully's eyes move from Sage to Selena. He raises his eyebrows at her bluntness. "I would be careful 'bout what you say round here, missy. You ever seen a tree grow twenty feet in two months?"

Selena narrows her eyes at him. "That still gives me no closure. For all we know, you're taking advantage of gullible teenagers." She motions to Sorin, who's standing right next to him.

"Okay," he starts, "I get that we're siblings, but can you at least *try* to be nice to me?"

"Y'all stop arguin'," Mr. Tully commands. "I'm just tryna help, but if y'all don't believe me, then I can go on my way and forget this conversation ever happened."

Selena sighs. "Fine. How does the *luck tree* work?"

I wait for Mr. Tully's answer, but he's left to light a new cigarette. We follow after him like a tour group.

"You give it an offerin', make a wish for luck, an' then it comes

224

true." He says this around his cigarette.

"So, like, wishing on a star?" I ask, raising an eyebrow.

"Right you are," Mr. Tully confirms with a nod in my direction. "But this ain't no fairy tale, you hear? People die. People get hurt. At the end of the day, you're the last person standing, and you realize that you've only got yourself."

I'm standing next to Ash now, so I can hear it when she mumbles, "Inspiring."

Mr. Tully's ears are better than expected. "True. Everythin' I've said." He nods in Ash's direction. "This here place is built on magic no different than yours. Why do y'all think the luck tree doesn't work? Give me an actual answer."

"It's just a myth," Selena argues. She's about to say something else, when Mr. Tully cuts her off.

He waves his hand and vines wrap around Selena's throat, threatening to choke her. Sage reaches for her dagger, and Sorin for his sword, but Mr. Tully just tightens the vines on her throat.

She chokes.

"Stop!" Milo yells.

"What are you doing?" I say.

"Let her go!" Sorin jeers, cursing. He steps forward and tries to claw through the vines on Selena's neck, but Mr. Tully just looks bored.

He flicks his wrist and the vines stop choking her. Selena gasps for air and her hands go up to her throat.

"There's magic everywhere, ya hear?" says Mr. Tully. He's glaring at all of us. "So y'all gotta learn that there's magic in that there tree. I'd expect y'all, of all folks, to better understand that."

We're all still shocked that no one responds. Not even Ash makes a sarcastic comment or insult.

Mr. Tully just grunts and lights another cigarette, leaving us for a group of kids weaving through trees and playing tag.

* * *

Sorin's still asking Selena if she needs him to heal her by the time the Tullys say it's dinnertime. She just ignores him and sits somewhere else whenever this happens, but it's starting to get annoying for the rest of us, too, and there are not a lot of places that Selena hasn't sat in yet.

"You're seriously okay?" Sorin's saying. Selena decided to sit next to me, so now I get an earful of his complaints and worrying. "No pain, nothing?"

"No pain, nothing," Selena repeats. "I'm fine, Sorin. Stop harassing me."

Sorin rolls his eyes. "Fine. But when you start choking again or start bleeding rapidly, it's not my fault."

Milo laughs from the other side of the campfire.

I shovel some food into my mouth. "Leave, Sorin."

"You too?" He looks defeated. "Fine." He pouts before leaving us and sitting by Sage, who smiles lightly.

There's so much tension between them. I know they're in *love*, but they act like they don't even know it, like the time I just met them, just a lot less anger. Sorin is awkward around her and Sage looks like a little girl, strange considering how independent she is.

It's hard to watch.

"They're cute," Selena says suddenly, and I have to nod. "I've never seen Sorin this happy. Well, I never saw him this happy when he was between the ages of zero and fourteen." She laughs lightly, but her words are heavy with guilt.

"I know we just met," I start, and I'm cautious not to make her mad, even though she doesn't have a sword with her, "but why did you want to be a soldier?"

She pauses before answering. "Simply? I wanted to be a hero."

"I wanted to prove to myself and others that I could do it, that I could help people." She lets out a breath, like that was weight on her shoulders. "So when the time came that I was the legal age to be a soldier, eighteen, I said goodbye to my family and I made my own way to the castle."

"You're twenty-three?" I ask.

"Yeah," she says with a chuckle. "Pretty old, huh?"

"No," I say quickly. "You just seem like you're younger."

We're quiet for a moment.

"I'm not evil, you know," she says softly. "I just worked for bad people. I've always wanted to help others, but I never knew how." She laughs, then she begins to tell a story.

"When I was eight and Sorin was just about to turn three, I went with my mom to the local store. I wanted to get him something I knew he'd like, but I didn't find anything. As we were about to pay, I saw this beautiful painting of the sun rising over a cluster of trees, the way the forest looks in the morning."

She pauses and I nod, even though I'm barely ever up early enough to watch the sunrise.

"I thought it was amazing for Sorin, considering sometimes he would make the sunlight do exactly that when he was curious. Sure, he blinded us a few times, but it was okay because he was a baby. When he started doing it as a preteen and teenager, that's when it became a problem."

She shakes her head. "Anyway, I wanted it, so I just picked it up. I didn't think about paying for it. It wasn't a big painting, just a small drawing. I tucked it into my pocket, and then I left with my mom."

"You got away with it?" I ask.

"It's hanging in Sorin's room right now, if you don't believe me. Well, it was when he was fourteen." Selena shrugs.

"That's really cute," I say, chuckling. "I wouldn't do that for my sibling."

Suddenly, my head hurts, like someone's pushing a pencil

228

through my brain. It's quick yet almost the most painful thing I've ever felt. I gasp and dig my nails into my forehead.

Selena glances over at me. "I—are you okay?"

When I don't respond, she jumps to action. She calls one of the passing Tullys over. It's Autumn's grandma.

"Sweetheart, sweetheart, are you all right?" Autumn's grandma leans over me.

I nod and take a deep breath. "Just a headache."

Selena stares at me strangely when I calm down. "What the hell was that?"

I shrug. It makes my head hurt briefly. "Don't ask me."

"What, do you have a sibling?"

I sigh. "Don't ask me."

"You—wait, what? You don't know?" Selena laughs, but there's nothing funny about the situation. It's more like a laugh out of confusion rather than anything else.

I shake my head solemnly. "*I don't know.*"

We're quiet for the rest of dinner.

* * *

Autumn's grandma has graciously offered her house for us to use while we're staying here.

"Hey, you okay?"

I'm making my bed made of twigs when I feel someone behind

me.

I recognize her voice.

I turn to face Ash. "What do you want?" I say neutrally.

She makes her way over to me. "You looked on the verge of passing out earlier. Forgive me for checking up on you."

"Everyone else is at the campfire."

"Sad, really." She averts her gaze to her fingernails. "It's not even that high."

"Careful, or Mr. Tully'll choke you."

"I'm terrified." She doesn't look terrified. She looks bored.

I smile. "Seriously. Why are you here?"

"Some of us have to sleep, Viggo." But Ash winks. She stretches her hand toward the makeshift fireplace, made of twigs, and a ball of fire springs from her to it, lighting up the house.

It's not too hot but not a dying fire either. Even with the humidity and heat, the fire feels good.

When she uses her fire, the thought of the dream I had before I woke up after I lost my memory comes to mind.

I've completely forgotten about it, but now, with this strange headache earlier and all these people we've met, with our deadline inching closer every second of every day, I want to ask about it. I *need* to ask about it.

"Ash," I start, and she turns around.

"Yeah?" She eyes me expectantly.

"Uh … have you ever—"

I'm cut off by the sound of screaming.

Ash's eyes widen.

We rush out the door.

There's smoke and people rushing into their houses everywhere, though through the chaos I can see something.

The silhouette of someone crouching over someone else. Someone shaking and crying leaning over someone limp, their chest barely rising and falling.

As I approach closer, my stomach rises into my throat, threatening to choke me.

I see the ghost of a grin, the dullness of usually bright blue eyes.

Sorin's usually bright blue eyes.

CHAPTER 17

SORIN

I'm sitting next to Sage. Her hand is covering her mouth, laughing at a stupid joke I've made.

She once told me, when we were kids, that she loved my stupid jokes.

I'm guessing this is proof of that.

Ash stands suddenly. "I'm going to bed," she says.

We nod.

Elysian's left the campfire to go to sleep, too. I wonder if this is just an excuse to see her, but the thought is so odd and out of place that I push it away.

Sage's hand hovers over mine. Then it drops and I feel butterflies in my stomach. Sage is ... perfect. Witty, clever, funny when she wants to be. She's everything I've ever wanted, and here she is, sitting in front of me, laughing with me, touching me. She's even kissed me.

"You're beautiful," I say. Sage turns to look at me, and I see her eyes. Gods, her eyes. A sparkling, vibrant green the same color as the things she controls. Her eyes hold so many things, so much wisdom. I could drown in her eyes.

"You're so in love with me," she says, giggling, and I smile just because it's true.

I'm in love with Sage, and she's in love with me (well, I think she is—girls are confusing, especially this one), and we're happy.

"You really are," says my sister. I almost forgot Milo and Selena were there. "It's going to make me puke."

"You sound like Ash," Milo tells her, and she laughs.

I see the way Milo looks at Selena. He has a crush on her, which is like, dude, my sister? But also like, that's cute. But like, she's going to burn you to the ground, too.

Then again, I see the way Selena looks at him, like he's something fascinating. So maybe not.

I wonder if she's told him.

I push the thought away. Now is a time for me to be with my sister and my friend and my almost-girlfriend, sitting under the stars with a nice, crackling fire. All of the bugs that come with the forest are gone. There are no gnats, no mosquitoes, nothing. It must be an enchantment Autumn's family put on this place. What was it that her grandpa said before he tried to kill my sister?

Oh, yeah. "There's magic *everywhere.*"

He sounds like a Disney princess.

"What?" Sage asks me.

I realize how quiet I've been. "Uh, nothing."

She passes me an unbelieving look, but I watch her let it go.

That's one thing about Sage. She's so easy to read. Like a book. Her eyes tell everything. Maybe it's just how many times I look into her eyes, but I always feel like I know exactly what she's feeling.

"You're doing that thing again," she tells me.

"What *thing?*"

"That thing where you look like a little kid in a candy shop."

I kiss the top of her head. "Well, you're so sweet, you're all the candy I'll ever need."

I expect her to retort with something snarky. She doesn't disappoint. "Gross, Torsney." But her eyes are teasing.

Easy to read.

"One second," Selena interrupts. She holds up a finger and leaves her spot next to Milo to pretend to puke in a nearby bush. I roll my eyes but Milo and Sage laugh. When she sits back down, she's smiling.

I can't remember the last time I saw her smile like that, genuine and not full of anything, not hatred or fear or hopelessness. Full of real happiness.

I can't remember the last time I saw my sister happy.

That's sad. *Really sad.*

"Could you actually support me for once?" I tease.

"No," she retorts. "Not when it's romance. Hell, especially when you're acting like this." Her eyes dart to Sage, who's laughing so hard her shoulders are shaking violently.

I hit her arm. "Oh, so this is funny? And I actually thought you liked me."

She laughs harder.

This makes Selena laugh. "Not even *her*, man? What did you do to yourself while I was gone?"

"Grew a foot, cut my hair, ditched the glasses—"

"Hold on," Sage chokes out. She turns to me. "You—you wear glasses?"

"Oh, yeah," Selena says with a smirk on her face. "Imagine super nerd, just with blond hair, lanky, and *horrible* bangs."

Sage erupts into a fit of giggles again. I roll my eyes jokingly.

"Oh, so all of a sudden, you're the funny one?"

"I'm the funny one when I have to be." Selena crosses her legs, that smirk still on her face. "Like when I'm making fun of you in front of your girlfriend. Priorities."

There's that word again. Girlfriend.

Sage tenses next to me. She stops laughing and her eyes travel down to the grass. I glare at Selena, who winces like Sage's reaction hurts her.

"Uh," she says to Milo, "let's go for a walk."

Milo gives her a confused look but follows anyway, and then it's just me and Sage, sitting together awkwardly. Tension hangs in the air.

"You know I'm not trying to push you into anything," I say. "We can—we can be whatever whenever you're ready."

Sage sighs. "I've never had a boyfriend," she admits. I resist the urge to tell her I haven't had a girlfriend, resist the urge to interrupt her just to try to make her feel better. "It's all surreal to me. Like kissing you, saying I love you, being affectionate. I ... need practice with those things."

I cross my arms teasingly. "Well, I can help you with those things."

"I know." She smiles faintly. "I know. Just. I know."

"Hey." I lift her chin so she's looking at me. Her eyes are conflicted, shadows in the beautiful forest of emotions. "I'm not going to give you some inspirational speech on how I love you and you need to be with me because of that. I'm not going to tell you to do anything, to force you into anything, to make you go too fast when you're not ready. Hell, I'll let you bully me until I crawl into a hole if it makes you feel better."

She giggles, and I smile. "I really, really like you, Sorin."

"Glasses and all?"

"Glasses and all."

Then, she does something surprising. She leans forward, closing her eyes slowly. I do the same.

Our lips meet for the third time in all of eternity, and it's like I'm on fire. Like my body's on fire.

Wait, wait.

No.

That's not happiness.

Oh gods.

That's *pain*.

We break apart, and then I feel it. There's a searing pain in my right shoulder, like it's coming apart blood cell by blood cell, muscle by muscle, bone by bone. I cry out in agony.

Sage notices. She tries to catch me as I fall off the log, but I land on the grass anyway. I smell dirt and the smell of fresh grass, and Sage is leaning over me. I'm gasping for air. It's like my throat is closing up, tightening with each and every breath I take.

I hear Sage curse under her breath, and I'm about to make a joke when I understand how serious this is.

With Sage's bullet wound, there were two Healers on the scene: me and Milo. Now, I'm down, and I know enough about injuries that it'll take two very talented Healers to heal me.

Sage cries out, something I can't understand, and there are footsteps pounding on the ground, getting closer to me. There are shouts from the rest of the people outside and I hear someone yell, "The king's guards!" but I'm so tired, so, so tired that I'm unsure if I heard them correctly.

Selena's leaning over me now, studying my face. I see the unmistakable fear in her eyes, gray, so gray, so, so gray, like storm clouds. The gray. The gray that made my father question if she was really his child. The gray that made people call her "Moonshine" for weeks in grade school. The gray. The unmistakable fear-struck gray.

"Sorin, Sorin," Selena breathes. "Gods, oh gods. What—?"

I open my mouth to tell her gray eyes something, but the words are caught in my throat.

Shouting and yelling, Sage crying above me.

Milo asking, "What the hell happened?"

He sounds like Elysian, when she found me and Sage.

Sage.

Sage is so beautiful. So, so beautiful. She was kissing me. She's kissed me three times now. Gods, I hate this stupid arrow. I could've held on to her tighter.

I feel like I'm in the air, though I stopped falling a long time ago.

I reach up to touch Sage. Beautiful, intelligent, difficult Sage. My love. Gods, I love her.

"Love," I force out. "You."

Sage laughs. It's broken. She's crying. Such beautiful tears. They roll down her face so perfectly. Perfectly perfect. That is Sage. She's perfectly perfect.

Gods, I'm so tired. Are people always this tired when they're hurt?

"You'll be okay, Sunshine," Sage says to me. She's copying Selena. That fear is in her eyes.

I know enough about injuries to know she's lying to my face.

"You'll be okay," she repeats.

Sage. My perfectly beautiful, perfectly smart, perfectly perfect Sage. Doesn't she understand she's said this already?

She's so perfect.

"Beauty," I whisper. "Beautiful."

She's breathing heavier. I want her to know that I love her. I want to hear her say it back.

"Love you," I repeat.

She smiles sadly. "I know, Sunshine. I know."

I told her, not too long ago, that I wouldn't force her into anything. But I want her to say it to me. I want to have that memory.

Perfect. That would be the perfect memory, with the perfect girl. "I do. Do you?" I realize she probably can't understand me.

Sage is smart. Beautiful, kind, smart. She will. She will understand.

"I love you so much, Sorin," she chokes out. She used to be laughing. Laughing that perfect laugh. I wanna hear it again.

I smile. She said it. I wanna hear her laugh.

"Sagey?"

She smiles again. There is nothing happy about it. I want her to be happy. Then she chuckles softly. It's sad. Still broken. She's sad and fearful, scared of what I've become. Scared of me.

"I'm right here, Sunshine."

I don't want her to be scared of me.

I reach up to touch her face, but the arrow in my arm makes it so painful I wince and drop my arm. Now my right arm is throbbing erratically, and I don't know what to do. I want Sage to know I'm not scary. I want her to remember me for being me, not for dying.

I want her to remember me.

"Poison," Milo is saying from behind me.

Sage looks up from me. Her gorgeous eyes are filled with concern. "The arrow's poisoned?"

Selena looks straight into my eyes. I forgot she was there.

"Don't listen to them. You'll be fine."

Her gray eyes are gray eyes of sadness and doubt and fear. I've never seen Selena like this before. As the older sister, she was always stable. But now … She breaks eye contact and Sage looks back down at me.

She's crying. Very clearly. I can feel her tears dripping onto my shirt, soaked with blood. *My* blood. My eyes cross for a moment and she's a blur, just a blur of red hair and beautiful green eyes. "I love you," she says to me, and her lip trembles. "I love you, and I can't lose you. Not yet, not ever. We—" Her voice breaks. "We were supposed to grow up together. To be together. Why—why are you leaving me?"

I shake my head and wince at the pain. "I'm—not leaving you," I promise her. She starts sobbing. "This isn't goodbye." It's getting harder to breathe. "This is just ... see you soon, huh?"

She doesn't respond. She just swallows roughly.

"Take out the arrow?"

"That arrow is the only thing keeping him alive. We take it out and he bleeds to death."

Selena and Milo are talking about me, about the arrow protruding out of my arm. Sage looks worried, so worried, and I know it's bad. I don't want her to be sad. I'm with the girl I love and here I am, on my deathbed (well, more like deathground) as she watches, and I hate myself for it.

"I'll see you again," I repeat. "I will. That's a promise."

Sage nods, and I'm suddenly tired.

So, so tired.

I want to take a nap right here, right now. My eyes droop.

"Sorin," Sage tells me sternly, though her voice shakes.

She smacks me across the face and I smile. Just like how we used to be.

"You have to stay awake."

While her smack definitely woke me up, it doesn't erase the tiredness I feel. Milo is leaning   over me now. His voice is soft when he speaks.

"Sorin, we need you awake. You can't go to sleep, okay?"

I nod. Sage clutches my hand. But then it returns.

That falling feeling.

It's ten times more intense, like I'm falling off a cliff. I feel it deep in my bones, and then, without warning, my eyes close.

I hear Sage's screaming and sobbing, and then nothing.

CHAPTER 18

ASH

I feel Elysian grab my hand.

Against my wishes, it makes my hand tingle.

Right now is *not* the time to be feeling … things.

Sorin is dead and I'm thinking about Elysian holding my hand.
Gods, I'm pathetic.

She's sobbing. Sobbing as the sun slowly rises over the horizon,
right into our eyes. Sorin would've directed it away, but he's dead. I
know it.

They took him to the little infirmary inside one of Autumn's
relative's houses. Sage hasn't left his side. Selena has been numb for
the past several hours, barely even reacting to things, and Milo has
been trying to heal him with the help of Autumn's relative. Elysian
hasn't stopped crying, and there's nothing I can do. I didn't know
him well, but he was like a little ball of sunshine, the thing keeping
us sane when things got bad. What are we going to do now?

They haven't confirmed that he's dead yet, but I saw his injury.
An arrow sticking out of his right arm. Poisonous, apparently. He
was barely breathing when we, Elysian and I, went to see what the
commotion was about. And now he's dead. I think Selena knows it,

too. She hasn't talked to anyone, hasn't looked at anything in particular, and it's like she's gone deaf. I think we all know, deep down, that he's never coming back, but some of us (Sage and Elysian) don't want to admit it.

"It'll be okay," I tell Elysian, and I'm lying through my teeth. "Everything will be fine."

She sniffles. "Milo told me."

"What?"

"It's your birthday, Ash," she says. A sad smile replaces the look of dread she had on before. "You're twenty now."

I bite my lip, picking at the skin with my teeth. "It's not important. It doesn't even feel like a birthday."

"Not important?" She looks at me like I'm crazy. "Twenty. Two zero." She holds up two fingers and makes an O shape with her other hand. "That's important to me. And I get it doesn't feel like a birthday, but come on." Her hand squeezes mine. "It's still your birthday."

"What are you going to do, make a cake?" I steady my glance at her.

"Possibly." She shrugs. "Once I know what's going on with Sorin, we'll celebrate."

I don't want to tell her. They will. Not me. But my stomach still twists at her words. She thinks he'll be okay. She doesn't know.

Great birthday, I think bitterly. *One I will remember forever.*

Not only that, but we have twenty-four hours at most to get to room 106 and save the prince. Perfect.

Sometimes I wish I hadn't come on this mission at all. And then Elysian looks at me the way she is right now, like she believes I've done nothing wrong, and I regret nothing.

Except I have done things wrong. So many things that she has forgotten, and the guilt gnaws at me every time she looks at me like that. Why does everything have to be so complicated?

She rubs her eyes and yawns.

"You should sleep," I suggest, though I know she has barely any intention of sleeping at all.

"I really should," she says with a sleepy nod, and rather than heading to her bed on the other side of the room, she rests her head on my shoulder and closes her eyes.

I feel my cheeks burning. Part of me wants to tell her that she should go to her bed, and the other part of me wants to let her sleep against me. Part of me wants to rest my head on top of hers and the other part wants to lead her over to her bed and make her sleep there.

But I freeze. I can't move, I realize.

Selena passes me a weird look over Elysian's head, and I'm about to glare at her when I remember her brother's just died and I stop myself. She doesn't deserve that, not now.

I smile awkwardly and her face turns into one of confusion, but

Sage comes out of the infirmary before she can say anything.

Her eyes are red and puffy. Her lip trembles dangerously, like she's about to burst into tears again, and her red hair is messy. Her clothes are bloody and ripped and she looks so pathetic that even *I* want to comfort her.

I know what it's like to lose a loved one. I would never wish it on anyone. Sage doesn't deserve this. Selena doesn't deserve this. Hell, Milo doesn't deserve working on one of his friends. And Elysian. Gods, it's breaking her apart. I can tell. Every minute that goes by she grows a little more antsy until she's almost jumping out of her seat. I've had to tell her that you can't go into the infirmary while they're working about five times, but even then, she looked like she would ignore me and go anyway.

Selena stands and rushes over to Sage, wrapping her in a bear hug.

"Are you okay?" Selena asks, and tears start running down Sage's face. She shrugs half-heartedly before collapsing in her arms.

I'm about to carefully take Elysian's head off my shoulder, when I realize she's already awake, staring at the scene with blank eyes. I stand and stride over to the two of them, Elysian following close behind.

"How is he?" Elysian asks hurriedly. "Can we see him? Is he—"

I know the next word out of her mouth before it comes, but it never does. Her voice breaks and falters and she stops, waiting for

Sage to respond.

"They did everything they could," Sage cries into Selena's shirt. "Medicine, blood, emergency surgery. Everything. But—but—"

"The arrow hit an artery," says Milo's voice from the doorway. "It was poisoned. We assume it was made for hunting animals. The poison infected his bloodstream, and … Well, there was nothing we could do."

It's silent for a second. The only sound is Sage's sobbing. And then I feel tears spring to my eyes.

When Selena talks, her voice sounds foreign, not like her own. "So—so he's dead? That's it? He's gone? You—you couldn't do anything?"

I watch her let go of Sage. I watch her storm toward Milo.

"I am so sorry, Selena," Milo responds solemnly with a slow shake of his head. "I am so sorry."

I feel the tears spill over. I feel them running down my cheeks, down onto my neck, making my face wet. I feel them hot and slow. I feel them, and then I feel ashamed. I wipe them from my face.

And then I watch Selena slap Milo.

I take a quick breath in and step toward him, but it's like everything's in slow motion. Sage's sobbing is slow and muffled. Selena's tears are gone the second they appear. Anger replaces her sadness, her disbelief, and Milo just stands in front of her, his head to one side, a bit of redness where she slapped him appearing.

"How could you not help him?" she screams, but her lips aren't forming words. It's more like her mouth is opening and words are coming out, slurred and choked and angry, filled with hurt and emotion. "You're the doctor! You're supposed to save him!"

"I'm sorry, Selena," Milo repeats. "I'm so, so sorry."

She rushes forward and I think she's going to slap him again, but then she clutches him like she's going to lose him, like he's the only thing keeping her holding on. Which he probably is.

She hugs him and sobs into his shoulder, and I watch in a daze as his arms wrap around her waist, stabilizing her, helping her. I've never seen Milo like this. Broken, sympathetic.

Confused.

"I never thought—" Selena says, but her sobs stop her. "I just came back and now—"

Milo holds her, even when I see her ruining his sleeve. "I know, Selena. I know."

Elysian, Sage, and I watch them. The shock from the encounter is more than needed, as it dries our tears and gives us a distraction from reality. Elysian grabs my hand again, and there's that burst of nerves again in my hand, like it'll explode at any second. But then she drops it and I feel disappointed, though I shouldn't.

Why, *why* does she keep grabbing my hand?

Why is she afraid of me?

How do I make her not be afraid of me?

Do I want to stop it?

I don't know.

A gust of wind from the open doorway reminds me that we're on a tight schedule. *Sleep is for losers*, I tell myself hastily, and I gather my things strewn across the room and my bed and the floor. I feel their stare on me, but I don't care. If we don't go now, Sorin's won't be the only life lost.

∗ ∗ ∗

That's how I find myself walking against the wind, struggling to make it who knows how many miles to the castle, watching the oak trees as we pass which are shining in the sunlight like someone isn't being held captive the next place over.

Sage is out of it. She hasn't checked her map at all since Sorin's death, which is so unlike her I don't know whether to laugh like this is just a cruel joke the universe is playing on us or scream until my throat runs dry and my vocal cords shrivel.

Any/all would be accepted right at this moment.

"You doing okay?" Elysian is walking next to me. Well, trotting. I'm very clearly taller than her and it takes a while for her to catch up to me when we're both walking.

I should be asking her that. There are evident eye bags under her gorgeous blue eyes, despite being bloodshot from crying so much. But of course, everything comes before her. "I'm fine." I slow my pace so she can catch up to me. "Are you doing okay?"

"I'm ... okay." She hesitates before answering, and I know she's lying.

Maybe the sun is getting to me, or maybe it's grief over Sorin, but I take her hand. She gives a small smile and though she looks away, she doesn't pull her hand away, for which I'm thankful. I think right now, after all the madness, we all need someone.

It's quiet. The sounds of birds chirping and twigs snapping under our feet are the only thing filling the air.

That and tension.

It's obvious. The way Sage recoils when anyone tries to touch her. The way Selena looks when anyone tries to talk to her. And the way Elysian reacts when I leave her side, like a lost puppy.

I lived with tension under the same roof for seven years of my life, and right now is almost just as bad.

It's making me impatient.

Well, more impatient than I already am.

"It's still your birthday," Elysian says suddenly, and I jump in surprise. Then I smile.

"Yeah," I say softly. I don't want it to be my birthday. Not today, not now. Birthdays are supposed to be happy, not sad and sorrowful and the other things death brings with it.

A feeling sets over me, like a cloud. I feel consumed by guilt, guilt that Sorin will never turn twenty, that I have this privilege when he doesn't. That I'm talking to one of his best friends as she tries to cheer me up even though she should be sobbing over his death right now. I feel like I've taken the spotlight off his death, like since I was born today, everyone will miraculously forget about him.

And past guilt. Guilt that I've pushed down so far I thought it didn't exist anymore. Guilt so strong, stronger than I've ever felt it. I find myself breathing heavily, like my throat's closing, and Elysian reaches over and wipes the tears that I don't know have fallen from my eyes, and I say to her, "You wanted to know about my tattoo."

She freezes. She wasn't expecting it. If I'm being honest, I wasn't expecting it. "Yes," she says carefully. "But I'm not forcing you into anything."

I stop. I swallow and clear my throat. "*Fuego y Luz*. Fire and light. I got it after ... Well, I got it after my mom died."

Instead of looking shocked, she just stares at me. "That's horrible. Can I—can I ask how she died?"

"Fire," I answer shortly. And then I suck in a breath at the guilt that threatens to consume me again, and I mutter, "Me."

Elysian lets out a short breath. "I knew it."

"What?" I turn so I'm facing her. She doesn't look scared of me or freaked out like most people do, and she's not making a move to run from me. She looks satisfied, and she crosses her arms over her chest.

"Ash, right after I lost my memory, I had a nightmare," she tells me slowly. "I don't know why, but it was of this little girl and her mother, on a beach, talking about Buit and Magics and execution. And then the little girl used her fire to kill her mother, and then she woke me up." Elysian glances at me. "From the moment I saw you, I knew you were the little girl. I don't know why I had that dream, or why it was of you, but I've been wanting to ask you this forever, and I—well, now I know."

I laugh, but there's nothing funny about the situation. "You knew?" *You knew what I did and you're still sitting next to me, talking to me?*

She places her hand on top of mine. "You're terrible at hiding things."

I lower my head.

"You're not a monster," she says quietly. It's like she can read my thoughts. "No matter how much of one you think you are, you're not. You're more than that."

I feel my cheeks grow red. Surely she can see it, but she says nothing and only tightens her grip on my hand.

"When I was a little girl, my mother was a *horrible* person. The sad part was, I thought I was the exception to her wrath. I was wrong."

My voice is beginning to become choked, and I quickly wipe the tears from my eyes. I shouldn't be sentimental. If anything, Elysian should be the one sobbing, not me. It's her who has lost her best friend.

"She taught me so many things, things deep down I knew were wrong, but I never said anything. And then she tried to kill me and all those things she taught me left my mind, as quickly as anything had ever left. I knew that I had to keep myself alive, but I didn't—" I sniffle. "I didn't think I would *kill* her."

Elysian sighs, and I feel she is pitying me. I don't want it. I don't want it, not right now, not when I'm openly displaying my feelings for the one person I thought I would never trust. Pity feels like a hit to the gut, and I want to double over, but I stay where I am, staring straight ahead at the gray stone castle that just sits there, sits there like everything's perfectly fine. Gods, I hate people who pretend. Misleading is worse, much worse than the truth.

"I'm sorry, Ash," she says. Her voice is heavy, and I understand why. She's lost her best friend. Surely the topic of death is not wanted, so I drop it. I drop her hand, the topic, the tension that's been building between us. At least, I hope the tension is gone.

The others are far ahead of us, walking silently with their heads hanging low. Sage turns to glance back at us and I see her. It's like I'm really seeing her. There are bags under her emerald eyes, earned from a sleepless night. Her red hair is messy and tangled, and I can tell she's been pulling it out all the way from where I stand. Her eyes are so tired, so, so tired, and so full of sadness and grief that I want to hug her, and I would *never* hug Sage Jobbs.

"Are you coming?" she asks. Her voice is low and defeated. Several different emotions flood into my senses, and I want to laugh and cry and try to perform a ritual to bring Sorin back for her and Elysian and Selena all at the same time.

I nod for the pair of us. Sighing, I reach out to grab Elysian's hand once more. We trudge forward toward the castle, which most likely will be the last time I get to celebrate a birthday.

Amazing birthday.

CHAPTER 19

MILO

It's noon by the time we stop to rest.

Ash has insisted, possibly out of the fact that the girl can literally survive on marshmallows and cheese (we tested it), that we keep going, but I can tell we can't. Sage and Selena are drained, both emotionally and physically, and if any of the three—Elysian, Sage, and Selena—were forced to walk any further, they would collapse before we got there, most likely pass out while saving the prince, and then we'd definitely be in a pickle.

Sage takes a sip of water from her hands. Unfortunately, the only thing we found water-wise that wouldn't give us dysentery was a running creek not too far from the castle. Selena said it's a safe haven for soldiers monitoring the woods, but since the disappearance of Prince Ameer, the soldiers have been busy searching for him rather than protecting the forest.

Elysian is leaning against a nearby tree. She glances down at her nails and at the sun, squinting. Then a look of sadness passes over her and she drops her head, staring at the ground.

Grief is horrible. It takes all the strength and power you used to have and turns it into sadness, anger, refusal, crappy things that control you. Everything reminds you of those you've lost until it's too much to handle. Overwhelming feelings tend to take over you, to change you, to prevent you from doing anything.

I hope that we make it to the castle before they spiral out of control.

Ash is messing with her hair. Her face is tense, expression set, like she's ready to test out her fighting skills on anyone who approaches, which, considering Ash and her behavior, she probably is. But then she sees Elysian, and she softens. It's like she's staring at a rainbow on a rainy day, like seeing new possibilities for the first time in her life.

I smile to myself. *She's hopeless.*

And Selena. Well, I'd be lying if I said Selena was okay. Her eyelids are red and puffy and her eyes are bloodshot. She's been crying so much. Sorin's death hit her the hardest, and after Sage's reaction to the news, that's saying something.

She rubs her eyes. When she sees me glancing at her, she glares at me. It's an appropriate response. She's grieving. Like I said earlier, she's drained, and the energy she used to have has been shaped into anger, so much anger. I have dealt with so many deaths, so many illnesses, so many injuries. And yet I couldn't save her brother. When I think about it long enough, it's like it's piercing through my soul, taking over *my* strength and *my* emotion. Sorin had become my friend, and then I couldn't save him.

Tears form at the bottom of her clear gray eyes, the ones I used to think were so strong. And they are.

You see, here's something that, no matter who, what, where you are, you'll learn: Everyone has a weakness. Whether it be comedy or sadness or an object or a family member, everyone has the one thing that makes them break. I have unintentionally found Selena's. Her weakness was her little brother.

Guilt claws at me and I turn away, looking toward the top of trees and the horizon, feeling the hot sun on the top of my head.

"Hey."

It's Elysian's voice, and, surprisingly, it's clear and pronounced, unlike last night.

I face her. "Hi."

She sits next to me and sighs. "Crazy. I never thought I'd be rescuing a prince or going on an adventure with a rivaling camp. It's—"

"Insane?"

"Amazing." Her head hits the trunk of the tree. "When you think about it, that is."

"I'll have to think hard," I mumble, and she giggles.

"Sorin really wore off on you, huh?" Elysian says. I expect her voice to waver or break, but it's just the same as before. Almost like she's speaking of a fond memory, not grieving at all.

Another thing you'll eventually learn: Some people are

incredible at acting okay. That doesn't mean they are.

I chuckle, trying to lighten the mood. "Yeah, I guess it has."

"I've been meaning to ask you ..." she says, and I ready myself to be struck by another pang of guilt. "Did Sorin ... did he make any final requests before he died?"

"You mean, before we operated on him?"

"Yeah." She clears her throat. "Yeah."

I think, trying to remember anything from that night except tears and the sting of emotions and the slap that Selena gave me. "He couldn't talk well, but I made out a few things. He said he wanted Sage to be happy. He kept mumbling about her eyes, and I think he said something about Selena."

"And ... me?"

I smile. "He said he wanted you to remember. I think you and Sage being happy was all he wanted."

Elysian sucks in a breath, and it's a little while before she speaks. "Well. I'll try my best."

I wrap my arm around her, sighing. We glance up at the sky. "I know it's hard when you lose a loved one. Trust me, I've gone through it myself."

Instead of emotion, curiosity fills her voice. "Your dad?"

"Yeah." I nod shortly. "My father was an amazing man. He was kind and gentle, patient and worthy of everything he had. And then one day, something went wrong in his work. Apparently, a device planted by the Royal Guard caught fire, and the building blew up. It happened pretty recently."

"And your dad," she says. "Where did he work?"

I can tell the subject's distracting her from the topic of Sorin, so I continue. "He worked at a bakery."

Elysian looks up at me. "*The* bakery? The one that—"

I nod. "Yes. Later into his life, my father had acquired short-term memory loss. It got to the point where he couldn't even remember me, his own son."

Realization dawns on her. "So, when you were in there all that time—"

"I was talking to him, trying to convince him that he was, in fact, my father, and that I was, in fact, his son."

"But Sorin mentioned an Evelyn, and you didn't even cry or—"

"Evelyn," I say, "is my mother. She lives across the street from my father's bakery. She would also try to convince him that they were married, but he never really remembered. Eventually, she stopped trying, saying she would just introduce herself to my father every morning as Evelyn, and every morning he would fall in love with her again. And everyone deals with grief differently. I knew it would be coming soon, so I had prepared myself for it. With Sorin …" Elysian looks away. "You didn't have much time to prepare."

She draws a breath. "You know, Milo, you're a really good friend." She stares straight ahead, avoiding my eyes. "I feel like I can trust you."

She's trying to get the subject off her mind, Milo, I scold myself. *Why would you talk about him?*

"Are you going to tell me you need to hide a dead body? Because, considering I'm a doctor, and that's *illegal*, I—"

"No." Elysian chuckles. "Gods, no. It's just—well, I feel like, with Sage hating Ash and you being Ash's best friend, you're the only one I can tell."

I raise an eyebrow. If she's going to tell me what I *think* she's going to tell me, then Ash is going to be jumping with joy. "Right."

"Well," she starts, "I learned something about Ash."

This catches my attention. Ash told her? Or she found out somehow? How? "Right."

"And it's like I was expecting it, though at the same time it's caught me off guard," she confesses, fiddling with her fingers. "I want a way to tell her she can trust me. I just feel like she doesn't tell me enough, and, well, I really want her to tell me things. I mean, since we're on this journey together and we'll be forced to be together, I don't want to die of boredom, you know? And once this thing ends I don't want to resume being enemies again. Or, I guess you could say rivals. But I don't want to lose the friendship that we've built when we go back home. Especially with Sorin and this news about—" She stops herself "Well, you get it."

I can almost feel the energy that would've drained out of Ash's bones at those words. I tilt my head to one side. "Is that it? Just friendship advice?"

Elysian takes a breath so I can see her shoulders rise and fall, and then, very slowly, she says, "Yes."

"You're sure?"

"Positive." Her voice is flat.

"Well, I can work with that." I rest my elbows on my knees and lean forward. "The main rule about friendship and bonds is trust, so you've got that right. The main rule about trust, though, is to *show*, not tell."

She nods, and I continue.

"The way you do that is by telling them something important about yourself, keeping whatever secret or information they told you to yourself, or supporting them if they need it. You don't want to change the friendship at all, because to show you trust them, you have to show this information you've gained has done nothing to change the relationship you have," I tell her.

She nods again. "So basically just support her, reveal something about myself, and keep her secret?"

"Well, you don't have to do all of those things. Just give her flowers, tell her she looks lovely—"

"Now I know you've *definitely* spent too much time around Sorin," she says, sending an annoyed look to me, and I laugh.

"Okay, okay," I say. "But about the last one—that's real. Nothing has changed, right? You don't see her any differently?" For Ash's sake, I hope she doesn't.

Elysian shakes her head quickly. "Of course not."

"Then show that," I advise. "Nothing's changed between you."

Elysian smiles lightly. "Thanks, Milo." But there is a hint of sadness in her eyes that only grief can bring.

I smile back, but it falters. "You're welcome, Elysian."

* * *

After that awkward encounter, I find a quieter place with not too much sadness. Don't get me wrong, grieving is healthy. But it gets depressing after some time and then you're trying to find a place where it seems like there's actual sunlight, despite it being everywhere.

Birds chirp above me, though I don't understand how they can chirp when it seems so dark right now. Can't they feel the sadness in the air?

It's nice to have the quiet, the calm after the storm, or before it, considering my current situation, where you can't believe you might die and yet everything is so peaceful.

That's exactly how I feel.

How dare the birds chirp when I'm willingly marching into a death trap, even though they have no idea about it.

Maybe I *have* spent too much time around Sorin. I'm definitely acting as dramatic as he is.

Was.

Peacefulness, Milo, I remind myself. *Isn't that what you're all about? Don't ruin it.*

"Hey."

Selena. Without my permission, my heart rate quickens. I try to calm it down, but then she sits next to me, and it's no use.

"So much for peace," I grumble, and then I realize what I've said. "Oh my gods, I am so sorry. I didn't mean that, I just—you're not a bother—you—"

Selena just chuckles. It's like the life has been sucked out of her. Her cold chuckles seem even colder, yet toned down, so it's not as harsh as a punch in the gut. Her hair is messy and she's tired, so tired, and I can tell from the way she looks at me, looks at everyone, at everything, like she's going to collapse at that very moment. "It's okay. You don't need to apologize," she tells me, and her voice is flat. "I get it. We all need a break right now. I just wanted to talk to you."

"About?" I already know where this is going.

"Sorin."

I wince. It was hard with Elysian, and now I'm practically setting myself up for failure with Selena. But I nod anyway. "Sure. What do you—"

"It wasn't your fault," she says.

I'm taken aback at first. That's definitely *not* what I was expecting her to say. But the sincerity in her voice and the way she's looking at me right now, with pity, almost makes me want to believe it.

Almost.

I come back to my senses just in time. "What are you talking about? It's like you said last night. He died because I couldn't save him."

"It was my fault he even needed saving at all." She gulps, placing her hand on my arm. It sends a jolt through me and I scold myself. *Not now.* "If I hadn't been so insistent on escaping and finding him, I wouldn't have gotten the guards angered enough to shoot him."

"It was good for him, you know, to see you before he died." I glance down at the ground. It's muddy and I suddenly regret taking a nice long break here. "He talked about you a lot. You're quite the painter, huh?"

She takes a deep breath. "I was. Before ... before I left. Sorin was the more active one, and I really spent most of my time painting, reading, anything I could to make my parents proud. And I guess, in a way, that's why I joined the Royal Guard."

"Selena." I glance at her. "You have, trust me."

"And you don't know my parents."

"Maybe you haven't made your parents proud," I say, shrugging, "but you've made someone proud."

She stares at me for a long moment. Her eyes never leave mine, and once I think I'm going to pass out from the intensity, she reaches forward and hugs me.

Her skin is cool despite the sun. Her arms wrap around my waist and she's hugging me, grabbing me like I'm going to leave her, like she thinks I want to leave her. Her fingernails are digging into my skin but I don't care. Selena's hugging me and there are no tears and I feel like I'm on cloud nine right now. My face doesn't sting from a slap and she's just hugging me, and that's all it is, a hug. *Maybe that's all she wants it to be*, I tell myself, but I push those thoughts away because, gods, Selena is hugging me, and it's probably the happiest I've ever felt.

Slowly, I hug her back. My arms find her neck and I'm hugging her back. I close my eyes, letting the sweet smell of metal and grass and fire hit me. It may not sound sweet when I talk about it, but, trust me, Selena makes it that much sweeter.

She sniffles. "I'm so sorry, Milo. I wasn't thinking, and now he's dead."

"It wasn't your fault," I murmur back. She's still wearing her outfit from yesterday, though it's covered in soot and stains from I don't know what. "It was the king's fault. If he weren't so cruel, we wouldn't have to worry about the guards attacking Sorin."

After Sorin was in the infirmary, we studied the arrow in his arm. It was poisoned. Either that or Sorin was allergic to something in it. But the nock of the arrow was painted with the king's colors:

red and black. We knew immediately, the doctors and I being "we," that the king's guards were behind the chaos.

And we panicked.

If the king was dedicated enough to follow us to this safe haven where Magics were thriving in the middle of an abandoned forest, then who knows what he'll do as we get closer to the castle, to finding his son.

I hope he's grateful, but he might have his guards kill us before we reach room 106.

I push the thought from my mind. Selena's still hugging me, and I'm pretty sure this is the longest, most awkward hug I've ever had.

I part from her. She winces, like it pains her.

"Sorry," she says. "That was probably the worst hug ever."

I shrug, smiling. "Not too crappy."

I'm telling the truth. It might have been long, but it was with her, so it's okay.

Selena tilts her head, studying me. It makes me slightly uncomfortable, and I direct my gaze anywhere else.

"You're nervous," she states, and I jump.

Well, yeah. You might slap me again.

I know that's not the reason.

"I don't want things to be awkward." I lean back on my hands, grimacing at the mud I know is going to be caked on there where I pull them back up.

"Why would things be awkward, Milo?" Selena raises an eyebrow. "Because you couldn't save my brother?"

She says it softly, but I divert my attention to the sky. I don't want her to know the real reason, especially not now.

I clear my throat. Selena's shoulders sag ever so slightly.

"We should start to get going if we want to make it to room 106 by tomorrow," I say, and she nods. "Do you know if Sage still has her map with her?"

"Most likely," Selena says. "I mean, I haven't seen her take it out of her pocket since ... well, she hasn't taken it out for a while, but I'm sure it's there."

I use my arms to push myself up, wiping my hands on my already ruined pants. They have Sorin's blood on them, I notice, and mud.

I gulp and walk away from Selena.

It's the "I'm mad but don't want to tell you" thing to do. The jerk thing. I feel instantly terrible. Her brother's just died, and then I'm ignoring her. But it's not like I can turn around and rush over to her, declaring my love dramatically at the top of my lungs. And it's not like I'm about to run away like Sage did, not when we're *this close* to getting the prince and leaving.

Which brings me to another thought. What are we going to do with the prince once we find him and bring him to safety? The last thing I'd think to do would be to bring him to the castle, not when it's that close to room 106. It can't be safe. But it's not like we can bring him to one of the camps. The villagers would get suspicious, and the king would want us dead even more than he already does, which is saying something. But then again, the king's guards don't know where the camps are, thanks to a talented pair of Magics. So it could be a good hiding place for him ...

"Milo?" Ash's voice interrupts my thoughts. "Are you okay? You've just been pacing back and forth this whole time."

I glance up from the ground. I hadn't noticed I'd been pacing, but suddenly my legs feel tired. Ash stares at me suspiciously.

"Fine," I respond shortly. She can tell I'm distracted. She's always been able to tell. "We should go before it gets dark."

She stands up and nods, but she doesn't move besides that. "What's up?" She looks over at where Selena stands by herself, leaning against the tree, her eyes closed, a look of regret on her face. My stomach drops and Ash turns back to me. "Did she do something?"

I shake my head. "Don't worry about me. I'm fine."

"No, Milo, you're not. What's wrong?"

I can't tell Ash. She wouldn't understand.

I shove the feelings down.

"Can you tell Elysian that we're leaving?"

I turn away from her, but Ash grabs my arm. When I look back at her, her eyes are sad. Heavy. Full of weight only a death can bring.

"Milo." Ash's voice is steel, yet her eyes are anything but. Her grip on my arm is tight. That and her voice combined are the only things keeping me there. And how scary she can be when she's angry. "You don't have to hide from me. I'm your best friend. We've been through all of this, and you're trying to ignore me? I know you, and I know something's wrong."

I gulp again, counting to twenty in my head. It's a trick I taught Ash that would help her calm down, but right now, I need it.

"Tell Elysian we're going, will you?"

Ash releases my arm, and I stalk away from her, even more guilt clawing at my heart.

Way to go, Milo, a little voice in the back of my head mocks.

Yeah.

Way to go.

CHAPTER 20

SAGE

I can't breathe.

The cold water hits my face. Milo promised I could have one last splash before we left. I think he knows how hard Sorin … leaving … hit me, how hard it still is. At this point, I am grabbing on to the last thread of sanity I have, and it's slowly unraveling.

The thing that hurts the most is how sudden it was. We were just kissing, and it was like Sorin and I were the only humans on the planet, and then—boom. Sorin went down and I saw the arrow sticking out of his arm and the last bit of hope I'd had that we might be able to make it out of this stupid death-wish trail you could call a mission vanished.

And then he died.

Selena's acting like it doesn't affect her, but if it hurts me as much as it does, then she has to be breaking to pieces inside.

Sometimes the thought hits me that I'm pathetic for being sadder than his literal sister, and then I'm even more sad, and guilty. I thought this rest stop would be longer than it has been, a way for me to relax and try to stop the thoughts from coming back, but now I'm glad. The action keeps me on my toes. It makes me think about things other than death and heartbreak and stupid love and stupid Sorin.

My mom told me when I was a kid that wallowing in self-pity wasn't good for the soul.

I guess she's right.

But going on a death mission, losing the person you love as soon as you've found one—those things can't be good for the soul, either.

"Sage." Milo yanks me up by my shoulder, which is a good thing, because I think if he hadn't, I would've drowned myself while I was thinking.

Or maybe that wouldn't have been so bad.

I take a deep breath, trying to calm my racing thoughts.

"Do you have the map?" Milo asks me.

Confused by his question, considering we can see the castle over the tops of the trees, I nod.

"Why?"

He doesn't answer and I pull the slip of paper out of the pocket of my sweatpants. Milo scans it slowly, then hands the yellowing parchment back to me. I put it back into my pocket, and he announces, "We'll go north for a while. Then east. And we should be at the castle right as the sun's setting."

"Are you sure?" Elysian asks. She glances over at the castle. "It looks more like we should go north, then west."

"No, I'm pretty sure we're here." Milo holds his hand out for the map, and I hand it to him. He points to a place labeled "woods" on the map.

"No, we're here," Elysian argues, pointing to a whole other side of the map.

"No, we're—"

"Neither of you are right, okay?" Selena rubs her forehead, exasperated. I feel the same way she does. "Is that better?"

"Can't we just, oh, I don't know, follow the direction of the literal castle?" Ash says. I notice that they all have a jagged edge to their tone, something keeping or getting them angry. "We can see it. There's no need to make complicated plans. We should just follow the castle."

"Or the direction of the sun," I offer, and several people shoot me dirty looks.

I lower my head.

Well, that was rude, says a voice in the back of my head. I don't argue with it.

Wordlessly, Milo hands me the map back. I stuff it in my pocket.

"I don't care what you all do," Ash declares. "I'm gonna follow the castle. Most of the time, that's the best way to get to the castle."

Elysian holds up a hand. "Wait, why are we arguing?"

"Because about right now, Sorin would make a stupid joke or

pun to break up the tension," Selena says, crossing her arms over her chest.

I nod in agreement. Almost all of his jokes are stupid, and don't get me started on the puns.

Were, the voice clarifies.

I push it away. The last thing I need right now is another reminder.

Ash walks off. Slowly, Elysian follows her. Not wanting to be stuck with Milo any longer, I do the same.

There's tension everywhere, it seems. Elysian and Ash are silent as we walk, the only sound the crunching of the leaves and twigs under our feet. I'm not complaining, as Ash isn't the best person when it comes to communicating, but it still would be nice to have a dumb-joke/pun-making Sorin around.

Without warning, tears spring in my eyes. I close them tightly and the tears run down my cheeks. I wipe them away fiercely. I'm so close. I am not about to delay us even more by crying.

We walk for a while. My legs begin to go numb, and the sun gets lower in the sky, hiding behind the castle. The forest is dark, and I barely notice when Selena and Milo start walking behind us.

Selena grabs my hand, and I almost pull away. But then I see her. I see her eyes. They're desperate for something, probably for someone to lean on. So I relax and let her hold it.

If I imagine hard enough, I can see Sorin holding my hand

instead of Selena, joking with me, laughing with me, calling me cute and gorgeous and other things like that.

There was this thing he'd do. He'd look directly into my eyes, like he could see my soul. And he'd stare at me like I was the most beautiful thing on planet earth, like he couldn't take his eyes off of me. And then he'd tell me I had the most beautiful eyes. I never thought much of it, but now I miss it.

I want Sorin to grab my hand, and I want him to make a stupid joke or a pun. I want him to laugh in the face of danger. I want him to stare into my eyes like that, like he's never seen anything more beautiful. I want to kiss him again like moments before he died, and I want to be happy just because he exists.

Sorin didn't live long enough. I feel so guilty for what I told him. I wanted to be his girlfriend, so bad, but I wasn't ready. I wasn't ready and now he's dead and I'm so ready, so ready to be the one he rejects other girls for. I want to be the one who he brings out to fancy dinner dates, the one who he treats like a princess because he's Sorin. I want to be the one who he tells first drafts of his jokes to, the one who critiques his stupid ones and laughs at the even stupider ones. I want to be the one who his mother smiles at because she approves of me. I want to be the one with him as we watch the stars, wishing tomorrow will never come. I want to be the one who teaches him to slow dance, the one who he tells first when anything exciting happens.

I want to be the one for him.

And now I can't.

I only realize I'm crying when Selena's cold hands wipe a tear from my left eye. She smiles at me reassuringly, but it's broken. I smile back, and I'm sure I look just as broken. She just grabs my hand tighter, like she's scared she's going to lose me.

I'm grateful for her. She's Sorin's sister. Of course I should like her. But when I met her, I thought she was a soldier for the king coming to kill us, just like the rest. But then I saw Milo behind her, and I stopped cold.

Sorin looked at her, I remember, and then realization dawned in his eyes. We discovered they were siblings when he rushed toward her, hugging her. I wish I could describe that hug. It was filled with so much emotion, so many things that were so obvious but so unreadable at the same time.

It was beautiful.

The energy is off without Sorin. Everyone's on edge, like we're waiting for another attack. I've seen Milo with that distant look in his eyes and the rest of us aren't better. My eyes hurt from crying and my voice is scratchy from the amount of screaming I did last night.

It's strange to think about. Only last night, I was with Sorin, and we were happy. Only last night. And now I'm not.

It really shows you how quickly things can change, even if you don't want them to.

How quickly time passes. And how alone you can feel.

We walk until the sun finally is gone behind the castle, when the stars appear above us.

Selena glances up at them. Something weird passes over her face, and then it's gone. Almost like a look of remembrance, mixed with disgust.

It gives me an idea.

"Selena, Sorin said you were a Magic, too," I say casually. Her hand clenches around mine, though, and I scramble to change the subject. "Uh, beautiful night, isn't it?"

She doesn't relax. "Yes."

"Do you like the night?"

"Yes."

"Why?"

"It's calm. It's quiet."

"You know what would make sense?"

"What?"

"If you were a moon-related Magic."

"Sage, I really don't think this is the best time for that conversation—"

"Since Sorin was a sun-related Magic, it would make sense."

"Sage."

"Why are you trying to hide it?"

276

"Sage, please—"

"Is that why Milo didn't die? While you were looking for us?"

"I don't want to talk about this." Her voice is firm, a warning, like she's telling me if I continue she will personally cut my arms off.

But I don't want to stop. I can't.

"Why not? Why are you so scared to put yourself out there?" I stop us, turning so I can see her.

She looks up at the moon, and as its rays hit her face. I watch as a calm washes over her, a sense of familiarity, a feeling that can only mean I'm right.

"If you want us to trust you, to help you, then you have to prove you can be trusted, that you want to be helped. Being stubborn doesn't get you anywhere."

She snorts. "That's rich coming from you," she says, right as I'm about to say, "I speak from experience."

I tighten my expression. I feel my mouth harden into a tight line.

"Just know we're trying to trust you," I tell her. "Try not to ruin that trust."

"I'll try," she mutters.

I say nothing, but keep walking. Ash and Elysian are farther in front of us now, yet I don't understand how someone could walk that fast. Right as a stitch forms in my side, they stop.

It gives me a second to think.

Selena can control the moonlight, manipulate it. Like the opposite of Sorin. Except she's more closed off about it, which is to be expected since she worked—or I guess she still does—for the most notorious Magic-hater in all of the kingdom. She isn't wearing her armor, which is good, since it won't make us a huge target. But there are still guards guarding everywhere, including the entrance to room 106. From what Milo told us, Finn wants Ash. Like, *wants* her. Wants to marry her. I doubt he'll harm her if given the chance, so we'll have to send her in first. But she'll have to be smart; otherwise, the guards will kill her instantly.

Milo told us, as he was retelling the story of what happened the very same night we found out the prince was missing, that Finn showed up looking holographic, like he used some kind of machine to find her and appear in front of them without actually being there. He said it looked like the image was coming from the hilt of Ash's sword, which means …

If we find a way to turn that holographic image thing back on, we can alert Finn that we're here, that he can tell the guards to stand down. We can get the prince and escape, using the fact that he wants Ash. We can have her distract him to the point where the prince can escape without Finn noticing, and then reinforcements can come behind to pick her up.

It's a good plan, but there are several faults. What if Finn's too strong? What if he has a whole army inside of room 106? What if he kills Ash? What if the prince doesn't take the hint and get out of there?

Then I scratch everything in my mind as I spot the castle and room 106.

Ash curses. It's breathy, but loud enough that we can hear it.

I understand why she does.

Room 106 is connected to the castle, like a distant room.

Like a dungeon.

I'm so stupid.

"The only way to get to room 106 is through the castle," I realize, and I want to kick myself.

"Yep," Ash says. She throws her head back in exasperation. "Ugh, I could just die."

"Well, don't." Elysian touches her arm.

I watch them. They move strangely. There's tension when it comes to them, a sort of awkwardness that comes from suppressed feelings. Like I said before, I speak from experience.

And then I tear my eyes away from them.

I don't have long to make a new plan. I need to do it quickly, before morning comes, and before the guards spot us.

"We can rest here," Milo declares, and the four of us spread out, finding different trees to rest against. I sit in the grass and take out my map as my brain starts working, scanning the castle every few seconds to make sure I have my facts right.

There are four guards, at least, guarding each wing. If we all separate, that'll be us all taking on four guards each, just to get inside the castle. Then we'll have to go through the armies inside and all the way to the right side of the castle, where the entrance to room 106 is. That will be way too many.

What I've learned is the guards tend to stick together. We catch them at a weak point and the rest will come to back them up. We catch them at a strong point and the others won't put their guards down. *Really? Puns at a time like that? I'm ashamed of you, Sage,* I tell myself. No matter what. They are their strongest when watched.

I make a mental note of that.

Then I remember. I reach into my pocket, pulling out Sorin's pen. The one he gave to me right before we were captured, the one that he wanted to call my pen. My heart hurts at the memory.

But I don't have time for pain.

I jot down the note on the side of the map.

If we attack the guards at their strongest, though, they will still be at their strongest. We need a period of time where they are distracted, but not distracted enough that they notice and help each other.

When we first saw Selena, she had armor on. That must mean she knows where to get armor. If we get her to dress up as another armored soldier, another unrecognizable soldier, claiming there's danger, then we might be able to lure the guards away from their posts.

That brings us down to four people.

I write it down on the map.

Now for the guards inside.

We need a way to take them down. I'm not sure how many will be inside once we get there, but I'm sure it'll be a large number. I write my estimate in the corner of the paper: "around 600."

Now that I have a good estimate, I make my plan.

Every plan I go through seems like it's a failing plan, a useless plan, and I'm so close to giving up.

Then I remember our powers.

Milo. He can bring peace. If he casts one of his "spells" on the castle, then that means the guards will most likely let us pass through if we ask nicely enough. We'll have to hurry, since he's mentioned that his powers wear off after a little bit, but by then, I pray we're at the entrance to room 106.

Ash can use her fire to burn the door down if it's locked. And once we get inside, with how tiny room 106 is, as it's only fit for one dungeon cell, I'm sure we can't fit too many people. If it does have soldiers, they will most likely be intimidated by Ash's fire performance. But it will also send them after her.

I scribble the main details of my plan down quickly so I don't forget, and I decide to tell the others about it tomorrow.

My hands hurt from writing so much. By this point, most of the parts of my map I've labeled "field" are filled with my plans and writing, even though I write small. I barely have time to tuck the map and pen back into my pocket before my eyes close and my head knocks against the trunk of the tree.

I fall asleep to the sound of the cicadas chirping above me.

* * *

"Sage, wake up," says Elysian's voice.

Someone shakes me awake softly. My eyes open and I see the four of them staring at me like I've been sleeping for an eternity.

Ash is bouncing from foot to foot, nervously playing with her sword. I get it. Today is the day.

Today is the deadline.

Today is the day we might die.

I rub my eyes. The sun shines bright in my face, and I feel a surge of power, like Sorin's looking down on us. It makes me smile knowing that, in a way, he's still here.

"Are we leaving?" Ash says. She fiddles with the hem of her shirt.

"Yes." I stand, using my arms to push myself up. I review the plan to them and they nod, repeating it to me.

"I'll find armor and distract the guards at the front of the castle," Selena says.

"I'll calm the guards inside using my magic," Milo recites.

"I'll break down the door with my fire, if needed," Ash mutters quickly. She's still bouncing.

"And I'll …" Elysian trails off, and I feel bad. I didn't have a role for her with my planning, but she is definitely powerful. She can cause tornadoes with her sneeze. That's worth something.

I place my hand on her shoulder.

"Are we ready?" I ask the group.

Selena takes a long, deep breath. Milo closes his eyes and opens them again. Ash doesn't stop hopping. And Elysian glances at the castle and her jaw clenches.

"Ready," they reply in unison.

I take a shaky breath, keeping my hand close to the dagger in my pocket. This may not go well, but I have not come all this way, lost my (almost) boyfriend, battled countless guards and enemies, and almost died several times, just to give up.

I take a deep breath.

"Ready," I murmur, and then we surge forward, bracing ourselves for death.

CHAPTER 21

ELYSIAN

"Sorry to disturb," I hear Selena say, "but I saw someone moving over there. Maybe a spy. It's not too big of a deal, but you know the boss. He'd want it to be safe if Ameer ever returns."

Ash grabs my hand. I can tell it's her because no matter what, whenever she grabs my hand, her hands are always warm. I'm guessing it has something to do with her fire powers.

She's still bouncing. She's been hopping from foot to foot since the sun appeared over the horizon, and she hasn't stopped pestering me and the others with questions. "Are you ready?" or "Do you think we're going to survive?" She's a good friend but it's hard to answer when I'm not entirely sure myself.

I turn my hand. She places hers on top and I intertwine our fingers. My cheeks glow red, but I try to ignore that. Now is no time for … whatever this is.

One of the guards nods, glancing off at the woods that Selena pointed to. He talks to his friend for a bit, and he nods too, ushering for the other guards to follow.

Sage smiles triumphantly. This is a part of her plan. We sneak around the edge of the woods, waiting until we can't see the guards to make a run for it. Ash is still holding my hand. Her face is determined, tense, and I realize I'm not any better. I can't relax my shoulders, no matter what I try.

"Intruders!" I suddenly hear a voice yell.

"No!" Selena says, and there are footsteps pounding closer. We duck inside the castle, the door shutting behind us with a loud *BANG!*

I pray to the gods that the guards outside don't kill Selena.

Fortunately, we're away from them. Unfortunately, now everyone inside the castle has their eyes on us, and that's not a good thing. Guards come from all different sides, closing in on us like a pack of hungry panthers.

I reach for my dagger, but there's no need. Milo places his hand on the wall, and very slowly yet very loudly, so it grabs everyone's attention, he says, "Stop."

The guards move in slow motion. A few have their guns raised, which I'm offended by, but I have no time to study anything else. Ash pulls me with the rest of the group and we're running, running as fast as I think I've ever run in my entire life.

But then, too quickly, Milo's magic wears off. The guards sprint for us, and they're faster than us. Some fire their guns, and the poison-infested bullets hit the stone walls next to us, burying themselves in what I assume had taken millions of dollars to build.

Ash is now holding my hand like her life depends on it, which it probably does. I don't mind. It's probably out of fear and not ... not what I think it is.

"Am I still burning the door down?" Ash asks Sage.

She looks behind us before answering. "Ash, you could burn the whole damn room down and I wouldn't care."

Even in the face of danger, she smirks. "Don't tempt me."

I'm breathing heavily before I realize it. We must not have had a lot of run-for-your-lives-from-bloodthirsty-guards classes at Camp Serenity.

Their footsteps draw nearer. There's the sound of yelling and as we get closer to the door, they get closer, shooting even more bullets with more accuracy every time.

Finally, we stop in front of it. There's a split second where Sage checks to see if it's locked and then I can't see anything else. Ash grabs my shoulders, twisting me so I'm pinned to the wall to the right of the door. She glances behind her, and I see the bullet hole in the door that's right where my head would have been if I stayed for a second longer.

"Thanks," I manage weakly.

She looks back at me. Not for long, but long enough that I notice the unmistakable glint in those beautiful gold-speckled eyes. She's getting a thrill out of this.

Ash draws her weapon, fighting the guard who's advanced on us. I reach for mine, but there's no need. He's disarmed in seconds, and when he goes to reach for his gun, Ash stabs him right under his armpit, the weak spot in his armor. He falls to the ground, writhing in agony.

She glares down at him, but then her eye catches on something else. Or, *someone* else, I should say.

"Can you handle yourself?" she asks me, bouncing again.

I'm still breathing heavily, but my hands wrap around the dagger in my pocket. "I think so. Go be a homicidal maniac."

She grins at me before following my orders, slashing through guards like they're made of butter.

There's suddenly a guard in front of me. I show her my dagger, but that seems to offend her instead of intimidate her. I press the button on the hilt right as she's about to attack, blocking her hit. Now my dagger is a sword, and that definitely confuses her. The grip on her sword weakens and I press harder with mine. She battles back, regaining her senses. Our swords scrape against each other. Finally, we make eye contact. I see gray eyes under her helmet, and— and I *know* those gray eyes.

It makes me want to throw up.

"Selena?" I breathe. My voice is pathetic.

She launches for me, and my instincts kick in. I feel horrible, but I manage to kick her stomach. She flies backward into the stairwell, knocked out cold.

I'm so shaken that I forget to pick my sword up off the ground.

Suddenly the tip of the blade is at my throat.

"Surrender now," the guard in front of me demands. Her voice is deep, like she's using a disorientation filter. "Or you and your friends die."

I'm breathing heavily again. The sounds of fighting behind us die and the only thing I can think of is the hurt of Selena's betrayal.

I close my eyes, ready for the soldier to kill me.

And nothing happens.

Click.

"You try *anything*," Ash's voice says, deathly quiet, lethal, "and I will kill you."

It's like a chain of death. The guard still has my sword pointed at my throat, but Ash has a gun pointed at the guard's temple. It's eerily quiet. Ash's face is stone, and the guard has gone tense.

I reach for the hilt of the blade, and I press the button.

It shrinks down into a dagger and, using her moment of surprise, I slash right under the armor, where Ash has been slashing this whole time. Her eyes widen and she falls back.

Ash keeps the gun at her side.

"We might need it," she tells me, and I have no doubt.

People will die today.

"Lys! Ash!" Sage calls, and I notice her dagger at a guard's throat. Her face is twisted into a snarl, and she takes her opportunity, slashing the guard's face so he stumbles back.

She rushes toward us. "Have you seen Milo at all?"

My heart drops to my stomach. "He's not fighting?"

"He tries to avoid all hands-on fights," Ash says. Her eyes go wide as she realizes, and she searches the room frantically. I use my dagger to cut down another guard, and I notice there aren't as many anymore.

I wonder why, but it's brief.

There's muffled screaming.

"Ash! Elysian! Sage!"

It sounds like Milo's voice.

Ash turns, stomping in the direction of the voice. Sage and I follow after her. I feel like biting my nails, though I've never done it before.

The sound leads us to the door to room 106. I glance around. The guards are closing in. Several are holding weapons.

"Now!" Sage yells over the noise.

Ash nods, and a ball of fire springs to her hand. She throws it at the lock and it falls off, easier than it should. The door falls down with a satisfying creak.

I can't believe what I'm seeing.

Milo is tied, bound with rope. He struggles against the tape around his mouth, fighting against the restraints. His eyes are pleading, telling us to get out of here while also letting him free, and I find myself wanting to do both. His dark curls spill down the sides of his head, reaching his ears.

Suddenly, there are footsteps from above. Either someone's on the roof, heading for us, or there's a whole other floor I have no idea about. Either way, it means they're coming for us.

I see Sage scanning the room from the corner of my eye. I search frantically for something to use, to hide behind or against, to save the others. My eyes fall on a tablecloth hanging from a coat rack, and I throw it over Milo.

Ash sends me a weird look, like she's saying, *You sure about this?* I nod and she ducks under the cloth, the only sign that she ever existed is the ghost of her gold-speckled eyes, blazed into my brain.

I grab the sword in its sheath. I have a feeling of anxiety settle in my chest, a feeling that's choking and suffocating and a feeling I want to get rid of.

But I'm too late.

The footsteps stop.

I see *him.* The man. He has brown hair, like me, but his eyes are a dark brown, almost blending into his pupils. He stands with confidence reserved for a leader. I don't know how I know this, but it brings a sense of familiarity with it. His skin is tan, like he's spent a lot of time outside, and he wears a simple outfit: the crest of Buit on a black, long-sleeved button-up, black dress pants, and a black jacket, even though it's August. He's ruggedly handsome.

I know instantly who he is without needing my memories.

"King Cirillo." I regard him with bitterness and anger in my words. I can tell he is a horrible person.

The King of Buit says nothing, merely chuckles at me. At first, I think he's making fun of me, but then he straightens his posture and says, "You are too much like your mother."

I freeze. "My mother? You know nothing about my mother. And we should not be talking about her. Where is the prince?" I demand.

Cirillo yawns, and I'm deeply offended. How can he yawn at a time like this? There's a ringing in my ears. "I wouldn't be too sure if I were you," he tells me, anger in his brown eyes. His jaw clenches, perhaps on reflex. I'm too angry to care. "The last time I checked, you had no memories, correct?"

I stiffen. *How does he know these things?* I ask myself, but I can't find an answer. "I won't ask again," I warn. "Where is the Prince of Buit? I know you have him."

"My dear," he says, his eyes skimming over to where Milo, Ash, and Sage are hidden under the tablecloth, "may we at least have some privacy? I'd like to talk to you about this truly ... devastating ... realization of yours."

He knows. The thought flashes through my mind. He knows where they're hiding, he knows I've lost my memory, he knew my mother. I get tense. "I haven't had any devastating *realizations*," I say.

He nods, the corners of his mouth tilting upward. He is like a shark, and I am one singular piranha, swimming alone. His eyes are cold. "Perhaps not. But you are going to."

His whisper sends a shudder through me.

"Where is Ameer?" My words are desperate, pleading, and Cirillo notices. He arches an eyebrow.

"Only when your friends go," he tells me.

I consider it, even though the last thing I want to happen is for my friends to go. And then I straighten my back and raise my chin. I *refuse* to take orders from someone like him.

"No," I say. "You tell me where the prince is, and we won't have a problem."

The King chuckles. "Your bravery is admirable," he says, though it's anything but a compliment. "But it is also incredibly stupid."

He stretches his hand. I raise my dagger.

I don't know how to use my powers. I barely ever used them before, and certainly not while fighting an angry king. I know how to use my dagger, but I still want to give up and die right here on the floor, crumple into a ball and be gone forever.

But I can't.

Instead, I grind my teeth together. I stare right into his eyes, praying my own don't show how weak I feel.

And I charge.

It doesn't take much for him to knock me over. I'm on the ground the next second, and I reach up to touch my nose. It's throbbing and bleeding, and I have a feeling that's what will happen to the rest of me if I continue.

He's too strong for you, a tiny voice says in the back of my mind. *You'll never make it out of here alive. Just quit, and this will be over!*

I don't listen to that voice. I have not worked this hard just to listen to a tiny, cowardly voice.

The wind blows harder. It's stuffy and hot inside these dungeons, but the little windows that are cracked open send huge gusts of wind into my face. It gives me a feeling of power. I brace myself for impact and try again.

Surprisingly, I manage to cut him before he knocks me over again. My dagger slices his cheekbone as he throws a punch. Cirillo's jaw clenches and he reaches up to touch the wound, staring at the blood on his fingers.

Then he laughs.

"You are so much like your mother," he says again.

What he says sends anger through me.

How *dare* he talk about my mother at a time like this.

"You're pathetic," I hiss.

He glances over at me and grins. It's sly, knowing. Taunting. "If I am," he starts, "then you are so much like your father, little girl."

I realize too late. He lunges at me, and I fall to the ground.

Then memories run through my mind.

A man standing over me, his hair dark and his eyes menacing. A plot of land, overgrown and overwhelmed with violence. A woman with the same blue eyes as mine. A photo book thrown in the trash can. Hands on either side of my face. A young boy with the same hair as Cirillo, smiling. A letter written in scrawly and messy script. Sage. Sorin. Campers. Ash.

Memories I didn't know I had.

A chill runs through me as reality sets in. As I remember.

"My father is evil," I mutter. "I can see that clearly. After all, he's standing right in front of me."

A gasp comes from the tablecloth. The wind grows stronger outside.

Cirillo chuckles. "You finally remember, little girl. I knew my potion wouldn't last long."

"Potion?" says a muffled voice.

Sage's muffled voice. She pulls the sheet off and then her voice is clear. "What—what are you talking about? Lys, he is your—"

"Father," Cirillo answers. He laughs darkly. "Remember that water bottle you gave her before she swam in that stupid little competition of yours?" he asks Sage.

I remember. That water tasted strange, but I didn't think anything of it. Sage advised that I be hydrated when we swam, just because "hydration is important." Right after that—I think, it's all a blur—I went swimming in the creek, and then I woke up against the tree after my dream about Ash. After I lost my memories.

Sage gasps. "There was no way you could've gotten in." Her voice shakes.

"I have my ways, child," responds the King.

Anger spreads through me. "You are just as much a monster as you have *ever* been, dear old Dad."

"Brave talk from someone on the floor." I can almost hear him cross his arms. "Stand up and we will fight properly, you dumb little girl."

I see red. I'm not sure how, but I'm up in seconds, glaring and fighting with such agility that Cirillo's eyes widen. He throws a punch at my abdomen, but I block it with the flat of my blade.

My anger fuels my fighting skills. I think about the suffering I've had to endure. I think about losing Sorin, about losing my memory, about the man in front of me leaving me to live on the streets by myself, about the things I've had to relearn and the friends I've had to leave and make anew, about the people I've confused and how confused I've been myself, and my blade cuts the sleeve on his jacket, leaving him with a large gash in his forearm. His blood drips to the floor.

He looks up at me. His lips are parted slightly in shock, but his eyes are angry and guarded. He wants to kill me, I can tell. He wants to kill everyone in this room, but he will start with me.

I look straight into his eyes. It's like I can see into his soul. He's angry and conflicted and sad, really sad. He's on the verge of a breakdown.

I imagine he's doing the same, looking into my eyes, studying my soul. Like father, like daughter, I guess, though most fathers and daughters don't have staring contests before a battle to the death.

I take a shaky breath. I can't kill him, not yet. I need information. And, even though I don't like it, there's a part of me that feels sorry for him.

"When I was a girl, you left me. I created my own camp, my own sanctuary and I made *sure* you couldn't reach me, because I didn't want the father I had never had to support me show up at the last minute and ruin the home he didn't give me."

My words are broken like my voice, but that's the worst of my worries.

"So how did you do it? *Why* did you do it? Because you were scared? Well, let me tell you something." My eyes fill with tears, even though I can't cry. "I was scared this entire time. I worried I would die and I worried as I fought for my life against the people you sent after me. I worried I couldn't trust the people around me who I had supposedly known since I was a girl, that they would betray me, because you wiped the memory of them. I worried that I would never learn how to survive, that every day would be a harder challenge that I couldn't face, because you took away the skills I had. I worried that I would never find the dungeons in time, that one of your guards would kill me before I got the chance. You might have been scared, but I was worrying out of my mind because of you. Because you were scared you were going to get caught."

He opens his mouth to say something. I don't let him have the chance.

"And *you* left me," I whisper, "and that is the most scared I have ever been in my entire life because the only person who could protect me, failed to."

He stares at me for a second, too stunned to reply.

"You are so much like your mother," he says for the third time.

I clench my jaw. My mother wasn't much better. She left me, too.

But at least she didn't give me false hope by staying at first.

"You can't trust anyone," he finally says. "You learned that over your journey. Did you not stop to think about your own camp?"

My eyes widen as I realize what he's saying. "There's a spy in the camp?"

"Xelma," Sage says suddenly from behind me.

I remember—that kid I sent to inform Ash about my wanting to meet with her, right after I woke up. A medic.

"She was—she was the one who handed me the water before we went swimming," Sage continues. She starts to breathe heavily. "I thought—I thought I could trust her."

I want to comfort her, but I'm stuck. If I move, the King will kill me.

"She's probably slaughtering the campers right as we speak."
Sage looks to me for permission. "We have to go back. Everything's there. Our home's there."

I'm torn. If I go back to my camp, the prince, my brother, will die. If I stay here, my camp will be ruined, everything in shreds, everyone destroyed.

The secrecy of the camp destroyed.

Absolutely everything I've built, I've loved, gone.

Cirillo seems to understand. He starts laughing. "Wow. This went better than expected."

I have no time to wait for him.

I make my decision.

I'm sorry, Dad, I think, though I'm lying. I outstretch my hand. It's shaking. I try to calm my nerves.

Cirillo glances at it.

"What are you doing?" he says.

He knows what will happen, I know he does.

I ignore him the best I can. I channel all my strength, all my anger and sadness and grief and pity and willpower into my hand, into my powers. I call on the winds to support me.

Outside, the wind grows heavier. The sky becomes darker.

"Stop!" the King yells. "Stop it!"

I ignore him again.

And then, I let go.

Relief. Like a weight being lifted off my shoulders. The King slams back into the brick wall so hard he makes a small crack. Blood streams out of his mouth slowly, dripping onto his expensive clothes.

For a moment, I'm frozen. But then someone's hand grabs my arm.

Their hands are warm.

Ash.

I turn. She stares at me with sincerity in her gaze, real feelings. She looks proud. "What you did was amazing," she tells me, and then she wraps me into a hug.

I'm stunned for a second. I hadn't realized how much I needed a hug. Now, it's like even *more* weight is off my shoulders. I hug back tightly, willing the tears not to fall.

The surge of energy and power has drained me. Right before I pass out, I hear a voice call out.

"Ash, my dear. You made it."

CHAPTER 22

ASH

Elysian falls into my arms.

I catch her, of course, but just barely, and her dagger almost cuts my leg. Sage removes it from her hand before her unconscious body can do anything to me and she twirls it in hers, bringing out her other one.

I glance up. I recognize the voice that said my name.

"Where are you, Finn?" I yell. "Your boss is dead! Come out! Surrender!"

Yes, it was a shock that the King was Elysian's dad, but the resemblance was there and the way he knew her mother was freaky—until we found out they were related.

Now, he lay on the ground in front of us. Blood trickles in a line from his mouth down to his armor, and I almost feel sorry for him, until I remember what he did to Elysian, and I grow angry again.

Elysian's heavy. My muscles ache after a bit. But she's worth it.

I know Finn is here. Ever since he took me in years ago, I've had a feeling whenever it comes to him. It's like I can sense him.

Sage has untied Milo. He stands next to me and unconscious

Elysian, looking around the room. He walks around slowly, taking in what we could use as defense mechanisms or things to get to the prince, no doubt.

When he speaks, it's in a low voice, so we aren't overheard. "From what I've studied on this place," Milo starts, "there is a basement. That's where the dungeons are located."

"When Lys talked about what she saw, she described a camera Ameer talked to and Finn talked *through*," Sage adds. "It was like they could hear each other, but Finn could see Ameer and Ameer couldn't see Finn."

"Do you think he's waiting for us behind the camera?" I ask.

"Depends." Sage's expression is sour. "How well do you know him?"

"Well."

"Then what do *you* think?"

I raise my eyebrows. This might be the first time Sage has ever asked me for my opinion. *I'll make sure to document this moment and brag about it every chance I get*, I tell myself. But a tiny voice at the back of my head says, ruining the fun, *If you make it that long.* "I think he won't hurt me."

Sage nods. "Exactly. Now, I don't know if he can shoot venom through the hologram or whatever, but I have a feeling that this method of communication is dangerous. He obviously trusts you enough to let you lead the mission that will most likely kill him. If you go in first and Milo and I make sure we aren't seen, then we might get away with taking the prince."

It's like this has been her plan all along. Maybe it has. I wasn't paying attention when she explained everything to us.

I take a deep breath, trying to calm my nerves. We're actually doing this. I know Finn won't hurt me, I'm sure of it. But I also know he wants me for himself. I know Ameer has been captured because of me, because his boss (the King, if you haven't caught on) wanted me dead. But his boss is dead now, and there's no telling what Finn will do—especially if he finds Sage and Milo.

A thought hits me hard. *Where's Selena?* I ask myself.

Panic runs through me. I've never been the girl's greatest fan, but she might be dead. She might be fighting for her life right now. Or worse—she might have betrayed us.

"Ash," Sage says. "It's now or never. We either go to the dungeons and fight if we have to, or we get killed by the mob of angry guards trying to break down the door right now."

I glance back. Sure enough, the wooden door creaks with pressure from fists pounding against it in a pattern. I hadn't noticed the yelling before but now it's all I can hear, suffocating me, reminding me that no matter what we do, we probably won't win. We'll probably die and the first friend I ever had will die and everyone at my camp, my home will die and the girl I strangely no longer hate will die and everyone will die and it'll be the end of the world.

With that thought in mind, I choose. "Find the stairs," I order, and Sage and Milo start looking around the room frantically.

Suddenly, Milo calls out, "I found them!"

I rush over, a limp Elysian in my arms, Sage following behind, and we sprint down the stairs.

Downstairs, it's cold. Very cold. The walls are gray, dark and stone, like a dungeon floor should be. Empty cells surround us, and in every one, I see what Sage was talking about—a black camera, tiny red light in the corner of it flashing every second, is pointed to the right corner of the room, where the beds are. Dirt and dust and grime are everywhere, and the scent of death and time hang high in the air.

I plug my nose. My arms want to fall to my sides, but now, we're on stone. If Elysian were to hit her head on that, it would be game over.

I hold tightly to her body. She still has a pulse, but it's weak, and I know she'll need attention from Milo after this is over, if we even make it that long. So far, I'm just hoping we make it long enough that I can even find Ameer.

"Your sword," Sage whispers to me. "It has a hologram feature in it."

"Yeah," I whisper back.

"Try to contact Finn. If you can't reach him, then we keep

walking. If you can, then tell him only you are here, no one else. But don't make it that obvious."

I nod. I unsheathe my sword, and Sage takes Elysian from me. I try my best to figure it out, when I notice a small round button on the very bottom of my sword that I know wasn't there before. Or maybe it was. I haven't spent too much time grabbing on to the bottom of my hilt before. Or looking at it, for that matter.

I press it. Nothing happens. I press it again, and still nothing happens.

From upstairs, I hear the door creak. Sage's eyes widen in a terrified message: *Hurry.*

From anxiety, fire appears in my palm. I set it close to the button so it can feel the heat radiating from my hand and press it again. This time, an image of Finn pops up.

He has a smirk on his face, like he's been expecting me. I can't say I'm surprised.

As I film myself, I make sure Milo and Sage are out of the frame.

"Finn." My voice is low, yet I still sound as pathetic as I did the day I met him—crying on his doorstep, begging for total strangers to take me in and help me, just to even feed me if they could.

Finn smiles. "Ashlyn. You heard my voice then?"

I say nothing. His smile grows.

"Now, now, won't you talk to me? We are not enemies, my love.

We are simply," he pauses, thinking, "separated. On other sides of the world."

"Where are you?" I say.

"Eager, now, are we?" He chuckles. "It wouldn't matter. You will never find me. I will outsmart you every time you try something." His grin is manic. "For instance, I already know about those friends of yours, and that crush you have."

Sage's eyebrows crease. Milo sends a knowing glance at me. I look away, blushing furiously.

Finn laughs. "So it *is* true! You have a crush on my boss's daughter! Ah, yes. Quite obvious. I have been tracking you this entire time, and I must say, it is cute the way you get flustered. Soon you will act the same around me, my dear."

"Get to the point, Finn," I growl.

He puts up his hands. His eyes dance with amusement. "Are you in a hurry, dear? I suppose I understand why. Your prince is slowly succumbing to his painful death, one moment at a time. You are lucky he has made it this long."

I grit my teeth, resisting the urge to wince. Has it truly been that long? I mean, we were delayed several times, but we still made it on time. Today is August fourth, Finn's birthday, our deadline day. We made it.

"You did this on purpose," I realize. "You knew—you thought he was going to die earlier, so you made the deadline ten days. You wanted us to fail."

"We are not enemies," he says again. "It was the boss's orders."

"Well, your boss is dead," I hiss. "And if you don't hand over the prince, then you're next."

Finn smiles. A malicious grin. He thinks my words are full of fake promises. "Is that so? Well, darling, I'd help, but then that would spoil all of the fun."

I smile back dryly. Inside my head, I'm planning how I will kill him—preferably slowly, so he suffers. But then I hear shouting from upstairs and my eyes widen.

Finn notices. His smile widens. "Better hurry, darling."

Then the image of him disappears.

Sage starts to run as soon as Finn's gone and I sheath my sword. She runs as fast as she can with a healing gun wound and Elysian in her arms. Milo and I run after her.

There's a dripping sound, like water falling from a sink. We continue running until the dripping gets closer, and then we find him.

Ameer.

My heart almost stops.

His hair is greasy. It's pushed to one side. His mouth hangs open, his head leaning back against the stone wall he's in front of. He wears ripped, dirty clothes, and there's so much grime and dirt on his skin that it amazes me how he hasn't died from his own filthiness yet.

There's a crack in the ceiling of the cell he's in. It must've rained here, because water drips onto the ground, the dripping noise we followed.

I gasp. How could they let him live like this?

A million thoughts run through my head, most cursing Finn. But others scream at me. The tiny part of my brain that's still listening to the commotion on the floor above yells for me to hurry, to stop gaping and get Ameer to safety and Finn dead.

Guess which thoughts I listen to.

I don't remember launching toward the lock. I don't remember taking a pen from Sage and picking the lock with it. I don't remember how I even learned to pick locks. But I do remember the low laugh coming from the corner of the room, like someone or something is watching, taunting us.

Milo holds Ameer, being careful with his fragile body. A dark lock of hair hangs over his forehead. It's not curly, but not straight, like Elysian's. I wonder how I didn't see the resemblance before.

No time for reflecting. We're halfway back when I see the guards.

They're stronger than the rest, all holding swords that may be taller than them, built for chopping off heads. Their muscles are visible through the cracks in their armor.

I hear Milo whimper nervously as the guards walk toward us

slowly.

"You are Ashlyn Kave," says the guard at the front. "You will die, along with your little friends."

The rest of his group laughs.

I look around, desperately searching for an escape. If we die here, that's that. Elysian's camp will be invaded, my camp will be discovered, and all our work, our time, our home—will disappear.

And Finn will win.

The guards are still laughing. I stand, paralyzed, next to my friends, the only friends I think I've ever had. Elysian, Sage, Milo. I feel Sorin grinning down on us, the doofus little smirk he'd get whenever Sage was around. It was pretty obvious they liked each other. Based on Milo's reaction, I'm guessing I was pretty obvious, too.

The embarrassment of that situation makes me remember where I am. I slash my dagger toward the group of soldiers, praying they'll take the hint and get lost.

Instead, they just keep laughing. My heart crawls up into my throat. I've never been this scared before, not since …

No. I refuse to do that again, to kill another person with my fire. Not only would it be damaging to my physical health, draining me even further, but it would also be damaging to my *mental* health, bringing up memories I buried in the depths of my brain.

The memories I buried until I found out Ameer was missing.

I try to calm my shaking hands. Standing here watching them will do no good.

I turn my head. I see Sage trying to form a strategy in her head. I see Milo grunting as he holds Ameer (my guess is he hasn't had much experience holding unconscious teenage boys). Briefly, the memory of Selena being lost enters my mind. *What if she's dead?* says the same little annoying voice in my head that's been there since the beginning. I silence it. Doubt won't do any good. I need to keep going.

I need to *think*.

I think back to one day a few years ago, way before Ameer went missing. Milo and I saw the campers in chaos, and we just … waited it out.

Waited it out.

An idea forms.

"Yeah," I say, stepping forward. "I am Ashlyn Kave. And these are my friends, Sage, Milo, Elysian, and her brother, Ameer. Ameer's the prince. Long story, and I'm sure you have several other duties you need to do, eh?"

One of the guards stares at me strangely. I figure he's not the smartest.

"Ashlyn Kave, why are you talking? You are about to be killed."

"Then do it already," I urge. "Or are you too scared?"

The one in the front narrows his eyes at me. "Not scared."

"Then prove it. Why are you waiting?"

Sage shoots me a look. I send her one, too: *Trust me.*

"Yeah," Milo adds, catching on. He's always been able to know what I'm thinking before I have to tell him. "Are you too slow to understand what we're saying to you? Kill us, you fools."

Slowly, a look of realization dawns on Sage's face. She readjusts Elysian in her arms and says, "Unless ... you don't want to. I'm sure you aren't *really* killers, are you? You're just misunderstood."

The guard on the left of the one in the front glances at him. "Sir—"

The first one nods slowly. "I—I am not a monster."

"The King was," I say, dragging it on. "And now he's dead. You can be whatever you want to be."

I realize what I've said as the first one's eyebrows narrow. "You have killed our king?"

"Uh—" Milo says.

"You must die!" the one on the left snarls.

"Run," I say, and we sprint away from the band of guards, running down a long corridor built of stone. Dirt finds its way to Milo's eyes and he falters for a second. Then he must remember we're being chased because he begins to run twice as fast.

Finally, we find another staircase. We climb it hastily, Ameer and Elysian's feet hitting the stairs as we run.

When I see the familiar first floor of room 106, I want to throw up from relief. And running so much. And stress. Then I see the scene in front of me—like, actually see it—and I want to throw up even more.

Finn.

His dark hair is long and messy. His skin is bruised and bloodied. His back is to us, but I can see the glint of a sword held out in front of him.

Someone whimpers—most likely the person in front of him.

"Finn," I say. My voice shakes with resentment, anger, sadness, exhaustion.

He whips around. I then see the person he's holding at sword-point.

"S-Selena?" Milo's voice squeaks. "What—what's going on?"

Selena Torsney's helmet has come off. Her hair, covered in dirt and sweat and leaves from the forest, is pushed back, revealing her pale face. Her breaths are heavy, shallow, and I understand.

She's injured.

"I tried to stall him," she tells us. "I did. I'm so sorry." A tear or a bead of sweat—I can't tell—drips down her face.

Finn pushes the sword against her throat harder. She lets out a strangled sound. "Do not speak, girl." His eyes flicker over to mine. They're different than what I remember—darker, sadder, more ominous. "Ashlyn, my dear. We meet again."

I flinch at my whole name. He is one of the only ones who has ever called me my full name, *ever*. I made sure of that my entire life.

"Let her go," I tell him. "She's innocent."

"Oh, I don't believe so." He grins. His teeth are yellow and crooked and disgusting. I would expect nothing less from him. "A traitor of the King, she is. Now that he's dead, I believe it's my responsibility to do him justice, don't you think?"

Selena shakes her head wildly.

In a moment of desperation, I say, "Would the queen approve of what you're doing?"

"The queen?" Finn literally laughs out loud. "You really need to keep up with your royal family drama, my dear. The queen is dead. Has been several years. Was killed by a Magic, if you're unsure."

He sighs.

"Tragic, really. I believe her killer was the son of a Plenty. Like you!"

He laughs again.

"How ironic. Anyway, she died around the time your mother did—before, most likely. The King ordered all Magics in the land be killed immediately, and, well, you were in the area. When he found out you were a Plenty, he wished for your blood even more, to avenge his wife. A sad story. How unfortunate that he never did get his wish."

My breath catches. He captured Ameer because of me, because he wanted to kill me so badly that he was willing to let his own son go to waste. I glance at his dead body, several feet from where we stand. "What are you going to do to me?" I ask.

"To you?" He chuckles. "No, my dear. Nothing to you. We will live happily ever after. But your friends—*they* are the problem. After I wipe them out, then the spy at one of those Magic camps you've built will alert me of the location of the rest of them. I'll bring in some reinforcements and you, my love, will get the pleasure of killing your own campers! Isn't that nice?"

"Nice?" I hiss. My throat burns. How could he do this? My campers are my family. My campers are everything I have left.

"How could you?" I don't realize I'm crying until I feel the wetness of the tears against my cheeks.

Finn looks confused. "My dear, once everyone else is gone, then it'll just be you and me. Don't you want that?"

"*You* want that, Finn," I retort. "I don't love you. Hell, I don't even *like* you! I am never going to be on your side, ever."

Now he looks hurt. "Ashlyn—"

I glance at Selena, then back at Finn. We don't have much time, and I need information. I need to destroy him, but first I need information.

"How did you put that hologram feature in my sword?"

"Have I already mentioned the spy?" he says, pondering it. He pretends to forget what I said earlier, but I can tell. Like I said before, when it comes to Finn, I have a sixth sense. It came in handy when I lived with him. "What was her name? Xelma, I believe?"

My heart drops. I hadn't been listening to their conversation before; I had been too nervous. Now, I'm listening so hard I feel like my eardrums are going to rupture. I remember the girl who was the messenger for Camp Serenity, the one who came to notify me about everything Elysian said—if she wanted me to hear it. With the information she has, she'll tear my world—our world—apart, along with everything and everyone in it.

"You've lost, Finn," I tell him, but my voice shakes, and he laughs. He knows he hasn't—not yet.

"Have I, my dear?" His expression hardens. "Whether you stand with me or against me, you will be my wife. You will fail, along with your friends, and I will make you repeat the exact routine over and over again until the day I die or the day you die—whichever comes first. We are not enemies," he says with a sense of finality, "as long as you understand this is a losing battle."

This is not over, I remind myself, no matter how many times he says it is. I will win or make him realize I'm not who he thinks I am.

Either way, I win.

Or at least, I *think* I do.

Because the next second, he plunges his sword into Selena's stomach.

She crumples to the floor, dead.

I gasp.

314

Milo rushes toward her, but Finn steps in front of her body. "I don't think so, lover boy. Back up, or you're next."

Milo, his face pale, his eyes brimming with tears, backs up until his back is against the wall. He breathes heavily, almost panting, and his eyes never leave Selena's lifeless body.

I want to throw up even more. My thoughts are jumbled, buzzing. Everything is red. How could he do this?

Selena.

Dead.

Selena.

She's innocent.

Was.

Selena.

Dead.

How is she dead?

Never give up.

Never.

Let.

Him.

"If I go with you," I say, tears blurring my vision, "will you promise not to hurt anyone else?"

I feel so powerless, the way I did when I was a scared seven-year-old on a dark beach. I remember feeling helpless. I was preparing myself for my own funeral. Now, thirteen years later, I'm doing the same.

He waves his sword at Sage, Milo, and Elysian lazily. "After what they've seen, I'll have to kill them. And I don't need the prince anymore, so he can die. But after them, then, yes, I promise, my dear."

White-hot anger fills my heart. I try to calm myself. I can't let them die. If I die, I die. But Elysian, Milo, Sage, Ameer—they don't deserve to die.

I step toward Finn cautiously. He's still holding the sword. I know he won't hurt me, but if I do anything wrong, he may hurt the others. "Okay. That's fair."

"What?" Sage whisper-shouts. "Are you crazy?"

I send her a warning look. "I'll go with you, I promise. I swear."

Finn smiles wickedly. "I knew you'd see sense, my darling. It only took a little push."

I step over Selena's body, trying not to gag. "But *you* have to promise *me* one thing, okay?"

I don't let him say anything.

"You leave the camps alone." I try to calm my hands, my voice, anything that might prove I'm scared out of my mind. "You leave the people alone. You send your spy back to the castle. You tape her mouth shut, or you kill her. You let me make orders, not take them. You let all the guards who don't want to be here anymore go."

I think of Selena below my feet, dead. At what cost? She only got to see her brother for a short amount of time, and she spent *five years* trapped here against her will. Now she's dead.

"You stop saying things that are false. And most importantly, you let my friends go. You let them go free. You don't hurt them. Otherwise, we have no deal."

I try to make myself sound confident, but inside, I feel my pride crumbling, my willpower shattering, my heart cracking. I feel everything I have left freeze as I await Finn's response.

He considers it. Really, truly considers my offer. "Perhaps ..." he says slowly. "Perhaps I will oblige."

I let out a gasp of relief. *I did it*, I tell myself. I want to shout in joy, and I want to celebrate.

Until Finn raises his sword. I hold my breath as the tip of the blade touches my throat.

"You wouldn't," I hiss. "You love me, don't you?"

"Oh, yes," he says, smiling cruelly. "I love *you*. But remember, my dear, who has the power here. And your friends, the people, my spy, your camp, the guards ..." He shrugs half-heartedly, like he can't decide where to go for dinner. "I don't particularly care for them much."

And he steps around me, sword still raised, to get to my friends.

CHAPTER 23

SAGE

I'm going to die.

I'm sure of it, standing here, in front of Finn, his sword pointed at me and Milo. I feel him tense beside me. My muscles scream from Elysian's weight in my arms, and I set her down gently next to me. She's still wiped out, but her eyelids have fluttered a few times, meaning she'll wake up soon. I hope so.

Well, I tell myself bitterly, *if I'm going to die, might as well make it worth it.*

I stretch out one of my hands and see, in my mind, the earth closing around Finn's legs, keeping him in place. I will that to happen, and the wooden floor curls around Finn's ankles, suspending him from walking any farther.

He cries out in protest. Then he chuckles dryly. "It's been a while since I met an earthbender. It's refreshing, really."

"I bet," I snarl. I duck around the point of his sword, drawing my dagger, but Finn's fast, and he's expecting it. His other arm whips out and he hits me in the stomach.

I suck in a breath and dig my dagger into his arm.

He grunts in pain, but his wound heals surprisingly fast. "You're not the only one with friends, girl," he says when he notices my expression.

I can't dwell on that. Finn tries to hit me with the flat of his blade, and, unfortunately, it works. I stumble back, almost falling, but at the last second I find my balance and I go for Finn again, this time for his face.

Once again, he expects it. He blocks the attack with the butt of his hilt and pushes hard enough that I almost go flying again, but I hold on to the hilt. My hands wrap around his gnarly, dirty ones, and I yank.

He yells as I hear the crack of bones. I'm sure I've just dislocated one of his fingers, but I don't care. I don't stop. I keep pulling until his fingers loosen around the leather and I have full control of his sword.

I throw the sword across the room and reach for Elysian's dagger in my pocket. I have a dagger in each hand, which is good, but I notice that the spell binding Finn in place is coming undone, the wood unfolding so it molds back into its original build. I suck in a breath.

Fortunately, he doesn't go for me. Unfortunately, he bounds for his sword, which is behind Ash. He grabs her hand and grabs her.

I watch in horror, petrified, as he pulls her toward the door. I'm now aware of the pounding on the stairs behind us. The guards have found the stairs. Finn picks up his sword.

Ash wills flames to her hand. Finn pulls back, burned, and wincing, and rubs his raw skin. Ash goes for his body, stabbing at his ratty clothes with her sword. He cries out, but his wounds heal quickly, so our efforts seem to be only irritating him, not hurting him. Not permanently, at least.

I begin to doubt that we'll ever win. Selena is dead. Sorin is dead. Finn has the strength and patience of any of us combined, and he has time. We have nothing. The last bit of hope I have left fades.

Not good, not good.

I see, in my mind, a giant wall of earth coming up behind us, blocking the stair entrance so the guards can't make it to us. I smile, satisfied, as I hear the sound of wood breaking and shifting to comply with my wish. I call on the earth to trap Finn again, but it's like he can see what's going to happen before it happens. He sidesteps as the wood tries to trap him.

"Your friends are weak, my dear Ashlyn," he says, but he's facing me and Milo. I glance behind me. There's yelling from behind the earth wall blocking the stairs and Milo has put Ameer next to Elysian, who begins to stir. "I have no idea why I expected more of them."

Ash bites back a retort. I watch Finn's hand find hers again and wrap around her wrist tightly. She looks more irritated. Her eyes light up, like she's going to burst.

But before she can, I hear a disoriented, "Ash? Sage? Milo?"

My breath catches. Ash freezes. Her eyes dart to Elysian, who's sitting up, blinking slowly, and glancing around the room cluelessly. She looks the way she did after she lost her memory.

"Lys," I warn, but she's already standing, walking toward the rest of us. Finn watches her with a sly expression on his face.

I feel my power draining, my vision turning fuzzy. The harder the guards struggle against my trap, the weaker my power gets. I know I won't be able to hold them for long, and when Finn realizes he has backup, he'll surely kill us and flee with Ash.

"So you're Finn, huh?" Elysian says bluntly. I want to tell her to stop, that this is irrational and irresponsible and will kill us all, definitely, but Finn looks amused more than anything. His smirk grows.

"I am," he responds, like they're having a casual conversation instead of a showdown. "And you're the boss's daughter, my Ashlyn's schoolgirl crush."

For a second, a surprised look flashes on Elysian's face. But then she tries to collect herself, despite her arms and face turning bright red. "I am your boss's daughter," she confirms. "Let her go." She nods in Ash's direction.

Finn laughs dryly. "I'm afraid I can't do that, Princess. But I'll tell you what. You collect your friends and go, if you know what's good for you, and no one gets hurt."

"Let her go," Elysian repeats, "if you know what's good for you, and we won't have a problem."

She looks so powerful, I want to listen to her and drop my weapons. Her hair is tossed back, messy, and her eyes are cold and ferocious in a way I've never seen. They demand respect, radiate power. I can really see how she and the King are related now.

Finn looks mildly impressed. "You are brave for your age. Or incredibly stupid. Either one. But if you wish to play that game, Lightning Girl, then that game we shall play."

Elysian moves faster now, bounding toward Finn in long strides. "*Don't*," she warns, "call me Lightning Girl."

Ash's mouth hangs open. She looks proud, like a mother sending her genius kid into school for the first time, knowing the teachers will be impressed. But there's something not at all motherly about the way she looks at Elysian. I can't understand how I didn't see it before.

Ashlyn Kave is in love with my best friend.

"You can't do anything," Finn says, but he still looks a bit on edge. There's a hint of fear in his eyes, and he grips Ash's wrist so tightly that his knuckles turn white—and her face twists into a pained look. "You are too weak."

"Am I?" Elysian chuckles. "I didn't realize." She yawns and covers her mouth, but she flicks her index finger and middle finger up. Wind howls in my ears and Finn's hand flies away from Ash's wrist.

While he's distracted, Ash uses her sword to slash at him. The guards yell from behind the earth wall. I let my dagger drop to the floor as I get a raging headache. Elysian, her powerful moment forgotten, runs just fast enough to catch me in her arms. She grunts in effort and sets me against the wall next to Ameer.

"Stay here," she says, and she starts to turn around to fight, but I grab her wrist. I can feel, deep in my soul, the barrier holding off the guards weakening, branches and twigs snapping, dirt being pulled apart as I get weaker.

"The guards," I manage. "They're at the stairs. They're going to kill us all."

And once she hears this news, she grins, an honest-to-gods Elysian grin that reminds me of Sorin, and she says, "I'd like to see them try."

She keeps going, charges on Finn. I take a few deep breaths, and, though reluctantly, I push myself from the floor. My power is drained, but I can stand now, and I reach for my dagger across the room.

"Sage!" Milo yells. He points to the earth wall, crumbling as we speak. My panic skyrockets, but my faith drops to the ground. Until he takes a deep breath, grabs a spare sword in a leather bag near the rest of the stored things and raises it threateningly. Milo, who avoids physical contact and fighting at all costs, is going to fend off guards much stronger, much better than him at fighting, and he's doing it for us.

Elysian's words echo in my brain. *I'd like to see them try.* I smile triumphantly. *I'd like to see them try.*

I push myself up slowly. There's no time for rest. I hobble across the room to grab my dagger. My injured leg screams in pain. It was dull for a while, but now I can definitely feel it—and it's the worst pain I've felt from it.

By the time I make it to my dagger, I'm breathing heavily from the effort. I glance over my shoulder at Milo, his face pale, the sword he's holding raised to the middle of the wall. He spreads his feet apart slightly and bends his knees, like he's playing a sport. I ignore it. Any help is needed.

I step toward Finn. I trust Milo. Even if he can't fight them, he'll calm them down. Ash and Elysian are sword fighting with Finn, and while they're exhausted, he just grins in triumph. Whatever Healer he used to help his recovery, it's a good one. Even if they manage to wound him, the wounds close immediately, and we only make him stronger. Meanwhile Ash and Elysian's faces are drooping, their breathing turning harsh. They're getting tired, and he's getting stronger.

"Surely you aren't going to keep trying, are you, my dears?" Finn asks the pair of them. He glances at Elysian. "You know, people would pay well for the daughter of the King. You could be valuable to me and my new wife, as soon as I eliminate the rest of you."

Elysian doesn't say anything, but Ash's face contorts into one of anger, and she goes for his abdomen. I make my way toward them slowly, taking my time, hoping Finn has bad peripheral vision. Ash knows Finn; she knows he would never hurt her unless he absolutely had to. I have learned how to read people (it's a survival skill) and I can tell that Finn would be losing, if it weren't for the magic that heals him. He's a good fighter, but even now he looks on the verge of exhaustion, until his power helps him. Ash and Elysian are better than him. He's all talk. These are the obvious things.

But what *aren't* the obvious things, the things he'd want to keep hidden?

I scan Finn. He walks with a slight limp in his right leg, but he doesn't wince when he uses it. That may be something. He has a scar on his face, and it looks like it's recent. I remember what Selena said once after an intense battle with Mrs. S: "All's fair in love and war."

It sparks an idea.

I picture myself in his shoes. Battling his crush's crush, going through mountains of pain, anger, embarrassment, resentment. I would have some mood swings, too. But this—fighting, sending spies after people, lying with every breath—seems a little drastic.

Still, I try to give him the benefit of the doubt. Even though he doesn't deserve it, Finn is still a person. And his anger (mixed with some ignorance) may do us a lot more good than he thinks.

I sneak around the back. Finn still hasn't noticed me, which is a good thing, but Ash and Elysian have seen me already. I wish for their eyes to move back to Finn, but when they don't, Finn turns around, and he notices me.

His expression is anger, embarrassment, and fear mixed into one.

"I thought I got rid of you," he breathes, and he reaches for my arm, but I'm quick on my feet. I dodge it, sending my dagger into his thigh, though I know it won't do any good.

He yells out, but the wound quickly closes, and he lunges for me again.

Elysian holds her sword to his throat. Wait, did I see that right? Yeah, her dagger is a full-fledged two-foot sword, the point at Finn's Adam's apple, which bobs nervously.

"You can't kill me," he says, though he doesn't sound too sure. My hand tightens around the hilt of my dagger as I watch the two exchange deathly glares.

"Watch me," Elysian threatens. She pushes her sword farther into his throat.

I glance back at Milo. He stares up at the guards, his face frightened, the sword he used to have thrown to one side.

My heart drops. There's no way we'll win, not by force. By wit, by luck. By magic. Luckily, we have just enough of that.

"Finn," I say, surprising myself along with Ash, Elysian, and Finn. And apparently, from the way the guards stop their fight with

Milo to pay attention to me, I surprise the guards, too.

Finn glances at me. His lips are twisted up into a sneer, like he's smelled something nasty. His dark eyes are conflicted, and there are eye bags under them—purple ones. He looks so helpless, but I know the last thing I can do is feel bad for the guy who killed Sorin's sister, the one who indirectly killed my Sorin. The person in front of me is a pathetic man-child. He deserves no pity.

I hide my anger behind hurt, using what Sorin implied about my eyes being readable to my advantage. I think about the way I felt when I discovered he died, he *actually* died, and then I channel it into my eyes. Finn softens, but only for a second, because then he remembers Elysian's blade and the fact that we're mortal enemies.

And it will stay that way. It'll stay like this until Finn's dead.

"Please," I beg. "Finn. You know Ash. We're her friends. And you've seen the way we fight. If you continue"—I sigh and shake my head slowly, like I care if he dies—"then we'll find a way around your medicine."

My eyes catch on Milo's. I walk across the room and yank him up until he's on his feet. The guards are too busy waiting for me to speak again to attack, and I carefully lead Milo back to Finn, where I'm sure he'll be safer than before. Not *safe*, per se, but *safer*.

"We have our very own Healer right here," I announce, putting Milo on display. It isn't the smartest move, but the guards avoid his eyes cautiously, like they're scared Milo can kill them in one blow.

"Whatever you try, he will be here to back us up."

I fully expect Finn to say something like, "*Then just kill the Healer*," but he doesn't. The battle must've made him more unstable than I realized. His face pales, and he gets this look on his face, like he's rethinking his entire life decisions. Then he swallows. His voice cracks when he speaks. "I will win this."

I intimidate him. It's such a strange thought, I want to laugh out loud. I intimidate Finn, the man who killed Selena Torsney? But I don't. I don't laugh, because then my friends would think I was going crazy.

"You will," I confirm, and I watch Elysian's eyes widen. It's like she's calling me a traitor without saying anything, and I wince internally. Externally, I try to remain calm. I continue with my plan. "*This* one, you will win. You know why?"

Finn raises his head in an effort to look intimidating, I guess. He only winces as Elysian's sword digs into his throat.

"Because as we speak, the spirits of room 106 are listening," I say. "They're listening. They're waiting for this to be over. So you win this battle. But you wanna know something, Finn Brocker?" I lean forward, dropping my voice to a whisper. "You win the battle, not the war."

And with that, I grab Milo's arm, mentally telling Elysian to grab Ameer. Ash ducks around Finn and before he can move, she digs her sword into his abdomen. Elysian is by us in seconds, Ameer in her arms. I notice her battle skills have kicked in.

Finn yells out in agony. His magic has apparently weakened, so he drops to his knees. Ash unsheathes her sword and pushes the door open with the hilt, and before Finn can heal, we run.

If my assumptions are correct, and if the spirits are on our side, then room 106 should be gone by the time we get outside.

There are guards waiting for us, their swords raised, some reaching for their guns. I drop Milo's wrist and cut through a few guards with my dagger, then run down the long hallway in an effort to get out of this castle. I feel my wounded leg screaming at me as the muscles flex. I've used it more today than I ever have since I got shot, and it's not reacting well. But I have to keep going; I have to do this. Not just for me, not just for Ash or Elysian or Milo, but for the prince. For Autumn and her family. For that old baker in the village. For the guards who are being forced to be here, like Selena was. For Selena. And most of all, for Sorin. It was all he wanted, and instead of feeling sorry for myself, I'll do this for him.

I barely have time to look back before I realize I'm right—room 106 is gone, along with Finn, along with the guards.

And even though I just had this internal monologue about saving people and all that stuff, I can't help but think bitterly:

Happy birthday, Finn.

CHAPTER 24

ELYSIAN

I don't know why Ash is still holding my hand.

Something must've happened. There's blood on her upper lip, blood that makes her grim expression even more grim. Her eyes sparkle in the sunlight, and even though we're running from the enemy as they're being taken to some other continent, I can't help but admire those beautiful gold-speckled eyes.

They match my stare. A grin breaks out on her face as she runs through the forest. I'm not sure this is the smartest idea with all the roots and things, but my mind is racing so fast I only hold on to the thought for a few seconds. "We did it, Viggo," she tells me, and there's a rasp to her voice.

I nod, a smile growing on mine. I laugh, either out of hysteria or the lack of sleep or the thought that we defeated my father, got my brother back, and sent Ash's stalker all the way to a different continent. "We did it, Kave."

Truth is, I barely remember anything.

I know I stood up to my father. I know I killed him. I know I was carried through dungeons somewhere. But I don't know anything other than that. And, if I'm being totally honest, I'm not even sure I *want* to. I'm fine with this, with Ash holding my hand and smiling, with Sage looking more determined than she ever has, even with Sorin not by her side, with Milo running like he'll never stop, with the fact that I don't feel winded at all, despite the fact that my adult brother is slung over my shoulder.

Which, I guess, deserves an explanation.

We cut through trees as outraged guards follow after us. I know exactly where we're going: home.

But the battle isn't over yet. I remember the spy. There's a spy at camp, waiting to kill the campers. If we get there in time, then we'll make sure they can't tell reinforcements where the camp is located.

Even now, with the thought of battle and death and revenge on my mind, I can't help but notice the unmistakable warmth in Ash's hands, the way she looks at me like the world is falling apart and we're the only ones left, the way I want to stop everything just to be *by* her. But that's wrong.

It's wrong.

Right?

Honestly, after everything we've been through, I *should* want to feel this way, right? I mean, sure, I don't feel like this with Sage or Milo, but Ash ... she's different. Somehow, someway, Ash is different. I don't want to know exactly *how*, but I don't find myself wanting to stare into Sage's or Milo's eyes until the day is lost. And I don't notice the warmth in Sage's or Milo's hands. And I don't wish I could spend all day with either of them, just listening to stories like the one of their parents' wedding day. And it's not like I find myself just talking with them about nothing just to hear their voices. And I don't sleep on their shoulders. And, yes, I love them, but not like … not like I love … Ash …

Oh gods.

Holy hell.

I love Ash.

I love Ash. Gods, I love Ash. How did I not realize it sooner? It's so obvious.

Not now, I scold myself, but with this new realization, I feel like a weight has been lifted off my shoulders. Now I know where Ash stands with me. But … does she like me back? Not every wish you have comes true, and I want to make sure this one does.

I glance over at Ash. The wind whips at her face as we run. Her lips are parted slightly, her hair being pushed back by the wind. Her eyes are lit up by the midday sun, the gold in her eyes turning to glitter.

She's gorgeous.

Yeah, even as I think that, I wonder how I didn't notice it earlier.

But … growing up, I'd always been trained from the thugs on the street that looking at a girl the way I did was wrong, that I was meant to like boys with so much gel in their hair that it made it stick up like a mohawk, that I was meant to like boys in general. Which I *did*, but I liked girls more. And since I had the controlling father who wished desperately to keep me from the public until he abandoned me as soon as I was old enough to defend myself, I never really learned that was "wrong" to other people until I met said street thugs.

I crane my neck to look at my brother. I drop Ash's hand so I can keep him quiet, as he's been groaning since we got away from the castle. Ameer could've been my brother. He didn't have to be a distant stranger who I only heard about through newspaper articles. But, then again, I had that controlling father. I never lived in that castle past seven. I wasn't like him, this—this famous prince who everyone knew the name of and everyone loved. I'm the rebellious Magic who left her family and started a camp for fellow Magics that was hidden from the royal guards. I'm the kid no one ever talks about. And Ameer—well, he's been the topic of every conversation that took place inside the kingdom.

What is this quest about? Saving Ameer. What had we been talking about since we left the camps? Saving Ameer. What had distracted Sage so she got shot? An article about Ameer. Who has always been the favorite? Ameer. Even now, as I strain to look at his handsome face, his eyes closed, mouth open slightly, I understand why.

Ameer is the golden child.

The "normal one." The one born without magical powers despite our parentage.

Yeah, I said despite parentage. Why'd you think my mom left in the first place? It wasn't just because *I* was *unnatural.*

Ameer may be *the* favorite, but he's always been a good brother to me. The few memories I had of him before I was taken away by my father were good ones. He was always a good big brother.

Ameer was born before I was. He was a little shorter, but he was ten months older than me, and since he was considered normal enough, my mother stayed long enough for me to be born. Then, once I was about three and my magical abilities grew and became more pronounced, my mom left without a trace. My father resented me for it. He trained me to fight and protect myself, yes, but deep down, I knew he always had a deep loathing for me. And then, at the ripe age of seven, he took me away.

Away from the castle, away from my brother, my family, my home. He left me on the streets. He didn't care.

He never did.

My stomach tightens at the thought. My father never loved me. Guilt claws at me, though, and despite the fact that he is—*was*—a horrible person, did he really deserve to be killed? Should I have spared my father?

I didn't mean to. My power grew out of my control. But, still …
I did it. I killed him.

I didn't mean to.

Didn't you? asks a taunting voice in the back of my mind. *You always resented him as much as he did you. Are you sure you didn't mean to?*

Of course. I wouldn't ever kill someone—not on purpose.

If that's what you believe.

The voice goes quiet again.

I swallow roughly. I know I didn't mean to. He is—was—my *father*. I could never kill him.

And yet …

And yet I did.

I shove those thoughts out of my mind. They won't do any good. My father is dead. There's no getting him back. There's no getting my mother back. But I can get my brother back, and I have.

And I will get my camp back, even if I die trying.

That's reassuring, the voice says sarcastically.

Oh, hush.

✳ ✳ ✳

We run until my legs grow tired. We run until we pass the same creek that Sage took a drink out of before we left for the castle. We run until Ameer begins to stir, muttering and whispering things about Finn, his lips cracking with every breath. We run until the guards fade into nothing, until we're sure we've lost them. We run until, according to Sage's map, we're in the middle of the forest, several thousand feet from the castle.

I catch my breath and rest my muscles by setting Ameer against the trunk of a tall tree. I crouch down to a nearby stream of water and splash it onto my face. Then, I take another handful and pour it in Ameer's mouth.

He swallows, which means he's okay. For now.

We're not done yet.

I meet with Ash, Sage, and Milo to create a plan. Sage brings out her map while Milo keeps looking around as he breathes heavily, like he's scared we'll be attacked at any minute. Which, considering the current situation, may not be such an absurd fear.

"Sage," Milo says quietly, "are—are you okay?"

I then notice how pale Sage is. She looks like she's about to cry. She swallows roughly. "Fine. Just ... just busy."

We give it a moment, then I say, "Where are we headed?"

Sage pauses. She glances down at her map, then at the three of us. "Camp Serenity. Xelma"—she clears her throat—"Xelma will be there."

I remember suddenly that Xelma is the traitor. I want to scream. I want to cry. Of course, now, none of those things are really options.

Ash lowers her voice, though it's not like the crickets are going to run to tell people our plan. "What if—what if she *isn't* there?"

Sage shakes her head frantically. "No. No. She *has* to be there.

She *has* to."

I want to hug Sage, but I know she's not in the mood. Now is not the right time. "Okay, then, let's say she *is* there," Milo says. "What do we do?"

I think about that. Xelma has always been quiet and reserved, but a leader. She's the one we send to tell messages, normally with a group of people in case something were to go wrong. But she can handle herself. That's what'll make this harder.

"We find her," Sage says. "And ... we just start fighting."

Ash holds up a hand. "As someone who's *just started fighting* their entire life, I don't think that's a good idea. What if something were to go wrong? The other campers you have don't know she's a traitor, right? They may try to stand with her."

My eyes widen. Sage's do, too. "Oh, no," I say. "What if they *do?*"

"We'll lose, obviously," Sage says. She looks like she's trying to swallow a bird. "Let's hope they have more sense than that."

I can tell she's trying her best to be positive. It's not like I can judge her, though, because at least she's trying, especially considering our current situation.

"Okay," I say carefully. "So say we defeat Xelma. What do we do next? I mean, it's not like the camp's going to be viewed as safe once the campers find out. And when we kill her, what will we do with the body?"

Sage winces, as if she's been hoping no one would ask that. "Well, I don't really have a plan for that. But *if* we kill her, then the campers will most likely be angry, and that's the last thing we want to do, make them angry *now*, when we have a literal prince with us. We need to just ... hope for the best."

Ash raises an eyebrow. "Meaning?"

"Sage, I know it upsets you, but we have no other choice," I tell her gently. "The newspaper said *non-Magics*. Xelma's a Magic."

Sage shakes her head. "No, no ... I don't want to—"

"Sage." I grab her hand. "You have to. It's our only choice."

Sage nods begrudgingly.

"Anyway," Ash says uncomfortably, glancing back at Ameer, who sits behind us, listening intently in on the conversation, "the real question is: What are we going to do with the prince?"

That has no answer. Awkwardness hangs in the air as Ash glances behind her at my brother, obviously not helping the secrecy we already fail to have. "We ..." I start, thinking of the way he was always there for me, no matter how mad my father got, no matter how much he yelled and threatened him for helping me, "we take him with us."

Ash's eyes flick back over to mine. "Is it safe? I mean, two camps, one with a known fugitive running it, the other with a prince who's apparently missing, won't it seem suspicious?"

Sage swallows. "They don't know our location, right? It may

cause suspicion, but it's not like they'll come after us. It's not like they *can* come after us." Even *she* doesn't sound so sure when she says it, though.

I want to agree with Sage. I want to tell her that even though the odds are against us, that it seems like the gods themselves are arguing with us, stopping us, everything will be okay. But I think an empty promise is as worthless as no promise at all.

"She's right," I agree, not just because I'm trying to lift her spirits, but also because she's made a valid point. "The campers' magic has already stopped the guards from finding us once. We can do it again."

Ash clicks her tongue. "Right," she starts, "but you're forgetting that we have a literal *prince* with us. Once the people see he's missing, they're going to get suspicious. Eventually, the guards are going to connect the dots and figure out where the camps are."

Ash, I want to say, *I love you, seriously, but can you not be such a pessimist?* Instead, I say, "There's also the fact that those guards are dead."

"Except that they're not," Milo says, realization dawning on his face. His mouth opens and closes for a bit like he's a fish before he continues. "We didn't kill them, just wounded them. The guards aren't dead. And Ash is right—eventually, they'll connect the dots, and then we're dead."

Sage glances up at the sky, the beautiful blue sky, the setting sun, the birds chir—wait, *setting sun?* My eyes widen. The day is almost over, and we still have to get back to the camp, miles away, get rid of Xelma, and live happily ever after. I'm really hoping we can make it to the last one.

"We have to go," I say to them, picking my brother up once I'm close enough to get to him. "We have to go now."

CHAPTER 25

ASH

Great, we're moving again.

Running is my favorite, can't you tell? The way it knocks the wind out of me and makes me feel like I'm dying all while my muscles ache and I gasp for breath. It's such a fun pastime.

But my all-time favorite is when we're running for our lives and there's nothing in sight except for sweaty friends, groggy royalty, and trees.

It's the best, it really is.

Elysian runs beside me as the sun slowly falls, edging closer to the dried grass behind us. I've always wondered how something as beautiful as the sun can be viewed as beautiful if it's something much more: deadly. But, I suppose, most beautiful things *are* deadly.

Speaking of beautiful deadly things, I glance over at Elysian. Her hair has come loose, hanging around her shoulders, acting as a brown halo. Her eyes are a darker shade of blue in the setting sun, and they are determined and set. She makes me wonder why she's even talking to me when she has so many other better things to do, so many other better things she's capable of. She is capable of everything, really.

And I hated her.

I can't believe I actually hated her. I don't know why. As the years passed, I forgot why I hated her. All I knew was that I did. I hated her, and that was that. We had been rivals because of our camps since the first day they were made—why? Because Elysian wanted peace and I wanted war?

Maybe.

Or maybe ... maybe I had never hated her, just wanted to think that I did. My mother had never supported me that much, and even after she died, I heard her sour words in my mind, infecting my ability to think clearly.

I was only seven years old.

But never mind that. Now, I have to rescue my ... friend? ... from this spy destroying her camp, everything she's loved. Ever. Great. There's no pressure in that.

But I'm willing to walk with Elysian to the ends of the earth if that's what she wants. She means so much more to me now, now that we've bonded, than I think she ever did before. I told her things ... I told her things I wouldn't tell anybody before. There's the story of my parents' wedding, and I told her my father was a Plenty. I told her about my tattoo and what happened to my mother. And I trusted her—I trust her—with my life.

I know how dangerous trust can be, how badly it can hurt you, how much it can backfire. But when it comes to this girl, I honestly don't care. Trust may be risky, but this is *Elysian*. She cares about me and I care about her, and I will run all the miles in the world if she wants me to, and I know she'll pick me up at the end. Because that's just how trust works.

And it may break my heart. Yes, it very well may. I know this. But I also know I'm willing to take that risk.

I'm willing to take it for her.

* * *

The lower the sun gets, the more Sage calls for breaks. We sit on rocks, against trees—pretty much anything we can find. My legs are cramped from the amount of running and even though we take *several* breaks, I can never catch my breath enough. It's like I'm running out of oxygen with every movement. It's very annoying.

And painful.

"Okay," I say, watching the sun as it lowers beyond the castle, miles away. The castle seems perfectly content, even though I know it's chaotic in there. We've escaped and sent some guards and Finn to a whole other continent. Now, we're on the run, and the guards still can't find us, even though I'm sure they're riding on horses instead of running (that would be nice. We should try it the next time we're running from guards). "What do we do next?"

Sage, who is bent over the creek, sipping water from her hands, turns to look at me. "What do you mean?"

"We're not going to be fleeing forever," I point out. "And we're already running out of daylight. Once we get to the camp and we defeat Xelma, what do we do next?"

Elysian looks up from her nails. She's using a part of her shirt that's torn and wet with creek water to clean the blood from under them. Milo, who is trying his best to strengthen Ameer without any of his normal supplies, glances up, too. They're both interested in this topic.

Sage notices the extra eyes, sighing deeply. "I ... don't know."

I chuckle, but there's nothing humorous about the situation. "What do you mean you *don't know?* All these plans, this preparation and you *don't know?*"

"It's been really stressful," she retorts. "I don't know if you understand this, but you're not the only one struggling with stuff, Ash! I'm not your personal plan-maker! Can you *ever* think for yourself?"

I clench my jaw, scoffing. "You know, I'm sorry. I just thought you'd actually be trying to fix this situation, instead of ... what? What are you doing to help?"

"You say that like *you're* doing something." Sage swallows and shakes her head with a dry chuckle. "I'm sorry I can't just do everything for you. I'm not your personal assistant, Ash!"

My throat runs dry. Hurt flickers through me, but then it's replaced by anger. Red-hot anger. Elysian glances at me, her mouth slightly agape. Sage swallows again as her eyes widen. She probably sees the attitude on the tip of my tongue, the fire in my eyes.

"You don't know *anything* about my mother, Sage," I hiss. "So don't pretend like you do." I clear my throat, wanting this topic to be dropped. It's my fault, and I know that. "I'm ... gonna go take a walk."

I stand from the grass, warning Elysian with a sharp glance not to follow after me. Her eyes follow me, though, as she watches me leave like an abandoned puppy.

I find a clearing eventually. I shouldn't have said that. It was stupid. I know Sage is trying her best, but I was just so *angry*. It's not that I want everything to be figured out for me. I just want to have a plan so we're not just walking into battle unprepared, unready. That would be suicide.

Still, I didn't have to snap at her like that. I consider telling Sage I'm sorry, but I decide to let myself cool off first. I scream into the sunset, cursing whatever gods had the idea to let me suffer like this, to go on this damn quest. What's the point? We saved the prince, but at what cost?

I shoot fire at a nearby tree. It burns the bark, turning it a satisfying black as it drops to the ground. I do it to all the trees around me, screaming with each burst of fire. I haven't been this riled up while using this much fire in a long time. Ever since my mother ... ever since I ... since I killed her. Since I killed my mother.

That makes me scream harder, that thought. By the time all the trees that I can see are burned, my throat is raw. I take a few deep breaths before returning to the group of them.

I don't say anything when I return. Elysian looks nervously from Sage to me, not saying anything. But I know what she's thinking. I'm thinking it too.

Okay.

We keep walking. Not running, not anymore. After running a few miles, we decided to just walk. I'm thankful for it, as it stops my lungs from burning all the time, but it's still giving my legs a good workout.

After a while, Sage says, "Is there something we should talk about?" She keeps her face forward, ponytail swinging behind her.

I keep my face ahead, too, keeping my eyes fixed on the scenery. "I'm afraid I'm not sure what you're referring to."

She sighs. "You're going to make me spell it out for you, aren't you?"

"Maybe. Depends what you're talking about."

"Fine. You were being sucky to me earlier. Anything you want to say to me about that? Maybe apologize?"

I pretend to consider it. "Yeah, actually. I forgot about that. But I was going to tell you that I was wrong."

"Yeah?" She arches a brow, turning to face me.

"And that I'm sssssssss ..." Honestly, now I'm just drawing it out

346

to annoy her.

"Ssssssensitive?"

"Ssssssssssssorrrrrrrr …"

"Sssssssssssssssssorrrrrrrrrting through emotional trauma?"

"Ssssssssssorrrrrrryyyyyyyyy …" I say finally. "I'm sorry. But that last one, too."

It takes a while for her to answer, like she's looking for something to say. Finally, Sage says, "I know. And I know you're stressed and I know that this whole thing is insane. But … we're a *team*. We have to work together to get this right, to win it. You might think that no one understands you because of how much weight is on your shoulders, but we all have that weight, no matter how heavy, and you're not in this alone. So I get it. You're under pressure. But so am I."

She lets that sit for a moment. I wait for her to speak, and when I realize she isn't going to, I say, "I'm sorry. Really."

She nods. "I know."

We walk in silence for the rest of the hour, thinking about each other's words, feeling the hot sun on our backs fade to a cool night breeze. The stars come alive above us and as they dance, I glance up, not wanting to miss a moment of their show.

It's remarkable, really, how the stars are so consistent. They continue to do what they do no matter what the world is doing. They're independent and constant, and maybe that's why I found so much comfort in them after my father died. They were always there, no matter if they died or not, and I just desperately needed someone like that. Someone who was always there and always would be. Wouldn't betray or abandon me.

For a second, I let myself forget. I let myself forget about the anger and the bitterness and the fighting and tiredness and the emotions building up inside of me, straining with every moment. I let myself relax and watch the stars as they twinkle in their beauty, and I let myself mutter the words, "Sage, do you think Elysian likes me?"

And then I realize what I've said. My eyes widen, and I glance at her hurriedly, trying to take it back, when I notice there's a hint of a response on her tongue.

Too late, I think miserably. I wait for the look of shock or disappointment or confusion or *something*, and it never comes. Instead, Sage says, "Yeah. Yeah, I think she does."

My breath catches. "What?"

"I *said*," she repeats pointedly, "I think she does." She says it like it's the most obvious thing in the world.

"Y-you're serious?" I ask. "No—no questioning looks, no surprised face? Just a straight answer?"

Sage shrugs. "What were you expecting? Please, Ash, she looks at you like you're a Saturday at the end of training week. She's *in love with you*. I can't believe that's so hard for you to realize."

I stare at her. "She—she's in *love* with me?"

"I think so."

I try to say something, *anything*, to prove that I understand her, but Sage continues, and only a little croak comes out of my mouth.

"During that battle, I saw the way you looked at her. And all this time, pretty much since the first day she saw you—well, the *second* first day, I guess—she's had pupils shaped like hearts. So, yeah, she's in love with you."

Still, I can't say anything. It seems surreal that *Elysian* could like me, much less *love* me, and I wouldn't know what to say if I *could* say anything. I let the information sit, and then I tackle Sage with questions. "Love me? How do you know? The way she looked at me? She's looking at me a certain way? Is it a bad way? Why didn't you tell me this sooner? Were you hiding this from me? How long have you known? All this time?" Finally, I end it with an agitated whine: "Sage!"

"Look," she starts, keeping her face forward, "I only just found out. I would've told you sooner, but I didn't know she ... liked girls, I guess. Not that I'm against it. You love who you love, and you can't change that. No matter what. But she never told me, and you were her mortal enemy for, like, forever. So, yeah, forgive me for not sensing that my best friend was in love with her rival of several years."

I consider going over there and talking to Elysian about this, but my fear doesn't let me, pushing the idea down. I can't find the words to say anymore, so I just keep walking, trying not to think about the fact that, yeah, *Elysian freaking Viggo is in love with me.*

I'm so drunk on this new information that I barely care when the bushes to the right of us start rustling. I barely hear the low snarling emitting from the bushes. And even as Sage shoves me to the side, screaming, "WOLF!" I can't register the danger of the situation.

Then I see its dark fur, gray and sticking up dangerously as drool drips from its jaws. The beast itself is a beautiful creature, with sharp teeth stained with blood, amber eyes with hunger in them, and fur the color of moonlight and gravel. But it's also dangerous, more dangerous than I can fathom before the wolf lunges toward me, eyes the color of lanterns trained on mine.

I don't know why I scream. I block the wolf with the flat side of the blade of my sword and the wolf backs away slowly, a warning. But I glance down, and panic overwhelms me.

There, on my left leg, is a gash as long as my calf. Crimson streams run down my leg, touching the grass with a satisfying DRIP. I watch in horror as the adrenaline fades away and I'm met with searing pain, pain worse than I've ever felt. It feels like someone is ripping my leg apart down the middle, and all I can do is watch as the wound slowly drips my blood onto the ground.

Milo is kneeling next to me in seconds. He asks me a few questions, but my eyes never leave the wound, breathing heavily and screeching in pain as I pray I'd never learned that Elysian loved me.

As he works on my injury, studying the gash, Sage says, "We need to get her to camp. *Quickly.* Sorin"—her voice breaks slightly as she says his name—"Sorin had all these tools that he used when he would heal people. I'm sure you know how to use them."

Milo nods. "Of course I do. But this cut is deeper than it looks. We need to get there *fast.*"

An idea sparks in my mind. Despite the pain, I manage to squeak out, "The horses."

Milo understands immediately. His face lights up with recognition as Sage studies the pair of us carefully.

"*What* horses?" she asks.

He stands, ordering Elysian to keep an eye on me. As Milo makes his way deeper into the forest, toward the royal stables, Sage trailing behind him with questions, Elysian leans down next to me. Her expression is plagued with worry, and wrinkles run down her face. I think it only makes her more beautiful.

"Ash," she tells me, and I can tell how much this pains her, "you're an idiot."

"You make me an idiot," I mutter without thinking. Elysian's eyes narrow.

"W-what do you mean?" Something weird passes over her face, and I wonder for a second if that's real fear in her expression.

I simply shrug, sending an echo of pain through me. I wince, and Elysian is quick to aid me. "Are you okay? What's the matter? Are you hurt?"

I stare at her for a second. She glances down at the ground when she notices what she said, then up at the sky when she sees my injury. I chuckle lightly. "No, I'm not hurt. Wolf attacks don't normally affect me."

She rolls her eyes playfully. "You know what I meant."

I'm about to say something else sarcastic when I hear footsteps, along with … hoofsteps? I've never really been sure what the proper word is, but I hear horses.

I raise my head higher. That's a good sign, hearing the clip-clop pattern of the horses' hooves. Milo comes out of the darkness hauling a horse and Sage behind him, who is also holding the reins to a horse.

The pair of them grin at us, then rush forward to get us on the horses. Milo gets positioned behind me and Sage on the other horse. Ameer gets on after her and then Elysian brings up the rear.

"Do you even know where we're going?" I question Sage and Milo accusingly.

Milo shakes his head, but before I can say anything about this, he pushes his feet into the horse's stomach, sending us flying forward into the forest.

I try to contain my breathing, try to keep it steady as we ride. I make sure not to blink too long, as tiredness is beginning to envelop me like a dark cloud, threatening me with death. Every time my breathing falters, Milo grabs on to me tighter, like he's afraid he'll lose me. Considering the severity of this gash on my leg, he very well might.

✱ ✱ ✱

By the time we come to a slow in front of the gates leading to our camps, my leg has been in so much agony that it has refused to work. The horses whinny nervously as they spot the guards at the gates, who have been talking about politics while not-so-secretly drawing their swords. I consider leaping off this horse and cutting through them with my sword just to get the job done, but my leg throbs annoyingly, like it's threatening me. So I refrain from doing so.

Instead, Sage simply sends them a strong glare. "I would suggest you move aside before you're killed," she says to the guards.

Noticing the way her hand hovers over her dagger, the guards' eyes widen and they move away from the gate, pushing the button that allows us to get through. Our horse goes first, and theirs next.

We lead our horses through the Camp Serenity entrance, causing all the campers in the camp to stare at us strangely. When they spot Sage and Elysian sitting on a horse, Prince Ameer behind them, they cheer.

But someone in the crowd that's gathered asks, "Where's Torsney?"

I wince internally.

Sage's mouth opens, then closes. She chooses to avoid the question. "We need two Healers in the infirmary immediately. We have a wolf injury."

I glance over at her, simply just to see she's okay, but as I do, I get a glimpse of what my leg looks like. The blood has dried around the wound, my leg stained with red. The gash is long but shallow, hopefully. Milo hops off the horse, then eases me off of it. But I can't look away from the gash. It's hard to. *How could such a tiny wolf do so much damage?*

I wince—externally, this time—as my leg touches the ground, sending pain ricocheting through me like a bullet (though I'm sure my wound doesn't hurt as much as Sage's did). Milo leads me toward a square building labeled INFIRMARY, which holds some teenagers sitting in bed, clutching their stomachs. Some are drinking a clear liquid that looks remarkably like water, except it's fizzy, like soda. Meringue, it's called.

Elysian follows after us, and I understand how important she thinks this is. She's abandoning her campers, her family, to help *me*.

Milo lays me down in a bed, then calls over the teenage Healers who have gathered in the doorway of the infirmary. He explains what happened, and then they set to work, studying my injury so hard I can feel their eyes burning into my skin.

Elysian holds my hand like she's afraid she's not squeezing it tightly enough—with every passing second, she squeezes tighter. Honestly, I appreciate the gesture, *more* than appreciate it, but my hand is beginning to lose circulation, which I fear is worse than a little scratch from a wolf.

"Lys," I say, my first use of the nickname catching her attention, "I'm okay. Really. You can let go."

She smiles slightly and drops my hand. "Sorry," she says, wiping her sweaty hands on her shorts. "I'm just nervous. I saw that wolf. It was so big."

I stare at her in confusion. "What do you mean? That's, like, the tiniest wolf I've seen in those woods."

Elysian looks like she wants to hold my hand again. Her eyebrows crease. "Ash, that—that wolf is a Mortel Wolf. It's the most dangerous wolf in all of Buit. You may *think* that that cut isn't deep, but, Ash, it's horrible."

Then I think about it. I've never understood French, but I'm sure *mortel* is a French word.

Before I can say anything, a Healer asks, "Wait, a *Mortel Wolf?*" His eyes widen. "Doesn't that mean 'deadly?'"

I swallow roughly as Elysian nods slowly.

"Wait, so I've been hurt by a deadly wolf?" I ask. "What the hell is that supposed to mean?"

Milo frowns as he works. "It means, Ash, that there's a very high chance you could die."

CHAPTER 26

SAGE

I can't find the words to answer the camper's question about Sorin, so I don't. Instead, I storm through the camp, searching for Xelma. If she's out of the camp, then we're screwed. I know my campers, and I know they're clever. But I also know they're good fighters, and that fighting and trying to kill her would be useless. We have to use wits to win this.

Which means I have to think like a spy.

She's working for Finn. If she knows about the fact that you forget the location of the camps once you leave, which I'm betting she does, then she'd write it down. But where …?

Of course.

The training areas. She's preparing.

I run across the field, ignoring the eyes that watch me as I pass. The campers probably think I'm insane, but I don't care. Not now.

First, I check her cabin. I know she's not stupid enough to leave any evidence, but I still need to make sure. And honestly, I want to stall. Facing Xelma means facing Finn again, facing my boyfriend's death, facing everything I've tried to push down. I don't know if I'm ready.

There's nothing, like I expected. Even her belongings are packed into a small suitcase. She knows today will be her last day. She knows it.

I take a deep breath and try to stabilize my shaking hands. I rest them on Xelma's nightstand, spotting an empty water bottle. There are a few drops at the bottom of the bottle.

Xelma must've been thirsty, I think, though I don't know why. I'm focusing on random things, trying to make sense of them, because nothing else has made sense. I tear my eyes from the water bottle and walk to the forest, paying attention to the branches above me and the paved path below me, searching for traps.

Surprisingly, there aren't any.

I keep walking until I find the training area. Everything seems perfectly normal, but then I spot her.

Xelma. Standing in the middle of the sandpit, looking around, paranoid. She holds her sword in front of her defensively, though there's something clumsy about the way she holds it. Like she can't remember how to hold a sword.

Anger fills me then. Just seeing her, thinking about the way she hurt my best friend, indirectly hurt my boyfriend, hurt me, I can't think of anything else but this blazing hot anger.

"Scared?" I question, rather threateningly. Xelma whips around, holding her sword higher: an idiot move. It gives me the opportunity to drive my dagger straight into her stomach.

While I'm grateful that this will make things easier, I know something's wrong. Xelma knows how to fight. She's smart. But this … this is not smart.

"W-who are you?" she asks, and I'm completely taken aback.

This must be part of her plan, says a tiny, menacing voice in the back of my mind, a voice I want so desperately to listen to. But another part, a more reasonable part, a bigger part, whispers, *The water bottle*, and everything clicks.

The water bottle. Elysian's water bottle. The one she drank before—before she lost her memory. The one Xelma drank from before coming here. There were only a few droplets left, and I understand now why.

She wanted to forget. She wanted to forget so badly that it consumed her, that she drank from the dreaded water bottle.

I lower my dagger, my anger fading. I know what it feels like to want to forget everything. I know so much about it, more than I should.

She notices, but it only makes her lower her sword a fragment of an inch. I take a cautious step toward her, and when she swings the sword at my face, I duck, and it gets stuck in a tree trunk instead.

"Don't hurt me," Xelma says, giving up on the sword. She decides to just put her hands up in a pleading motion, which I ignore. How could she—our best fighter, our strongest enemy—be so *clueless?*

"I'm not going to," I respond, putting my hands up as well. I drop my dagger, letting it make a satisfying *thump* on the grass. I step into the sandpit and reach for her, but Xelma backs up. She doesn't trust me. That fact makes my heart stop beating for a second, because, betrayal or not, we were family once. "I'm unarmed. I'm not going to hurt you, Xelma."

Her face pales. "How do you know my name?"

"I—" I choke on my words. "I knew you. I *know* you. I'm your friend, Xelma."

Tears brim in her eyes. She's scared. Unbelievably scared. "Why did you try to attack me?"

"You've done some pretty bad things, Xelma," I say slowly, carefully. "Even if you don't remember what you've done, I do. And I was trying to kill you for it."

If it's possible, her face goes even paler. "Kill—*kill* me?"

"Xelma, let me talk to you. Let me get you out of here."

She yanks her sword out of the tree. "No, I don't think so." Her hands shake. "You—you were going to *kill* me. Now I'm going to kill you."

I then realize the danger of the situation I'm in. Gods, why did I throw my dagger to the side? She may not remember how to fight, but her reflexes will save her. I'm standing right next to her with a bullet wound in my leg, and my dagger is behind me, and one thing you're taught, the most important thing you're taught, while training

359

is: *never turn your back on your opponent.*

I back away from her, stepping over the edge of the sandpit once I get there. Xelma swings for me again, but I duck, grabbing my dagger once I'm near the ground. Then I continue to back away from her, all chances at being kind and understanding leaving my brain.

Should I kill her? I ask the menacing voice in my brain, the one that is desperate for blood. I know what it will say before it says it.

Then, after a long moment, it says, *No.*

I almost freeze, but then I remember I'm in battle, and I block another swing with the flat of my blade.

What do you mean, no?

I mean, *no. Be reasonable.*

Oh, that's rich coming from you.

I wouldn't say that to a god, if I were you.

That makes me literally freeze. I block another hit as Xelma walks toward me, backing me against a tree. *What do you mean, god?*

I mean, god, *Sage. Exactly what I said.*

Why is a god in my brain? Which god even are you? And do you really have to be telling me to be reasonable when I'm in the middle of a fight?

Hey, lady, you called me. And trust me, you'll figure it out soon enough.

And the voice disappears. There's no warning, no goodbye, just a "you'll figure it out soon enough." Like *that* clears up anything.

But I'm still fighting. I wrestle with my blade for the offense instead of the defense side of this, when I realize Xelma isn't confident at all. She doesn't know how I fight. She doesn't know how *she* fights. All she's doing is throwing random swings and hope they hit something.

Which sparks an idea.

Suddenly, I redirect my hits. Instead of going up and down, I go to the side, which sends her off her rhythm. She barely blocks the strike when I send it to her stomach, leaving a tiny cut on the side of her abdomen. She sucks in a deep breath, showing she's in pain. Another thing you learn in training: *never show your opponent if you're getting weaker.*

I strike to the other side, but she's expecting it. She blocks it at the last second, but my dagger isn't there anymore. It's in her front, and I run my dagger down her stomach, resulting in a nice-sized gash down her front.

She cries out in pain, searching around her for something—*anything*—to help her. And she makes the final mistake of turning her back on her opponent.

I plunge my dagger into her left side. It cuts through tissue and nerves, finally piercing a lung.

I don't pierce her heart. I keep in mind what the god said: *Be reasonable.* Xelma doesn't know any better. I'll take her to the infirmary to heal her and then kick her out of the camp for good—if she lives that long.

Even now, her breathing is starting to slow. Before her eyes flutter close, she manages to mutter, "S-sorry."

Now you've done it, says the god's voice.

I quiet it.

* * *

That night, I lie in bed, silent. Xelma is trying to heal in the infirmary, and I haven't heard from the god since the woods incident. The welcoming dinner we had was fun, yes, but it was strange. Almost everyone there seemed annoyed, and I was so tired that I decided to go to bed early, so here I am.

It seems like sleep will never come to whisk me away into a world of nightmares. That's all I've been having since Sorin's death, just nightmares. Most are short, but others are long. Some make me relive his death, and others are about me living alone forever. But most are about the time we had in front of the campfire, right before that arrow plunged into his shoulder. Our kiss. And then everything just goes dark, as it lets me remember what happened.

I've tried everything—lullabies, counting sheep, staring at the stars through my window—but nothing is working.

So I do the only thing I can: I close my eyes and wait, and I listen to the chirps of crickets outside, and I wait, and eventually, I hear nothing at all.

CHAPTER 27

SORIN

W hen I open my eyes again, all I see is a flash of light.

Blinding light, light that makes me want to go back to sleep like I did that night at the campfire. But then the light fades, and a tall man, around seven feet tall, appears.

His dark hair is slicked back. He wears a bright red suit with a black shirt, and his face and skin are incredibly pale. My eyes widen as I recognize him from the stories on my mother's shelf: Adar, god of fire and war.

"What—?" I say, but my voice is scratchy and I can't make any words other than that "what" come out.

The god smirks. "I see you're stunned. Lost for words?"

After a few moments, I regain my voice. "You—you're a god."

"Yes," Adar says, rather impatiently. "What else?"

"Aren't—aren't you Ash's dad?"

"Ash, *who?*" he asks. "I have several children, kid."

"Ashlyn Kave," I clarify. "Aren't you her father?"

He raises an eyebrow, then chuckles lightly. "That girl? The one who took your little kingdom by storm? Ah, yes, I have to say she has my spirit. Most fire-blessed Magics do. Yes, I blessed her, but, technically, I'm not her father. It's that damned Plenty, the one with all the money and the kind heart." Adar rolls his eyes. "I've always hated Plenties. Like, why don't you just put your money somewhere else, save it for things more valuable than saving the world? You see, kid, you can never really save the world. No matter what you do, the earth will always be broken evidence of human carelessness."

I swallow. "If you're just here to give me life lessons, then why are you here? And, more importantly, why am *I* here?"

The god laughs, but there's nothing humorous about the situation. "First of all, you're here because you're dead. Second of all—"

"Wait, I'm *dead?*"

"Second of all," Adar repeats with a glare, "I'm here because I have to show you something. Someone. Boss's orders."

Before I can ask who could be a god's *boss,* he fades, and I'm alone, surrounded by white light somewhere in the universe, dead.

I'm dead.

And the god of war and fire just said he had to show me someone.

Okay, that's a lot to take in.

I try to sit, but I'm frozen. All I can do is stand and breathe, just wait.

I'm getting tired of waiting. I want answers.

Right as I'm about to find a secret passage, a door out of here, anything, I see something out of the corner of my eye: a flash of orange. I turn, expecting the god to be back, but then my breath catches at what I see.

Sage.

Her red hair is messy, framing her face like a beautiful halo. Her green eyes are wide and alert, except they follow my movements messily, like she's half-asleep. Her pale skin is dotted with more freckles than usual, proof she's been out in the sun. When she spots me, her lips part slightly and I find myself wanting to run into her arms, to hug her until I can't feel my arms, to kiss her until I can't feel my lips.

And then she starts to cry, and it's the most heartbreaking sound ever.

I'm running toward her, and I don't even know why I'm able to. I wrap my arms around her body as it shakes, and she hugs me back, gripping my shirt like she's afraid I'm going to fly away.

"I thought I lost you," she murmurs into my shirt, choking on her tears.

I hold my back as I respond. "You'll never lose me, Sagey. Never."

I grab her chin and pull her tear-soaked face back. And then I kiss her, and it feels like a breath of fresh air after being packed in a stuffy room. Sage is my fresh air, and all I want to do is inhale and inhale.

I put my hands on either side of her face, pulling apart to rest my forehead against hers. Her arms are still around my torso, and I can feel the muscles she's gained from her quest.

I make eye contact. I watch as new tears brim in her eyes, beautiful tears that cloud in her eyelashes, her beautiful dark eyelashes. "So." I chuckle. "I'm dead."

She laughs, a broken sound. Then she sniffs. "Don't joke about that, you idiot."

There you are. I hug her again, simply because I can, simply because she's here and I'm here and she's here with me. I kiss the top of her head. I want her to know I love her, so I mutter it with every movement. "I love you," I say, over and over again, until they don't sound like words. Our lips meet again, and fireworks go off in my stomach, beautiful fireworks, the best kind.

I can't believe this is happening. If I'm really dead, then I'd love to stay here forever with Sage, just talk and touch because we can. It'll be my personal heaven.

But of course, the gods are cruel. And I know that not being with Sage for longer will actually be my personal hell.

"I love you," I breathe against her lips. "I want you to know that. I want you to know that I'll never really leave you, no matter what. You are my angel, Sage, and I'll never leave you."

Something between a disbelieving chuckle and a heart-wrenching sob escapes her lips. "I love you more than anything,

Sorin. Without you … I don't know how I'll do it."

I kiss her lightly. "You'll do it. I know you will. You're strong."

"Not—" Her voice breaks. "Not without you."

"Sage." I bring my face away from hers so I can look her straight in her eyes. "Trust me. I love you, but you can't change fate. You and I are destined to be together, but not in this life. And maybe that's just the way it will be. But you will see me again. And it will be like this. I will kiss you and I will hug you and I will love you more than I did the last time I saw you because you're you and you're so incredibly perfect. Impossibly perfect. And yet you make it possible."

A tear trails down her cheek. "I'm not perfect. I'm broken. I'm a monster. I—I killed someone today. She's not going to make it; I know it. I don't deserve this. I don't deserve *you.*"

I kiss the crown of her head. "I love you, Sage. And I'm so sorry. I'm so sorry I couldn't be there longer."

I feel my power fading, this moment ending, and then Sage is gone, just a memory, a wistful longing I can't forget. I love her, more than anything else, and I don't know how I'll stand being dead when she isn't.

She is *my* girl, and it will stay that way.

It will stay that way until forever ends.

EPILOGUE

ELYSIAN

The morning comes crisp and cool. I pull a sweater over my regular training outfit, and I make my way to the infirmary.

Healers have been working tirelessly on Xelma, trying to fix her lung before it collapses and she dies. I don't understand most of this, so all I can do is watch and pray she'll be okay, pray to whatever gods exist that she'll live.

Deep down, I know she won't make it. But still, hope is a weapon. A tool. A savior, if that's how you choose to use it.

Still, when they announce that she's died at breakfast as I sit with Ash and Sage and Milo and Ameer, name tags discarded on the spotless marble floor, tears spring to my eyes. I knew this was coming, but it's still disappointing. Xelma was like family, and now she's dead.

It's as easy as that sometimes.

You love someone, and then they're just gone, just like that. No goodbye, no see you later, no I love you, no warning, nothing. They're just ... gone.

I decide to have a real funeral for her. Spy or not, Xelma was a fighter, and as much a deserving person as any other camper. They carry her body out to the training area, where she spent most of her time. They bury her sword with her, which we found in her cabin along with a crammed suitcase and an empty bottle of water.

I hold Ash's hand at the reception. I don't care how it looks. All I know is I need some form of comfort, and since Ash is out of the infirmary due to her injury healing quickly and well after the Healers worked on it overnight, she's the best kind.

No one says anything about Sorin. It's an unspoken rule: Don't talk about the obviously dead guy. Don't talk about the best Healer Camp Serenity has ever had.

Sage seems more closed off than usual today, distancing herself from people and conversations, like she's afraid of something. I briefly wonder if something happened, and then I realize it doesn't matter. I just need to be there for her.

So I am. And I let her cry into my shoulder as she talked about her dream about Sorin, how she got to say her final goodbye, about his reassuring words, about Adar, the god of war and fire, the voice in her head, coming to visit her. I let her spill everything, because I know how much it hurts to keep everything in. How explosive it can become when you finally have to let go.

And after that whole morning, it's still cool. It seems as though the gods are allowing us to have a break after the sweating and stress that the hot sun has caused.

I find a good spot in the forest to sit, bringing pieces of paper with me and beginning to write a story I've been wanting to since the day I lost my memory, hence the papers that were spread all over my room that terrible day that started it all. The branches hang above me, acting as extra shade, protecting me from the bursts of sunlight that occur every few minutes. It's like the sky is at war with itself, but with all the war and fighting I've had to endure, I think I'll pass on joining in on this one.

Ash joins me under the shade after a few minutes. She sits next to me, waiting until I'm done scratching down outlines and notes and random ideas to talk. I'm grateful for it, because it lets me know that she's here, even when I'm busy. Maybe I'm looking too deep into it. Either way, she's here, and isn't that all that matters?

"Hey," she says finally. "I—uh, I was wanting to talk to you."

I notice her serious expression and I'm about to say something along the lines of, "Does it include death?" when she beats me to it.

"It's nothing bad," she assures me. "Don't worry. It's just ... Sage told me something."

My eyebrows knit together. "*Something*, meaning?"

"She, uh, she told me you loved me?" She says it like it's a question, and then she glances down at her nails, picking at the skin around them. "She told me you loved me," Ash says again.

I resist the urge to smile. "Did she?"

"Uh, yeah," Ash confirms. "She definitely did. I remember it. It was right before the wolf attacked. She said you loved me."

370

I chuckle breathily. "She's not wrong," I say after a while.

Ash freezes at that. She swallows. "Really?"

"Really."

She doesn't speak for a moment. Then, she grabs my hand. The soft grass tickles our hands as they intertwine. I finally understand why her hands have always been so hot around me. It's not just her fire. "I—I think I love you too."

"Really?"

She takes a deep breath. It's more of an "admitting" sort of deep breath, rather than a "considering" sort of deep breath. "Really."

She rests her head on my shoulder. I feel her soft hair touch my skin, but I don't care. Right now, at this very moment, all I care about is Ash loving me and me loving her. I don't care about war or peace or death or living. All I care about is this moment—these feelings.

All I care about is her.

And now, as I sit in the grass, my project below me, the source of my happiness sitting next to me, I'm sure.

This is when my nightmare ends.

ABOUT THE AUTHOR

E.G. Keith is a young author that, until recently, has never mustered up the right amount of patience to write a full novel. With a debut novel that several have good opinions on, she hopes to make a splash in the author world with her punny jokes, witty remarks, and evil way of thinking. She is very into Greek mythology and spends a lot of her time looking for books on the old stories, and she is convinced that her story, no matter how unique, has already been told by an old Greek writer. She strives for perfection in everything she does, and the several annotations in the first draft of this novel can prove that. E.G. is an adamant reader, and you can find her mostly wherever books are read or sold.

Follow her at egkeith.com for all of her next steps, including the sequel to Havoc, Serenity, coming soon...

ACKNOWLEDGEMENTS

While there is only one name on the cover, there are several that have worked long and hard in order to get me where I am now.

Thank you to *John B. Jamison* for being my writing coach/professional mentor during these past few months. You pushed me to work hard and get what I needed to get done, and for that I will be forever grateful.

Thank you to *Ryan Keith*, my father, for creating my website off a simple Google Doc and a stray idea, and the funding to fund it, as well. Thank you for blessing me with your writing skills when I was born— clearly I am benefiting from them. Thank you for the press kit that you made for me to get my name out there, and thank you over all for being supportive in your own special, sarcastic way.

Thank you to *Emma Moylan* for copy-editing my train wreck of a first draft. If it weren't for you, I'd still have quotation marks in the middle of a word.

To *Damon Freeman* for your beautiful work on the cover for this book. Initially I wanted something completely different, but you persuaded me into choosing something else by using the talent that you so evidently possess.

To *Sarah Lowery, Kathy Stoyak, and LeeAnn Gilbert* for turning my first-draft French and Spanish into something that doesn't make the reader wonder what they got themselves into.

To *Mallori DeSalle* and *Jacob Mason* for taking stunning pictures of me using your very, very fancy cameras. Thank you for taking someone naturally awkward (me) and turning them into someone a little less awkward.

To *Alyssa Bishop*, for BETA-reading this book. It definitely needed some shaping and you made sure of that. (P.S.: When the next one comes out, at least *try* to cry. For me?)

To *Andrea Runge* and L.E.A.D. for organizing the launch party and welcoming me as a new entrepreneur in our county. I appreciate the support you showed me—and the enlarging of my head as you continued to compliment me. Maybe my mother was serious when she said I should try to fit my head back into the room.

To *anyone* else who has supported me and my family through this journey that I am simply overwhelmed and have neglected to mention, please know I am so grateful for all the love, support, and pride felt by others. I could not have done this without that.

To *my readers*, I hope this book makes you *feel* something.

And finally, thank you so much to my mother, my manager, my greatest supporter, my BETA-reader, my money supplier, my editor, my typist, and one of my first readers—I owe everything that I am to you, literally. You are an inspiration. I try to live like you every day because of the wonderful person that you are. Though we've had our heated discussions and creative disagreements, I still believe that you are one of the best people that I have ever met and ever had the pleasure of loving and being loved by.

PRAISE FOR THE AUTHOR

I really have never found one (fantasy novel) written so well
by someone so young. I'm really kind of amazed.

ACCOMPLISHED WRITER JOHN B. JAMISON

A well-crafted and irresistible page-turner throughout,

it's an impressive contribution to the genre,

which I'm sure will be well received.

BOOK CRITIC/EDITOR LOUISE CROSS

Havoc was a phenomenal read.

I loved it so very much.

It's the perfect mix of romance and action. E.G. has a gift.

VORACIOUS READER ALYSSA BISHOP